THE ROAD TO LISBON

THE ROAD TO LISBON

MARTIN GREIG & CHARLES McGARRY

This edition first published in 2016 by
Arena Sport
An Imprint of Birlinn Limited
West Newington House
10 Newington Road
Edinburgh
EH9 1QS

First published in 2012 by
Birlinn Limited

www.arenasportbooks.co.uk

ISBN: 9781909715394
eBook ISBN: 9780857901903

British Library Cataloguing-in-Publication Data
A catalogue record for this book is available from the British Library

Typeset by Iolaire Typesetting, Newtonmore

Printed in Great Britain by Clays, St Ives

To Charles Anthony McGarry, 1931–2007

Acknowledgements

Our appreciation goes to all at Birlinn, especially Pete Burns, who bought into the idea and proved a knowledgeable and trustworthy sounding board throughout. Thanks to agent Mark Stanton, who believed in it from the start. Hugh 'The Mamba' MacDonald steered us away from perils and pitfalls, as is his way.

Martin: Huge thanks to Nicola Middleton for loving support, and George and Eileen Greig for doing what they have always done for me. To Neil White for ludicrous football analogies and Alan Partridge-isms . . . and Graeme Broadley, who liked an early draft and fell for Delphine. To John McGeady who provided vital feedback in the early stages. Michael Gormley's love for the written word first inspired me as a teenager at St Thomas Aquinas Secondary in Glasgow. Without his formative influence, this book would not exist. Finally, to Charles, an exceptional writer and friend. It was an absolute pleasure.

Charles: I am indebted to my family, especially my mother Anne and my late father Charlie, and my dear friend Stuart Rivans, for their unstinting support and encouragement. Thanks to my brother-in-law Bill Wright and Paul Coulter for their invaluable help with our promotional film, and to my sister Clare for helping set it up. To my Uncle Jimmy, whose kindness freed up so much writing time. To Des Mulvey for his inspirational stories. To Mr Gormley, who once advised 'write what you know'. To Martin for the original idea of *The Road to Lisbon*. His determination and positivity ought to be bottled and widely distributed.

Day One

Friday, May 19th 1967

Particles of dust swirl in the shaft of sunlight. Steam rises in gentle wisps from the mug in front of me. Outside, in the corridor, footsteps grow louder, louder . . . then fade away. Silence. I look up at the board, read out the names.

Simpson, Craig, Gemmell, Murdoch, McNeill, Clark, Johnstone, Wallace, Chalmers, Auld and Lennox.

The team. My team. My wee team. European Cup finalists. Four down, one to go. Inter Milan. Helenio Herrera. The best team in the world.

I smile to myself, but I have never felt more serious.

I can sense it, see it in their eyes. Confidence, presence, a lightness of spirit. Belief. A steady, unshakeable belief that I have nurtured but that was there already, part of their characters. Belief greater than gallusness – built on expectations of excellence and success.

Two years in the making. Two years of searching, honing, crafting. Panning for gold. Putting the fear of God into them, physically and mentally. I think of the casualties, the ones who wilted, who couldn't stand the heat, the lash of my tongue. I'd get in their faces, scream, threaten, abuse.

"I'm the boss, I'm the fuckin' boss. Can you handle that?"

I'd look right into their spittle-flecked faces, into the whites of their eyes.

"Can you fuckin' handle it?"

Some would crack. Look at their shoelaces. Fold.

"You can't handle me? I'm just one man. How the fuck are you gonnae handle 100,000 baying for your blood?"

Weak men. Hearts the size of peas. No good to me. No good to Celtic Football Club. Kick them aside, like garbage in the street.

Then, the ones who held your gaze. Not defiantly. Steadily. Who looked right at you. Through you. Never flinched. Then went out and proved you wrong. Went out and rammed those words down your throat.

I needed to know, to search deep into their characters, to get inside their heads. Know what made them tick, what they could handle, whether they would be ready when the moment came. The moment is now.

I have said it all along. Nine months now, banging the same drum. "I think this could be a season to remember."

1966–67. The season where it all comes together. I watched for the looks on people's faces every time I said it. Nods. Disbelieving nods.

It's gone to his head.

Getting too big for his boots, the Big Man.

But it wasn't swagger. For 18 months, I watched the pieces coming together. Our moment in history awaited us; this was no time for false modesty.

The signs were there. Off-field bonds there for all to see in an on-field unity. An unspoken understanding of each other's games, controlled aggression, instinctiveness, imagination.

A knock at the door. It is Sean Fallon. The Iron Man. My former playing comrade now my right hand. He speaks in his familiar heavy Sligo accent.

"This time next week we'll be European champions, eh?"

"Too right, Sean."

"That's the boys ready, Jock. Well, Jimmy's still in the bath. He was covered in suds and singing *The Celtic Song* when I left him."

"Tell him if he's not washed and dried in five minutes flat I'll fuckin' drag him out the front door with his trousers round his ankles in front of all those fans."

Celtic to the core, is Sean, solid as a rock. We have come a long way together. From the moment we met in the Parkhead dressing room in 1951 I could sense his character. With some others I felt a coolness in the handshake, a failure to make eye contact. Not with Sean. Since he first held out his hand, nearly crushing the bones in mine, and I watched those features light up, I knew I was dealing with someone different; someone who would look past background, age, everything; someone whose look searched for the humanity in others. A couple of years later he made me his vice-captain. Our friendship was cemented in Ferrari's restaurant in Sauchiehall Street, lost afternoons shuffling salt cellars around. Myself, Sean and Bertie Peacock, me talking 19 to the dozen and the other two listening closely, only occasionally interrupting.

"You've got it all worked out Big Man," Sean used to say, as the waitress rescued her salt shaker from the makeshift tactics board.

Now here we are on the edge of making history. The Press having been trying to second-guess my selection. The fans talk about little else. I give nothing away. Before I leave the office, I will wipe the names off the board in case someone spots them. I am completely settled on my starting 11. No injuries, no dilemmas. They have only played together six times, but proved themselves more than capable of coping with anything. It is the same 11 that clinched the title away to Rangers and the Scottish Cup against Aberdeen. Their disciplined performance in the second leg against Dukla Prague in the semi-final was further proof that these were players capable of delivering when the pressure was at its most intense.

I look at the board, scanning the names again. The chosen few. I repeat them.

Simpson, Craig, Gemmell, Murdoch, McNeill, Clark, Johnstone, Wallace, Chalmers, Auld and Lennox.

Silence broken again, this time by the phone.

"John, Bill here. How you feeling?"

"Prepared, Bill. We have the players, we have done the work, and the rest is down to the big man upstairs. And wee Jimmy, of course."

"Well, at least you know you can rely on wee Jimmy," laughs Shanks, but then his tone changes.

"John, I'll never forget two years ago against Inter in the semis. We hammered them in the first leg. The boys were glorious that night. Poetry in motion. Hunt scored early and Anfield exploded. Never heard anything like it, John. 3-1 it finished. We had a goal disallowed too.

"Then the second leg. Two of the worst refereeing decisions in history. They win an indirect free-kick and the boy chips it straight into the goal. The referee gives it. A sick joke. Then Tommy Lawrence bounces the ball on the ground as he prepares to punt it upfield. Their man sneaks in, takes the ball off him and scores. I had to be held back. If I'd got my hands on that referee I would have throttled him.

"I can see his face now, John. As I'm sitting here talking to you, I can picture his face in my mind's eye. We could have been the first, John, but now it's up to you. You and your boys."

"I hear you, Bill. I want to win this trophy for so many reasons. I want to do it in style, too."

"Ah John, this is your moment. I can feel it. I'll be there to cheer you on. See you after the game. With that big cup." He laughs and rings off.

Shanks knows where I am at this moment. He knows the journey. The journey from the blackness. The darkness. Two miners taking on the world; Shankly and Stein, a friendship that has survived no little meddling from the football gods. It is just over a year since we were denied a place in the Cup Winners' Cup final by Shanks' Liverpool. I close my eyes and think back to that fateful night. 2-1 down on aggregate but then Lennox scores in the last minute at Anfield to put us through on away goals.

Through to the final in Glasgow. No question in my mind that we will win it. Hampden Park. Imagine the size of the crowd! I am hugging Sean when I glimpse it from the corner of my eye. The offside flag. An outrageous decision. Then the final whistle, the recriminations, the bottles raining down. Anger. Disgust. I stand at the side of the park and wait for the Belgian referee, waiting to unleash my fury and desperately trying to avoid Shanks; shunning the handshake that would feel like a dagger through the heart from an old friend.

Bill has his pain. I have mine. Football has decreed that they are intertwined. But redemption is on hand. The phoney war will soon be over.

"How do you go about breaking down the most stubborn defence in world football?" the Press ask me.

Every day the same question and every day the same answer.

"It is not all about the Italians and how they set themselves up. We have a plan, we have a way of playing, we have a philosophy."

I leave one part out. We have Jimmy Johnstone. I close my eyes again and watch him go, driving at them time and time again. Wearing them down, crushing their spirit. The best defenders in the world reduced to rubble by a little red-haired Scotsman. I can see the joy in his face as he attacks again and again and again, streaked in sweat, skin pinking in the Portuguese sun.

"This is your stage, son," I will tell him in the minutes before we leave the dressing room. "This is your destiny."

And Jimmy will respond because the bigger the stage, the bigger Jimmy becomes. A 5ft 4in giant.

January 1965, Stein's Hibernian reserves v Celtic reserves, Easter Road, half-time.
"Jimmy Johnstone."
He glances round at me, cautiously.
"Mr Stein," he replies.

"Jimmy Fucking Johnstone."

"Yes, Mr Stein."

"What the fuck are you doing here," I say.

"Peeing, Mr Stein, same as you."

Then that wee smile. Part charm, part defiance.

"I know you are peeing, son, but it's your football talent you are pissing on. What I want to know is what you are doing playing in a reserve game in front of two men and a dog? Never mind pissing into the fuckin' bowl, you're pissing your talent down the drain. Not one of those clowns out there could lace your boots, but here you are, on a fuckin' Tuesday afternoon, running rings round the stiff-ersed defenders that aren't even good enough to make the Hibs bench . . . and making yourself feel good. Well, you may be happy kidding yourself son, but yer no kidding me. I know you. I've seen you play. You should be somebody. You'll know by now I'm coming back to Celtic. Mark my words, when I get my hands on you, Johnstone, you'll no know what's hit you. Now finish yer fuckin' pee, the second half is about to start."

I leave him there, still hovering over the bowl. Not smiling anymore.

The road to Lisbon.

Two hours on a plane. Seventeen-hundred miles. The European Cup. The pot of gold at the end of the rainbow. Estádio Nacional. The marble terracing, the perimeter moat, the eucalyptus trees. The coliseum waiting for the lions to be unleashed. And unleashed they will be. This is more than a match. This is attack v defence. This is me v him. Stein v Herrera. Stein's Scots v Herrera's world stars. This is the match I have been waiting for, the moment when everything I believe in will hopefully be expressed on an immaculate patch of grass in Portugal. This is about those 11 names on the board but it is about more than that. It is about who they represent. Who I represent. They will travel in their thousands. Planes, trains and any vehicle, roadworthy or not. Anything with wheels will be pointed in the direction of the Portuguese capital. People who have never been beyond Glasgow Cross will be digging out maps of mainland Europe. They will be hanging off cross-channel ferries, careering down country roads in France and serenading bemused Spanish senoritas with their songs.

Ay Ay Ay Ay
Simpson is better than Yashin
And Lennox is better than Eusebio
But Johnstone is better than anyone

Then, the friendliest, most boisterous occupation the city will ever have seen.

I can hear them now, outside the entrance to the stadium, milling around, that low murmur of voices, tense, exhilarated, rising to a roar as their heroes emerge.

It is time. I throw my jacket over my arm and close the office door softly. As I pass down the corridor, my secretary calls me back.

"Mr Stein, it's very busy out there. Would you like me to organise for the bus to get you at the side entrance? It'll save you time."

I look at her and smile.

"No need for that. This is the best bit. The day I slip out the side entrance of this place is the day I chuck it."

I walk through the front door, emerge blinking into the glorious afternoon sunshine and a huge roar rises up to greet me. The hairs on the back of my neck rise too, my back straightens. I look at their faces. Young men, mainly, hundreds of them. Young, working-class men who have invested their money, their time, their hopes and their dreams, everything in this football club. In its players. In me. Celtic, the centre of their lives, the core of their beings. I plunge in among them. I sign every piece of paper and politely acknowledge every goodwill gesture because I know that these people will make the difference. These people believe in me and believe in my team. My wee team.

"Good luck, Mr Stein. We are with you every step of the way," cries one young man, his face flushed with excitement.

I shake his hand and look into his eyes.

"Thanks for your support, you have no idea how much we appreciate it."

"We'll see you over there, Mr Stein," he shouts after me. "We'll see you in Lisbon!"

I get on the team bus bound for Seamill and sit at the front with Sean. As the coach pulls away I glance in the rear-view mirror at my team. My wee team. I see the rows of heads, laughing and joking. I look past them through the back window and see Celtic Park framed there. Then, I whisper to myself again . . .

Simpson, Craig, Gemmell, Murdoch, McNeill, Clark, Johnstone, Wallace, Chalmers, Auld and Lennox.

~~~

I approach Paradise, daring to daydream of adventure and glory.

I wander through the large crowd of well-wishers that has gathered in the car park. We are all charged with this strange new excitement that has been around ever since we reached the final.

Mark – my shadow lately – is easy to pick out due to the fact he's waving a copy of Aquinas' *Summa Theologica* at me. Total redneck in front of all these punters.

"M-m-mind we were discussing God's essence as being identical with H-H-His existence?" he asks with his familiar stutter.

"Vaguely."

"W-w-well I think I've c-cracked it!"

"I'm pleased for you."

Now I am known to visit church now and again myself, but tell me later. Much later. Three and a half thousand miles later.

I am rescued by a massive, throaty roar as the squad emerge, but they are off-limits and club officials usher them towards the waiting coach heading for Seamill, the Clyde coast retreat; Celtic's Lourdes, they call it. I try to pick out the 11 I feel certain he will start with in Lisbon.

Tommy Gemmell, the gallus full-back with the distinctive hooter waves enthusiastically towards us. Jim Craig smiles and gives us the V-for-victory sign. There's Bertie Auld with his trademark grin, giving the thumbs up.

"Wee Bertie. He's a hard wee bastard."

"Aye. H-h-he would kick his granny."

"He's a definite."

Bobby Murdoch, the engine of the side, waves over, a down-to-Earth guy despite being world-class.

"Boaby's arguably our best player."

"B-b-better than Jinky? You must be kidding me!"

"Alright, alright. I said arguably."

John Clark, the classy left-half, looks serious and thoughtful. Then there's Billy McNeill. Cesar. Our captain. Straight back, dignified, commanding – a massive presence beside Wee Clarky. They're both on the team-sheet, for sure.

I see Willie Wallace, our prolific inside-right, Stevie Chalmers, the classic Celtic centre-forward, and big John Hughes coming out in a cluster. Any two from three.

"If B-B-Big Jock wants to rummel them up he'll go with Y-Y-Yogi. But I've a f-f-feeling he'll play S-Stevie and Wispy," says Mark.

"For once, I think you're right."

There's the goalie, Ronnie 'Faither' Simpson, with that wizened face; Scottish Player of the Year. An absolute stick-on.

Not just fine footballers, but fine men too. Men you are glad to believe in, proud to have represent you. Men who all hail from either Glasgow itself or the surrounding area. It's a bloody miracle. Who do they think they are taking on the might of Inter Milan!

There is Bobby Lennox, always cheery, loves the fans – as skilful and graceful an outside-left as you will ever see, and with the kind of pace that defenders hate. That makes 10 . . .

Jimmy 'Jinky' Johnstone bursts from the stadium's main doors, and a crescendo of good-natured ribaldry goes up from fans and players alike. His shirt tail is hanging out and he grins as he dashes across the car park, stopping to shout over to us. He is hustled away by a steward as a familiar chorus, to the tune of *Ging Gang Goolie* fills the air:

We've got Jimmy-Jimmy-Jimmy-Jimmy Johnstone on the wing, on the wing.

We've got Jimmy-Jimmy-Jimmy-Jimmy Johnstone on the wing, on the wing.

He gets onto the coach, waving at us, and I wonder at this cheeky, reckless, ginger-haired midget who strikes terror into the greatest defenders in Europe. Mesmerising, flamboyant, imaginative, and in terms of sheer skill, utterly sublime.

Mark can't contain himself.

"Jinky's the m-m-man. If we do this, Jinky will be the man. Eh Tim, know what I mean? Know what I m-m-mean?"

"I think, if I hear you correctly, you are saying Jinky's the man!"

We burst out laughing and join in again lustily.

Jimmy. Oh Jimmy Johnstone, oh Jimmy Johnstone on the wing!

That's my side. It's got everything. Balance, ability, courage, fitness, strength, invention and belief. Belief in one another. Belief in their captain. Belief in their manager.

Belief instilled by their manager. Jock Stein. Big Jock. The Big Man. My hero.

Finally he emerges from the stadium, shaking hands. Including mine. The hefty steward doesn't even try to stop him. He knows better. My mouth is dry. I am struck temporarily dumb. Then I find some words.

"Good luck, Mr Stein. We are with you every step of the way."

"Thanks for your support, you have no idea how much we appreciate it."

He says it like he means it. He does mean it. I catch the look in his eye as his huge paw envelopes mine. A look that says he wants to win it for the people that matter. Really matter. Us.

"We'll see you over there, Mr Stein," I shout after him, as he hurries towards the coach. "We'll see you in Lisbon!"

I turn to Mark. Offer him my hand.

"Want to shake the hand that shook the hand of God?"

He bursts out laughing, grabs my hand and then hugs me. We bounce up and down manically like the couple of star-struck kids we are.

I walk Mark to his home in the Gorbals. Gives me a chance to score some blaw. Afterwards I will head back over the river to court. We cut through Glasgow Green to avoid any Tongs but a few of them are hanging around the wee bridge, guarding their border.

"Tim! W-w-what are we g-g-g-gonnae do?" Mark hisses urgently.

"Keep your knickers on. Get ready to do whatever I do."

The leader is a serious-faced individual with a terrible scar who looks a bit like a youthful Jack Palance. I recognise him from the summer, when the Tongs ruled the waltzers during the carnival. He knows who I am. But he lets us pass unmolested. A miracle.

"H-h-how come they didn't have a g-g-go?"

"It must be 'cause of the gemme. It's mesmerised every-one."

The Gorbals seeps into my nervous system like a narcotic. It's only a year since we flitted from here to nearby Toryglen but already I sense the hostility from the younger team, not helped by my lengthening hair and increasingly outlandish clothes. But I'm six foot and known.

A Gorbals tenement seethes and teems and pulsates and throbs and hums and buzzes and screams with human life. The air is continually punctuated with the sounds of people. Doors slamming, children shouting, couples fighting, babies crying, dinners cooking, radios blaring, the groans of copu-lation. Wakes, receptions, parties and sing-songs. Now lots of these buildings have been demolished and the land they stood on lies vacant or is being prepared for high-rise developments.

"I love this place. But they're murdering it. They're mur-dering the Gorbals. The whole community."

"So w-w-what?"

"Don't you care?"

"It's alright for y-y-you. You don't have to live here any m-more."

"Fair enough. But what about those auld yins?" I say, nodding towards a boarded-up, half-demolished tenement, where some former residents have congregated. "I saw them dragging auld kitchen tables and chairs into that parlour for a bevvy, just so that they could be together again. Except the parlour no longer has a ceiling, or a roof. Poor bastards. They're scared."

"Of w-w-what?"

"Of what's gonnae happen to them. Of where they're gonnae go."

"They'll get a n-nice house in the schemes."

"They don't want to go to the schemes. They want to stay in the Gorbals. Where the spirit is."

A wee old woman is walking by pushing a pram full of laundry to the steamie, a rain-mate on her head. She has overheard and turns to me with tears filming her eyes.

"They're knocking down the greatest place on Earth, son."

"You see?" I ask Mark, vindicated.

He shrugs his shoulders. Mark has a boyishly handsome face, light-blond hair and intense, clear-blue eyes.

"You realise what's going on here? Why they're really knocking this place down? They're tearing apart the auld Irish neighbourhoods. The Calton, the Gorbals, the Garngad. Splitting us up."

"They're s-slums, Tim. They need to be torn down."

"No. We've got ourselves educated, radicalised. They're scared of us. They hate us."

"You're being p-p-paranoid."

"Just because I'm paranoid doesn't mean they're no out to get me. Understand this. An entire era is about to end, auld Glasgow is about to slip over the horizon. And something precious will be lost forever."

Just then we happen by a gaggle of bedraggled, malnourished children, playing in a filthy puddle. They watch plaintively as an ice cream van, painted baby blue and tinkling a cheery tune, motors slowly by.

"Hauw! HAUW JIMMY!"

I run and bang the side to catch the driver's attention. He stops and clumps towards the serving hatch.

"Five pokey hats pal."

"You want raspberry?"

"Aye."

"Two and six, my china."

I give the children the cones and they skip off merrily back to their puddle.

Mark looks at me. Now it's my turn to shrug my shoulders. Deep down I know he's got a point . . .

. . . The darkness. I am 11 years old. The Gorbals. Fifty thousand people crammed into the most densely populated place on Earth: a ghetto of less than a square mile of filthy, rat-infested, jerry-built slums. Our tenement blackened and browned by poverty, worn down by four generations of hard living. The January gloom, the relentless cold. The stink of sewage. I can *see* it, for Christ's sake, snaking down the stair. I don't belong in this place. Hold on a minute – who do I think I am – better than these people? No. Nobody belongs in a place like this. But they see it in my eyes, hear it in the way I try to talk that bit clearer and use a bigger vocabulary, tell it by the fact that I go to the library, the fact that I ask the old Jewish intellectuals in the bathhouse about Marx, the fact that after the summer I'll be going to Holyrood instead of St Bonaventure's. The fact that I paint. *You think your shite disnae smell!* . . .

. . . We amble to Hell's Kitchen Cafe. Steam, the smell of hot fat, orders being shouted in warm, rough accents and The Who's *So Sad About Us* blaring from the wireless. We sit by the window, the bustle of Gorbals life comfortingly close. I choose, Mark takes ages, I make lines with spilled sugar. Eventually he makes up his mind and the waitress comes over; fake gold, a fag on. Friendly but unhygienic.

"Hullo boys, what yous for?"

"Two rolls and sausage, and a mug of strong tea for me; just a plate of soup for the lady," I grin.

She flashes a row of crooked teeth at me and goes.

Mark's nose is bothering him. Wants a bloody heart-to-heart.

"How are things between yourself and D-D-D-Debbie?"

It's been 12 days and . . . 22 hours since it happened. But the question is: was it actually a break-up? I don't really know because she avoided me for a week and then went to Saltcoats on holiday. Now I'm off to Lisbon. Bloody hell. I cast my mind back. Analyse the events for the hundredth time, events in this very café . . .

. . . She walks in. That familiar feeling. Excitement. The universe is fretted with meaning and I know this because Debbie Sharkey is my girl. Because she is in the same room as me. Because she exists.

She comes over, a serious expression on her face. She looks businesslike and determined in her raincoat. I regard her figure. She is wee and slim, so her breasts are fuller than you remember. Sometimes my eyes are drawn there, in unexpected appreciation.

She smiles weakly. Sits down. No kiss. Excitement turns to dread.

"You okay, Debbie?"

"Yes."

"What would you like?"

"Coffee please."

"Cup of coffee over here please, Agnes!"

Smalltalk follows, skirting the issue. What issue? What is it that is troubling me? The coffee is brought over and Debbie stares into it, stirring relentlessly. Usually her eyes, which are hazel, large and clear, fix whoever is addressing her, impressing upon them her quiet self-assurance, honesty and genuine interest in others which I've always loved. Not today.

"So what's this good news of yours?" she asks languidly.

"I've got a new job, at Hargreaves!"

"Hargreaves on the Clyde?"

"Aye. They do refitting for merchant vessels. What's wrong? You don't seem too impressed."

She sighs slightly, then looks at me directly. "Tim, this will be your fifth job in two years."

It's actually my sixth, but I won't correct her.

"So?"

"You obviously don't like it. Working, I mean."

"You think I'm lazy?"

Her gaze returns to her coffee. "No. I just think you hate working in the yards."

She's right, of course. I'd be happier painting. I'd work 80 hours a week doing that – for two bob an hour.

She looks away from the coffee cup and stares out of the window abstractly. I love it when she wears her lovely chestnut-coloured hair up like that. She has a button nose and her chin and mouth sit ever so slightly pronounced forwards. I hate to boast but people say that we make a very handsome couple. She's got a hundred times more class than the wee hairies Rocky knocks about with.

Rocky. At that moment I become more aware of his presence in a nearby booth. It might be my imagination but I fancy that he's trying too hard to make out that he's oblivious to us, talking self-consciously loudly to Iggy and Eddie about banalities.

I need to ask. I don't want to – Christ knows I don't want to – but I need to broach the subject.

"Is there something wrong, Debbie?"

Finally she makes eye contact, falteringly.

"I'm really sorry, Tim. But I'm having . . . doubts."

I try to swallow but my mouth has gone dry. I take a gulp of tepid tea.

"Doubts?"

"About . . . us."

I should be moved to a torrent of protest, to great feats of logic and persuasion. I possess a canon of evidence as to why we should be together – two glorious years' worth. Yet I am silent. Only later will I realise why; because deep down I know that you can't persuade people to feel such things. Because I know that it's hopeless.

She rises quickly.

"I've got to get out of here."

"But we need to talk."

"I know. But later. Somewhere else."

"Debbie!"

She comes back for her handbag. It's then that I detect it. A glance, no more than that, in which they catch one another's eye. I know that the bet is lost. I feel a wave of rage. For a split second I fantasise destruction; my smashing the fuck right out of the place, banjoing Rocky, teeth and blood, fearful faces, then self-pity and booze. Anger, livid and ugly, finding its release like poison being drawn from a boil. Then, later, the darkness, except worse this time, much worse.

But my wrath is restrained by the realisation that I might simply be being paranoid – it has been known. I need real proof. And even if it is true, maybe deep down I don't even blame them . . .

. . . Mark looks subdued. I feel bad for thinking he was just being nosey. There is sadness in his eyes. He cares about me. Cares about a lot of people in fact. I'm always doing that. Thinking the worst of folk.

~~~

1966–67. We hit the ground running. Manchester United in town for a friendly. Charlton, Stiles, Law, Crerand and Best. Charlton strutting, elegant, an aura of greatness; Stiles, all toothless

tenacity, the opposite of Charlton, but just as vital; both fresh from World Cup glory with England. The incomparable Denis Law. Greased lightning has nothing on the leaping Lawman, but it is his aggression, his lionheart that makes him the player he is. Crerand, the midfield warrior with the unsinkable spirit. I had him in my Celtic reserve team; I honed his character, polished off the rough edges, sent him in to buy me chips on the way home from training. Look at him now. I would gladly take him back. But the question now is, would he get in the team? My wee team. Then Best, the incarnation of a football god. The long hair, the glint in his eye, but substance as well as style – speed, control, courage, mental and physical toughness; an artist as much as a footballer. United have everything; a great manager too. Matt Busby. A fellow Scot and a former miner. A kindred spirit. A man whose hopes and dreams lay in ruins on an airstrip in Munich eight years ago. A man who lost the core of a great team, but never lost the life-force; who glimpsed the other side, but fought his way back, to health and, ultimately, greatness. A man I am honoured to be in the presence of on this sun-kissed day in the east end of Glasgow.

"Should be a close one today," says Matt, before kick-off.

"We'll see Matt, we'll see."

But it is not close. We annihilate them. We are faster, stronger and more ruthless. McBride scores and then Murdoch adds another. Bill Foulkes' own-goal sums up their disarray, before Lennox adds another. 4-1 going on 10.

I watch Charlton look at Stiles, Stiles look at Crerand, Crerand look at Law, Law look at Best. And Best shrug his shoulders.

"It's just a pre-season friendly, don't read too much into it," I tell the Press.

I lie. Manchester United, the great Manchester United, do not play friendlies. It is not in their nature. Every match is a battle. We won the battle fair and square. "Well done, Jock," says Matt after the game. "Your boys are in good shape."

"I think this could be a season to remember, Matt. A season to remember . . ."

The fixture calendar has pitted us against Clyde on the first day of the league season. I have not even considered it yet. It is irrelevant. Our season starts against Rangers in the Glasgow Cup.

"Forget about Clyde, forget about the league," I tell the players. "The summer is over and the season starts now. Today. Against Rangers."

We may have won the title last year, but the memory of our Scottish Cup final defeat still rankles. It's sat in my stomach all summer. Like a poison that's gradually seeped through my whole system, disrupting my sleep, destroying my holiday. Always there. Whenever I closed my eyes all I could see was Kai Johansen sauntering to the edge of the box and firing in the winner. That moment. It's not just about losing. It's about losing to Rangers. It fuckin' destroys me. Overwhelms me. It's personal. But it fires me up. By God, it motivates me like nothing else in this world. *Never again. Never a-fuckin-gain.*

Rangers have strengthened over the summer, but we are stronger, too, more confident and better prepared. Before the game, there is none of the usual pre-match banter. The players drift around quietly, going through their preparations. They can see the fire in my eyes. The madness. They know what this means to me. This is war.

I spell it out to them.

"Gentlemen, I want you to think back to the Scottish Cup final last season. I want you to remember Johansen's goal. I want you to remember how it felt. Remember your disappointment, but then think about how Johansen must have felt. Johansen doesn't score. It was a one-off, but he will want to do it again. The crowd will want him to do it again. He'll be charging over the halfway line like a bull. We must be ready for him. Every time he gets up a head of steam, we will be on top of him. Bobby Lennox, you will be up against him, but don't track him when he goes forward. Sit in that space and when we get the ball back, we will get it to you. Use that pace to tear them apart, Bobby.

"Now, go out there and win. Fuckin' tear them limb from limb. Destroy them. Or you'll have me to answer to."

Billy McNeill opens the scoring and then Lennox starts to enjoy himself. As Johansen pushes forward, Lennox bursts from the traps like a greyhound, time after time. At the final whistle, Lennox grabs the match ball. The hat-trick hero. 4-0.

The season has started . . .

~~~

Iggy has a habit of 'borrowing' motors. Jaguars, Triumphs, Rovers, Austins, Fords, ice cream vans – he isn't fussy. He even nicked a steamroller one time, just a half-hour nocturnal jaunt round a building site.

"Nice throttle action but the steering's a bit on the heavy side," he mused.

I suppose he just loves cars but knows he is never going to own one. A couple of times the polis put the chase on him but he was too daring, too resourceful, too quick.

Iggy's skills meant he was recruited to help the South Side mob on a few jobs. When I heard about this I was worried sick but he played it all down as though he was taking part in Sunday trips down the coast. I think he was seduced by the excitement of it all, the fun. The dough – I don't think he was particularly interested in it. He ended up giving it away to poor souls or to his poor parents. Anyway, he started to avoid me, tired of my lectures.

On Wednesday he was at the wheel of a 1965 Mark II Humber Sceptre, waiting to cross the Jamaica Bridge into the city centre. The traffic moved off except for the vehicle immediately in front. It was an unmarked car and the cops inside had decided that the face and the paintjob behind didn't go together.

I take my seat in the public gallery. He is drowning in an oversized collar and tie. Nice to see not one of his big-shot compadres are here. I'm the only one. Got to make sure he's okay. Got to look after him. Can't have him ending up like his poor wee brother. Killed climbing a scaffolding trying to escape from the polis when he was 13. The thought of *losing* him!

"Ignatius Patrick McCargo, you are hereby to be remanded in custody . . ."

That's it. No Iggy at Lisbon. Just me worrying about him getting sent down for a long stretch. You fucking *eejit*, Iggy.

As he is led away he looks up at me, a picture of innocence in his ill-fitting suit and grubby plimsolls. But I know that he's no innocent. I know that he embodies the madness of the Gorbals, even though his family didn't move there from the Calton until he was 14.

I remember the first time I met him. I was walking along Thistle Street one spring evening, feeling quite merry, when I heard the distinctive tuneless chorus of Gorbals community singing.

Que sera, sera. Whatever will be, will be . . .

The sound was getting steadily nearer. Intrigued, I turned round. A double-decker bus was crawling along behind me.

The future's not ours to see. Que sera, sera. What will be, will be.

The driver was a striking looking little fellow. With a mop of thick, jet-black hair that almost obscured his vision, and a wide, inane grin, he exuded cheerfulness and mischief. His features were all slightly too large for his face, like the product of a cartoonist's pencil, and he was clearly drunk. This was the bold Iggy. He brought the bus to a standstill alongside me to let an old woman off.

"Thanks, son. You've saved my poor auld legs."

"No bother, missus," he slurred, touching the peak of his hat which was tilted ludicrously to one side of his large head. The bus was heaving with people. Everyone singing and having a good time. The party bus.

His attention turned to me.

"Standing room only – no spitting, swearing or calling the driver an eejit!"

As I considered my next course of action my attention was drawn by shouting from down the street.

"HAUW! HAUW! HAUD THE BUS! HAUD THAT FUCKIN' BUS!"

A fat, sweating man dressed in the drab green of Glasgow Corporation Transport – *sans* peaked hat – was racing up Thistle Street as though his life depended on it. This was the real driver. Iggy, it would transpire, had stolen – or "borrowed" as he would later insist – the bus while the driver, on his way back to the depot, had popped into *The Britannia* for a swift half. While he was in the lavvy Iggy had swiped the driver's hat and keys, which he had imprudently left on the bar-top. Iggy then proceeded to nip outside and drive the vehicle away, stopping regularly just like an official service to take on board passengers, most of whom were drunken revellers like himself.

"RIGHT EVERYBODY – GET FUCKING OFF!"

Such was the real driver's shame at the theft that he didn't report it, and instead merely relieved Iggy of his duties. Iggy shambled along Thistle Street and his passengers all duly shambled along after him. The pied piper of Gorbals Cross. He stopped and turned to me.

"Are you coming?"

"Too right!"

~~~

The road to Lisbon.

Where did it start? It started in the darkness. The blackness of a coalmine in Lanarkshire. The moment that lamp went out and the blackness closed in. When I could see nothing. Not even the hand in front of my face, nothing but the inside of my head. And the ever-present threat of death, lurking in every darkened crevasse. A growing sense of fear. The fear of a 16-year-old boy. Terror. Silent terror. Then, finally, the flicker of something else. A determination, a will, a desire to overcome. To stand tall and take my place in the company of men. Real men. Men whose characters were hewn from the black walls of that mine. Men who needed each other, trusted each other, thousands of feet below the ground. Petty feuds and religious rivalries were left on the surface. They silently taught me how to be a man myself.

When the boy became a man . . . that was when the first steps were taken on the road to Lisbon.

And now . . . now I tell my players, "You're here to entertain. You're here to make people's lives better. People who work hard all week. People who work down the mines, in factories and in the yards. People who barely glimpse daylight during the week, who come along and spend their hard-earned money to watch you play. You have the ability to raise their spirits, to give their life meaning. You can be lights in the darkness."

The darkness. The blackness.

Burnbank. Protestant Burnbank. Protestant Burnbank with its corner of Catholics. Divided communities. 'Don't stray into the wrong street . . . don't look at them.'

'Them.' *Them and us.* Protestant and Catholic. I remember the Cross. Burnbank Cross. The centre of our community. The pubs, the chatter. I remember July 12th. The noise, the colours, the pageantry and the sense of belonging, of community. But I remember something else. An edge, a sneer at the end of sentences. A flash of the eyes. *Them and us.* I remember the no-go zones.

'Pope's corner' we called one of them, where the Catholics met. Them at Pope's Corner. Us at Burnbank Cross. *Them and us.* Protestant Burnbank. Catholic Bellshill. Protestant Larkhall. Catholic Blantyre. Divided communities. Worlds apart.

'Keep your distance,' they said, so I did, unquestioningly at first. But things change. Lives change, and you meet people. I met Jean one summer's evening in Cambuslang. Jean Toner McAuley. The woman who would become the love of my life. A Catholic.

I knew what it meant. From the first moment, I knew the consequences. It meant slinking down back streets on our way home because it was not a good idea to walk down the main street. It meant steering away from the Cross. From the pubs, the chatter. It meant whispers and disapproving, disappointed glances. *Turncoat. Jump-the-dyke.*

It meant rejection. But rejection by who? People who choose to hate you because of your religion? Fuck them. Fuck them all.

It also meant something more powerful, more meaningful. Not hatred, but love. Not them and us. Just us. Myself and Jean.

Football, my other love, was always there, a constant. Blantyre Victoria then Albion Rovers. Cliftonhill was where I made my name as a centre-half. Where I started to think about football, really think about it. Where I would question everything, study the opposition, find out their strengths and weaknesses, learn to compensate for my own weaknesses. And I had no shortage of those. With my left foot, I had a kick like a mule. My right was only of use for standing on. I developed a neat trick of using my right knee rather than my foot to clear the ball, but even that was capable of letting me down. 'Yer a one-footed mug,' would sound from the terraces at Cliftonhill, usually when we were getting beaten. But I had my ways of ushering nippy centre-forwards down blind alleys, of encouraging them to turn the way I wanted them to. It was all thought out, analysed, planned in the most minute detail. It did not make me a world-beater, but it did allow me to cope, even to flourish on occasion.

I looked around me and everywhere saw more naturally gifted players. Players who were born to play football, who knew the game instinctively. Players with the ability to do things out of the ordinary, but who could never quite explain how or why they did it after the event. That fascinated me. I wanted to get inside their heads. I wondered how good players could become even better and how great players could become world-beaters . . . how their natural instincts could be honed to make them an even more potent force. I thought a lot. About football, about tactics, about what motivates different people and about what undermines their confidence. God knows I had plenty of time to reflect on such matters.

Bothwell Pit, Monday to Friday. Cliftonhill or an away fixture on a Saturday. A week spent in the darkness, but a week spent thinking and planning, picking the team in my head. I was not the manager but it became clear that a well-timed word in his ear from me would sway his judgement. He knew that I knew more than he knew. He was right. Soaking everything in like a sponge. Directing play from the centre of defence. And the players looking to me for leadership. The manager looking to me for leadership. A leader of men. It came instinctively and it surprised me at first. It was the first realisation that I could do something different, but I did not know what it meant, what it could lead to.

Albion Rovers v Rangers was the highlight of the season. Cliftonhill bursting at the seams. The blue strip carried an aura. Most of us were Rangers men but we were all footballers, too. I saw no conflict between the two. I looked at my team-mates and I sensed a level of respect that went too far. I did not like it. I was my own man. A professional. I ploughed into 50-50s with relish, took no prisoners. They didn't like it, the Rangers players. They looked at me as if an unwritten rule had been broken. I just shrugged my shoulders and tackled even harder. Fuck them. It was not about loyalties. It was not about religion. It was about football. Always football.

~~~

The wireless is murmuring something about Muhammad Ali refusing the draft. Other than that there is only the sound of crockery gently clanking and splashing in the sink. She doesn't hear me come in. I watch her for a while in her tired, solitary routine, surrounded by sad brands, mocked by the faux cheerfulness of cheap detergent labels. I watch her muscular arms as she washes the lunch dishes and some of my painting things, absorbed in thought. Her movements are sluggish and resigned.

"Hi Ma."

I kiss her.

"Hello son. How are you?"

"Fine. Yourself?"

"Not bad, not bad."

She sighs.

"What's up Ma?"

"Nothing son."

"Where's my da?"

"In bed."

"Is he asleep?"

"No. Just a wee bit tired. Go through and see him."

The room is shaded. Christ crucified looms above the headboard. My father's odour fills my nostrils. He stirs, aware of me. I speak into the cool silence.

"Why are you in bed Da, are you tired?"

"Naw son. Just a bit cold is all."

"I'll put a fire on."

"It's alright. There's no coal anyway."

"That's no good Da, staying in bed 'cause you're cold."

I want him to complain. I want him to tell me how to make it better.

"Are you going then?"

"Aye. Leaving soon."

"That's grand, son."

I feel bad leaving him.

"Will you see it?"

"Aye. Your Uncle Joe's bringing round a telly. Might even have a wee dram!"

"That's great. Think we'll win?"

"I know we will. The good Lord didn't bring us this far to lose. Believe me son, Celtic's special. Anointed."

The doubt is written on my face.

"Have faith."

Suddenly he begins coughing violently, bent over, hacking phlegm from his lungs. I rub his back.

"Pass me that linctus son."

He takes a sip and the coughing abates. His chest heaves; a discordant harmony rises and falls with every breath. He relates a familiar story, as though he has to explain or apologise for the way his health is.

"Those fibres, it was lying around everywhere in the yard during the second war. We used it for fireproofing on the battleships. We even had a snowball fight with it once. It seemed so harmless, like kids' stuff. Then this new gaffer told us he reckoned it was dangerous, that it gets into your lungs. So after that we didn't touch it unless we had to. I forgot all about it, then years later, when I started getting breathless, an old workmate of mine made the connection. He had it too."

Da and Ma – they've done so much for us, never complaining. Sometimes I dread having a family. I'd be so

worried that I couldn't hack the graft, on account of the fact
that I find it so depressing and boring. Plus I hate the way it
fucks up your health. I mean, just look at Da.

"Now, go into my top drawer for me . . . take out that
envelope."

"What's this?"

"A wee minding. From me and your mammy."

"I can't take this; you with no enough for coal!"

He tuts impatiently in his particular way, then speaks with
mock sternness.

"There's no question of us no having enough for coal! Now
take it. Enjoy yourself. And make sure you thank your
mammy."

I walk towards him. Grasp his thin, leathery hand. Touch
his soft white hair. Kiss his forehead. That wee shrapnel scar,
so familiar to me, so emblematic of him. Close my eyes and
hold the moment. Remember it. Treasure it. Want to keep him
forever.

"Good lad."

He closes his eyes. I go to leave. Then turn back.

"Da. One question. Favourite-ever Celtic match?"

He instantly comes back to life in a series of grunts and
gasps.

"Help me sit up . . . put the wee table light on . . . now,
take the bottle out o' the dresser . . . naw, the next door . . .
that's it."

He pours us both a whisky, mine in the wee crystal glass,
his in his medicine cup. The meagre light illuminates his
grey, haggard face. I try not to look upset. At least those
hazel Donegal eyes are still sparkling. We raise our drams
and drink, me pretending that the spirit doesn't burn, trying
not to choke, trying not to spoil this precious moment of
togetherness.

"September 10th 1938. Celtic 6 Rangers 2. I was there, in

the Jungle. Celtic scorers: McDonald hat-trick, Lyon double, Delaney. Malky McDonald was magnificent that day, he was a player, son, believe me."

The room now is a hotchpotch of 40 years of marriage. Relics of five children and umpteen grandchildren, odd books and ornaments, things misplaced and mixed up during half-a-dozen flittings.

He is wistful now, almost whispering.

"But then there was Jimmy Delaney – he was a class apart. Watching a wee winger in a green-and-white hooped jersey take the baw past a big ugly defender – it's a beautiful thing to watch. It's Celtic. It's . . . romance!"

My eyes wander along the ever-growing line of medicines on his bedside table. None of them seem to *work*. I feel a wave of anger, then a sensation of helplessness and sorrow. My eyes film with water. Luckily he's not noticing; he's too focused on his story. I blink and pretend to have been listening.

"Anyway, it all started when McDonald smashed the baw in on the rebound. The half-backs, Geatons, Paterson and Lyon, were out of this world. The Huns couldn't live with them. We were three-nil up by half-time – played them off the bloody park! Then the Huns came back at us; before we knew it the score was 3-2, it was a bloody travesty! You should have heard their dirty mob chanting, they thought they had us on the ropes. But we just kept on singing and then Jimmy nets the fourth and we know it's all over. McDonald got the last two, superb goals they were. What a day. We sang *Hail Glorious Saint Patrick* all the way down the Gallowgate, all the way through the town and all the way to the Gorbals!"

~~~

Every life has its moments. Moments that are burned in the memory forever, that change the direction of your life. My moment came as I was sitting in my chair in a small house in a small village in a Welsh valley, reflecting on how my ambitions as a full-time professional had apparently seeped away.

Six months earlier I had ended my eight-year spell at Albion Rovers to sign for Llanelli, a forward-thinking club with intentions of entering the English football league. The club had trebled my £4 wage. I was 27, a full-time professional for the first time in my life and could not have been happier. No more mining. Just football.

But then things started to go wrong. The whispers of financial mismanagement at the club reached full cry. Then the wages stopped. Then the worries started. Jean was back in Scotland. The house had been broken into twice. I wanted to be with her. But with a return to Scotland came a return to mining. A return to the darkness. The blackness.

Then came the call that changed my life.

"Jock, it's Jimmy Gribben here, from Celtic Football Club. I hear you are looking for a move back to Scotland. You fancy signing for us?"

With the phone still glued to my ear, I began to laugh, waves of mirth washing over me.

"You can't be serious Jimmy," I said, after finally composing myself.

But Jimmy was serious.

"Jock, we want you to sign for Celtic. Have a think about it, speak to the family and call me back."

The phone went dead. Decision time. I stood there. In a small house, in Mansell Street, Llanelli, a tiny village in the Valleys. No steady income. No family beside me. No prospects. Until now. But this was no ordinary prospect. A Rangers man signing for Celtic? *Turncoat, Turncoat. Traitor, Traitor.* I thought of the friends I would lose. The family members who would shun me. I thought of the men at Burnbank Cross. I thought of it all. Fuck them. Fuck them all. Then I picked up the phone.

"Jimmy, you have a deal."

~~~

Mark and I have arranged to meet Eddie outside the cash and carry. He is waiting, leaning against a lamp-post, smoking. He grins at us through a spider-web of scars, his bogey piled high with booze. He takes a slug from a tin of lager; he's already getting torn in.

"Alright Tim?"

"Alright Eddie."

"Alright Olive?"

"A-a-alright Eddie."

We head to where the Imp is. We are struggling to fit all the booze into the car when Rocky finally turns up, looking effortlessly like a movie star, an entourage of his numerous younger brothers in his wake, each a smaller and slightly different version of himself. Wraparound shades, suede shoes, five o'clock shadow on his hollow cheeks, crisp open-necked white shirt beneath his chocolate-brown *Tailorfit* suit.

"I've no got the seat, by the way," he says.

"What?"

"Got let down. No my fault."

"Well what the fuck are we gonnae sit on for Christ's sake?"

"Sit on your bags."

"Sit on our bags? Are you fucking joking? I wonder how much of the journey you'll be spending in the back!"

"Haud the bus, Tim. Remember, it's my fucking car."

"So it's like that then is it?"

"Come on Tim, t-t-take it easy," intervenes Mark.

"Well he just breezes on in and mentions it as if in passing, as though he was telling us he had forgotten to bring his fags or something."

"Well shouting about it isn't g-gonnae help."

"Okay Mark – what do you suggest?"

Mark looks at his toes.

"Keep your drawers on, I've got an idea," says Rocky. "I know where there's a pile of auld railway sleepers."

"Jesus Christ!"

So we jam a railway sleeper into the Hillman Imp, where the back seat should be. First we drag it into a back court and Eddie hacks at it with a saw he lifted from a demolition site. His wiry brown hair moistens. His face becomes flushed. Ugly scar tissue from 50 gang rumbles and square goes divide it up into different zones. The skin might be discoloured purple or angry red in one place from a rash. Another section might be marred by acne or pockmarked from old spots. Another part is shiny from his close shave. It's funny, he and Rocky are both big-time tough guys in the Cumbie yet I don't think Rocky's got a single mark on his pretty fizzer.

"It's a surprisingly good fit."

"Aye Rocky, you try telling that to whoever's arse has been in close connection with it after 50 miles or so," says Eddie, wiping the sweat from his brow.

"At least Iggy's no being here will give us more room," says Rocky.

I just glare at him.

"Come on boys. Let's hit the Blarney for a couple. Get into the mood," suggests Eddie.

The Blarney Stone is a total cowp. The bar is made out of chipped Formica and the constant fug of cheap tobacco smoke just about masks the smell coming from the lavvy.

"Here," begins Eddie. "Did I tell yous I got bumped?"

"Naw!"

"Aye. That Hun bastard Christie says, 'If you're no here

next week you needn't bother turning up again.' The tube knows fine I'm a Tim. He just can't stand the thought of us going away to Lisbon."

I think for a moment of Eddie's colleagues at the packing factory. Dour, self-assured, silent men.

"Dirty Orange bastard," remarks Rocky.

"I had to go to MacFarlane for a sub to fund the trip," says Eddie, before necking a whisky and chasing it with his pint. We are silent. Going to a money-lender is not generally considered to be a prudent course of action.

"What about you, Mark? How did you get the dough together?" I ask.

"I'd to go to the p-p-pawn . . . D-D-Da's stuff."

His voice trails off and his eyes glaze over. He shakily reaches for his glass.

Coco Costello pops his head into the shop.

"You boys should get a swatch at your motor!"

We rush out.

Some kids have decorated the Imp with green-and-white bunting.

"Thank Christ for that, I thought it was something bad!" says Rocky.

Streamers are tied to the radio aerial and an Eire flag of a golden harp on an emerald background has been fastened to the bonnet. There are two other groups in the street due to leave that evening, Mickey Zamoyski and his pals, and the Murphy brothers. Their vehicles have been similarly festooned in Celtic colours. It was the Murphys' wee sisters who have done the decorating. The Murphy boys must have supplied the gear. I nod at Big Dessie in appreciation. He nods back in acknowledgement.

My ma descends.

"Here, boys, I've got you a few messages. It's just some pieces and some tea and things."

"Thanks a lot Mrs Lynch."

Then Rocky's ma arrives.

"Here's a few tins for yous."

"Thanks a lot Mrs Devlin."

Then Mark's ma.

"I've got yous a bag of bagels from Fogell's and some ginger. Now don't get sunburned."

"Thanks a lot Mrs Halfpenny."

Eddie's ma doesn't come.

All the local characters assemble to watch us depart. Every window is occupied by wifies out for a hing. Scores of working men returning from their shifts spend a moment taking in the proceedings before heading to the pub or up the stairs for their tea. My Uncle Joe and a wheen of my cousins are there. Father Breslin happens by and is commandeered by Mark.

"Hey F-F-Father – could you give the Imp a wee b-b-blessing please?"

We all bow our heads as the priest dubiously makes the sign of the cross over the car. "God bless this car and all who . . . drive in her. In nomine patris, et fili, et spiritus santi."

Suddenly – and I mean in a single instant – a carnival atmosphere breaks out in the street, as a hubbub of laughter and excited voices wells up in the early evening air. Mr Brannigan, who is one of the top men in the local Hibernians, brings his melodeon down and begins playing an impromptu version of *The Merry Ploughboy.* Some of the Tiny Cumbie provide the lyrics with gusto.

And we're all off to Dublin in the green,
Where the helmets glisten in the sun,
Where the bay'nets clash,
and rifles crash,
To the echo of the Thompson gun

We climb in. Mark is still saying goodbye to his mammy and his sisters. Rocky leans out.

"Get in the car."

Mark obeys.

So here we are. One moment in time. Even an event of immense significance must occupy just its single, arbitrary split second in history. So live in that moment when it comes. Live in the now. Breathe deeply and think: *here we go!* Keys in. Turn. Ignition. Accept fag from Eddie. We all do. A celebratory smoke. Camaraderie. Accept light from Rocky. Draw in the smooth blue smoke. Hold it. Bliss. Exhale. Pump accelerator gently. Give her a little gas, get her ticking. Depress clutch. Shift gearlever. Release handbrake. Bring up clutch. Biting point. Almost there. Last glance into rearview. Eddie and Mark perched on the edge of the sleeper like excited kids. Look left. Rocky grinning, basking in the warm sun of history. The Imp vibrates, agonisingly occupying the brink of two dimensions: stasis and adventure. The throng of well-wishers mob the vehicle but I'm in the zone; I can't even hear their cheers and songs. Here it comes. Exhale tension. Inhale.

"This is it fellas – LISBON HERE WE COME!"

"EEEEEASAAAAAY!"

Let clutch fully out. We are moving. The moment. The first imperial foot of the road to Lisbon.

The road to Lisbon. Seventeen-hundred miles of possibilities.

We're lucky if we make it 17 yards before I have to stop. We get as far as the corner of – ironically – Portugal Street when an immense rattling sound makes me panic that the exhaust is knackered. Then I am aware of the young team hooting and laughing at us and I stop – right in front of the local wags loitering by Lena's chippy – get out and unceremoniously sever the collection of old tin cans they have tied to the rear bumper. Everyone is pissing themselves. Christ, what a red neck! I climb back inside and this time I chew the ignition and grind the gears and screech the tyres. Fuck the big meaningful exeunt – I'm offski, and pronto!

We drive towards the main road south, out towards the edge of the city. A bunch of jakeys, who are clustered round a wood fire, notice our Celtic bunting and wave towards us and toast us with bottles of cheap wine. I sound the horn and we wave and raise our communal bottle of *Lanliq* in response. Then something a wee bit weird happens. One of the jakeys, a short man in his mid-50s with jet-black hair and a Celtic scarf steps out into the road and stares straight at me. He has these piercing, sad, intelligent eyes and he raises his fist high in the air in salute. I swerve round him.

"Hold the wheel for a wee minute Rocky."

Keeping my toe on the gas I lean out of the window, right out, and raise my fist high in the air. I see him still there, smiling.

"What the fuck are you doing? Get back inside for Christ's sake!"

As we travel through the Southern Uplands, glowing gold in the gloaming light, the sun sets in a gorgeous harmony of amber and purple and crimson. I take a moment to ponder the meaning behind my gesture. It was as though I was saying, I, Timothy Mario Lynch, will root for the Celtic in Lisbon on behalf of all the millions of Tims back home and dispersed around the world. Especially my old man and daft Iggy.

Christ, I can talk a good game when I put my mind to it . . .

Day Two

Saturday May 20th 1967

The tide lapping gently on the shore. The sea like a millpond. Not a breath of wind. The sun slowly rising over Arran. Dawn breaking.

The calm before the storm.

The players asleep. The coaches asleep. Everyone asleep. Apart from me. Another restless night spent staring at the ceiling. Playing the game over and over in my mind. Every eventuality. The tactics. The team-talk. The players' faces. The fans. The Celtic fans. The songs. The colour. The glory . . .

Inter Milan. Helenio Herrera. How to unlock an eight-man defence? How to draw out the greatest defenders in the world? How to get in behind them? How to destroy them? How to crush their spirits and trample their negativity into the turf? Herrera will be ready. His team drilled to perfection. We have the ability to break them down but I'd be lying if I said I had no doubts. The creativity that surges through my team is matched by their ability to stamp it out. Like a boa constrictor Inter squeeze the life out of teams. It is dull and monotonous, a crime against football; thrilling unpredictability reduced to a tactical numbers exercise. But it works, and they have the trophies to prove it. European Cup winners twice in the last three years. We, on the other hand, are novices. Fitter, stronger, but novices all the same. Our day in the sun hinges on more than our own abilities. What if we lose an early goal? What about the Portuguese heat? Will it all conspire against us?

The doubts. More than doubts. Fears. Huge fuckin' tidal waves of fear. What if it all goes wrong? What if the wheels come off? I could be a laughing stock. All those bastards that want to see me fail. They would crawl out from under their stones. Laughing. Laughing at Big Jock. I can hear them. I can see the fuckin' sneers on their faces. But I cling on. I try to trust the other voices in my head. The good ones. The ones that sustain me, give me hope. My team. My wee team.

Whatever happens, they will keep at it, keep driving forward, searching out new ways to break them down. They will be relentless, dogged, their heads will never go down, shoulders never slump. Inter will have to concentrate for every second of the 90 minutes. And Herrera will have his own concerns. There is a suspicion that his team's best days are behind them. That is why the last half hour will be so important. I will tell the players before the game, again at half-time, 'The game lasts 90 minutes, keep going forward, keep at them, don't let them off the hook.' Then, on the hour mark I will be out on the touchline driving them forward again. When the sun starts to lose its heat and Inter begin to relax, when the thought of a third European Cup starts to creep into their thoughts, that is when we must keep at them. That is when Auld's tackles must be crisper, Murdoch's passes slicker. That is when Gemmell and Craig must start to stretch their legs, and Johnstone's dribbles crush their spirits.

I want to win it. God knows I want to win it. But more than anything I want to win it with style. I want to win it by attacking. I want people everywhere – neutrals – to want us to win it. To be inspired, to remember it. Forever.

Today, a beach on the west coast of Scotland. Tomorrow, Portugal. Lisbon.

The road to Lisbon.

~~~

We arrive on the rain-slicked streets of London with Rocky at the wheel. A city brimming with the confidence of the age, sure of itself in its vastness, in its moment in time. In the brutal dawn, embryonic hangovers and sleep deprivation have put paid to last night's boisterousness. Eddie breaks the silence.

"Give us that bottle over ya bandit."

"I-I-I'll give you it if you address me properly," replies Mark.

"I-I-I'll give you it if you address me properly," mimics Eddie.

"Eddie," I say.

"What?"

"Favourite-ever match."

"Easy. Celtic v Aberdeen, Scottish Cup final, April 24th 1954. We had just won the league title for the first time since before the war. We had some fine players back in they days: Tully, Peacock, Mochan, Fernie; but something had arrived that had been missing previously – leadership."

"You're right there Eddie," I say. "Without Jock Stein as captain we would never have won that league."

"Aye. Anyway, the final had sold out – 130,000-odd tickets – but I managed to sneak in with wee Peachy Callaghan."

"Sadly missed!"

"G-G-God rest his soul!"

"You did him proud, Eddie. Gave that Orange bastard what he had coming."

"So did you, Rocky."

"Aye, but you did the time."

"What's right is right," Eddie says matter-of-factly. "Anyway, what a match it was. Celtic played great from the kick-off, attack after attack, but the Aberdeen keeper was on great form. Then, no long after half-time we scored with an own-goal. But Paddy Buckley equalised straight away for Aberdeen. Apart from that, Big Jock had Buckley in his back pocket. Then Willie Fernie hit the byeline and jinked his way inside before rolling the baw back. Sean Fallon was there to knock in the winner with his left foot. The crowd roared with joy but there were so many folk crammed together you could hardly get your arms up to celebrate. When the Big Man lifted up the cup it felt like heaven had come to Earth!"

The joint is in Chalk Farm. It is a shabby Victorian terraced house, innocuous in the grey morning light. Yet I feel a wave of melancholy – the darkness – wash over me at the banality of this place, the meaninglessness of it as a single address set against the indifferent and infinitely complex flux of time, amid such a vast ocean of people. I feel sick for home, for my mother, my father. I look around me. Thank God I have my pals with me. Just wish Iggy was here too. And that Da was okay. And that Debbie was waiting for me. Wish I could curl up with her right now. Turn my face away from it all. Please, Celtic, win this thing.

My smiling big cousin Nicky welcomes us in his rather tired, croaky voice.

"Alright boys? How's tricks?"

Nicky has a very intense, simpatico quality about him. His handsome face is lined with experience, his eyes are slit-like, his brown hair is shaggy and he is growing a beard. He is wearing sandals and his shirt, cut from a geometric-patterned fabric, is unbuttoned almost to his waist, exposing a hotchpotch of beads and medals.

"Christ Almighty Nicky, what happened to you – did you rise from the dead after three days?"

"You're still as wide as the Clyde, Eddie."

He turns to me and we grin at each other.

"How's it going wee cousin?"

"No bad. Yourself?"

"Grand. How's that auld uncle of mine? I heard he wasn't keeping so well."

"Ach, he's surviving."

"Tell him I was asking for him."

"I will, Nicky."

We are shown into the living room. I nose approvingly at a work-in-progress, a study of a nude redheaded girl lounging on a couch, set on an easel by the window. Above the mantelpiece hangs a large Bauhaus reproduction. An ancient mantle clock ticks away, five minutes slow, alongside which sits a jumble of ornaments. A miniature Blackpool tower, a brass Shiva, a plate with a lurid painting of Cobh waterfront, a picture postcard of the Bay of Naples, a Virgin Mary perched inside an oyster shell with fake carnations at her feet and around her neck, a wind up musical drinking decanter with a rotating dancer, a dusty portrait of King George V.

"How's life in the enemy camp?"

"Fabulous. What a fucking place this is Timothy. Fucking amazing. It's a grand time to be here. Anyway, you still going wi' that cracking wee girl of yours – what's her name, Donna?"

"Debbie."

"Christ," interjects Eddie. "Imagine riding that wee darling! Ya lucky bastard!"

I shoot him a glance.

For a split second Rocky and I make eye contact. I take a seat. We hear the front door opening and closing, and then Nicky's flatmates file in. Albie: small, bespectacled, earnest; Barbara: floral, smiling eyes, cascades of gorgeous chestnut hair; Nicky's girl Margaret-Mary: rotund, introspective, long straight blonde hair; Austin: charming, foppish, quintessentially English. They descend like exotic birds into a drab British garden. Genial introductions are made but I can sense a mixture of awkwardness and scorn from Rocky and Eddie.

Then she walks into the room.

"Ah Nicky, these must be our house guests – welcome everybody!"

Her confident French tones instantly invigorate the atmosphere. Her hair is auburn. It is loose and wavy, and it perfectly frames her exquisite wide cheekbones. It is parted in the middle, then it falls to her shoulder blades and over on one side onto her bosom.

Rocky is quickest off the mark, as usual.

"Raymond Kevin Barry Devlin at your service!"

He leaps to his feet and kisses her hand for fuck's sake.

"But everyone calls me Rocky."

"*Enchanté*. Delphine Marie Robin," she smiles. What a smile. The whole room lights up. Something moves inside of me. Christ, I'm a sucker for a redhead. I'm a sucker for a pretty girl. And she is really pretty. I am surprised at my reaction; I didn't think it possible in the immediate wake of Debbie's harsh truths.

"I am so embarrassed to meet you like this; we have been at an all-nighter."

"Oh really, where?" asks Rocky.

"At the UFO club."

"Who was playing?"

"Tomorrow, Arthur Brown. Have you heard of Pink Floyd?"

"Aye, he's terrific. Good auld Pink."

Her lip curls slightly and she turns away from Rocky. She looks at me. Smiles at me. She is smiling right at me.

"Delphine, this is Eddie," interjects Nicky.

"Hello."

"Hi."

". . . and Mark,"

"H-hello."

"Hi."

". . . and Tim."

She walks over to me. She is walking right over to me.

"You must be Nicky's cousin."

"Yeah . . . p-pleased to meet you."

I take her hand nervously in mine. Don't know whether to kiss it or not, or to stand up and kiss her cheek, like I've seen French folk do in the pictures. So I just sit there like a fud holding her fingers as she stands there in limbo. Fuck. I glance over at Rocky, who looks as though he is about to explode with mirth. I could happily smack him in the mouth right now.

"I can see the family resemblance. Nicky has told me loads about you. You are an artist too? Nicky says you are very talented."

How *sexy* is her accent!

"That's very nice of him. I just daub away, really."

"Aye, he's a *right* dobber," suggests Rocky to snorts of laughter.

One-nil to you, Rock.

~~~

1966-67. We hit the ground running. Domestically, we are rampant. The template is laid down. Every player knows his role, the standards required, the expectations to be fulfilled. Unity of purpose. Fellowship, friendship, systematic success. The first Old Firm league game of the season. Bertie Auld scores in the first minute and Bobby Murdoch strikes three minutes later. Auld and Murdoch then start to take control; keeping possession, spraying passes short and long, opening the game out. Rangers chasing shadows; out-fought and out-thought.

Auld and Murdoch.

I played them together last season a couple of times, but it was in pre-season that they finally cemented their partnership in central midfield. A match made in heaven. Auld, aggressive, dynamic, swaggering, bristling with self-confidence, but not just a ball-winner; gifted, a great passer, too. I moved him from outside-left to a central role beside Murdoch, where he could be in the heart of the battle and get forward more.

I brought him back to the club before I had even returned myself, the deal done while I negotiated my exit from Hibs. The chairman wasn't sure about it. They had history, but it wasn't about personalities, it was about winning. The chairman wants to win more than anyone. He wants to win playing attacking, attractive football. The Glasgow Celtic Way. He believes in the Corinthian spirit, the concept of fair play and respecting your opponent. I share all those beliefs but I know the realities, the harsh realities of the professional game. I know that not everyone shares those same beliefs. There are some who set out to ride roughshod over those principles, who interpret fair play as weakness. My team always sets out to live up to those principles, but they must always have an edge. We need men who can impose themselves mentally and physically when battles start to rage; men who know that the path to playing the kind of football we excel in can be a tough, physical one; men like Auld.

I needed winners and Auld was a winner. In my first game back, on March 10th 1965, he scored five.

"Auld played well today, chairman," I said afterwards. He just nodded but I held his gaze, long enough for him to get the point.

Don't ever question me on football matters. Don't ever try to pick my team. This is my team. MY fuckin' team.

Then there is Murdoch. Cool, calm, elegant and authoritative, a beacon in the middle, directing play like a conductor directs his orchestra; then, trotting off after 90 minutes with barely a bead of sweat on his brow. The engine of the side. He was an inside-right when I arrived. Bobby Murdoch. A bloody inside-right.

I said to Sean: "Can you believe anyone ever thought Bobby Murdoch was an inside-right? We've got a visionary on our hands, a bloody sea captain not a galley slave. He should be in the thick of it, dictating everything with that range of passing. Plus, he's physical. Look at those shoulders, Sean. I wouldn't like to be on the end of a shoulder charge from Bobby. He's no afraid to use his strength. He's our man, Sean. Inside-right, indeed! What a joke. He's a wing-half. I can build my team around this boy, Sean. Just watch me. Just fuckin' watch me."

At the start, the chairman wasn't convinced. Before the 1965 Scottish Cup final, he called me on it.

"Murdoch at right-half? He's not a right-half."

I looked at him and smiled.

"You'll see on Saturday that he is."

Auld and Murdoch. Murdoch and Auld.

I watch their partnership with growing excitement and realise that I can take a step back. Poetry in motion. The team that manages itself.

A season to remember . . .

The anticipation is building. I can feel it. Christ, I can see it. I am standing in the boardroom looking down Kerrydale Street and watching the huge crowds snake up London Road towards the stadium. There is a carnival atmosphere as supporters sway along, shoulder to shoulder, a sea of bunnets, their tones cutting through the drizzle.

"Are attendances up this season?" I turn to ask the chairman.

"Up? Yes, Jock you could say that. We got 41,000 last week for Airdrie. It takes us twice as long to count the gate receipts these days."

"That's good news because we need them. We need them all. This is going to be a long season and the players will need all the encouragement in the world. We can't create history on our own."

Europe. No-one mentions Europe. But I can think of little else.

"The league will remain our priority," I tell the Press before our first-round tie with Zurich, playing along with the myth that Europe is a sideshow, a mere distraction to the real business of domestic dominance. But even as I speak the words, as I watch them scribble them down intently, I am looking over their heads, gazing on some distant European horizon. Silently raising the stakes. A greater prize shimmers in the distance. The European Cup. Celtic has its legends, but we don't want to live with history, we want to become legends ourselves. The only way for a team to be considered truly great in modern football is to be victorious in major European tournaments. That is where the real quality is. That is where we deserve to be competing. This might be the first time we have entered the European Cup, but we are ready. Does anyone suspect what I believe this team to be capable of?

My team. My wee team . . .

The first leg of our tie with Zurich. The Press have written them off as no-hopers. Seven Swiss internationalists in their squad, along with two Germans and an Italian, is proof enough of their quality; as is their domestic trophy haul and the fact that they reached the last four of the European Cup two years before. Their manager, Ladislav Kubala, has done his homework. He pinpoints Auld, Murdoch and Johnstone as the main threats to his side's chances. He is right. They try to stop us by any means. Johnstone spends most of the early stages face down on the Parkhead grass after being sent spinning in tackle after tackle. The early goal we hoped for doesn't come and the game slips into a familiar pattern. I glance at my watch, willing the arrival of half-time. That is when a manager earns his money. I have to instil confidence and organisation. I have to find solutions to problems the players haven't realised exist yet. With any other team that could be a tall order. With this team it simply involves a shift in emphasis. My half-time message is short and to the point.

"Get the ball out wide to Tommy Gemmell and Willie O'Neill. Let's drag them into different areas, make them think, get them turned."

After 64 minutes, John Clark switches the ball to Gemmell, who thunders a shot from 40 yards into the roof of the net. The game starts to open up and, soon after, Joe McBride scores our second. The result gives us a cushion to take to Switzerland.

The plane grinds to a halt on the tarmac at Zurich airport. The seatbelt light goes off. The players start to get their bags out of the overhead lockers, stir crazy after a seven-hour journey from London. I tell them all to sit back down and pay attention.

"Gentlemen, if you are feeling anything like me then you'll be knackered. You'll be stiff as boards and you'll be desperate to get some fresh air. Well, there's only one solution to that. We're going to head straight to the stadium for a training session. Get that bloody stiffness out of your legs."

A gasp of disbelief sweeps around the plane. Their faces fall.

An hour and a half later we are putting them through their paces inside Zurich's stadium. The Swiss weren't expecting us but our surprise arrival has attracted an audience. It must be 80 degrees. The players troop out. They can't even look at me. They fuckin' hate me in this moment. Hate me with a passion. But they know better than to mess around.

They respond to the presence of the Zurich officials. The edge is there, the statement is clear. *We're here to do a job on you.*

"I told you this was a good idea," I say to Jimmy as he jogs past.

"No bother for me, boss. Better than being stuck in that bloody plane for hours."

Our visit to the stadium allows some last-minute preparations. I pace out the size of the pitch and am pleased to discover that it is only one yard smaller in length and width than Celtic Park. That means there will be no need to adjust the tactics that I have already settled on.

We have 17 players in the travelling party. Too many. The Press think that the extra bodies mean we will pack our defence.

The presence of reserve centre-half John Cushley leads one to suspect that Celtic's policy in Switzerland will be one of containment, read one report.

I had a quiet chuckle to myself at that one.

After the training session my secret weapon comes out. The magnetic tactics board that has been gathering dust in my office.

The 6 × 4 board that holds the key to our European success. The canvas on which I can fully express my philosophies and beliefs.

The first leg had been a bruising affair. Zurich defending like demons and kicking everything that moved. Us probing patiently before the two late goals. The Swiss claimed Joe McBride had committed a foul in the lead-up to the second goal. They will be out for revenge and I don't want to risk McBride getting caught up in anything. For that reason, Bobby Lennox will replace him. They can kick Bobby all day – if they can catch him, that is – and he will never react. His pace will be important, too.

I watched Zurich carefully, scrutinised every player, their strengths and weaknesses, technical abilities. I concluded that they were a busted flush. What they showed at Celtic Park is all they have in their locker.

I tell the players the night before the match.

"Gentlemen, here is what is going to happen. Zurich will play the same way they did in Glasgow. They will play their 'sweeper' system. They will chase and harry, kick and scream. The game will be a carbon copy of the first leg. You may expect them to attack because they are at home. But you would be wrong. They will defend like their lives depend on it."

I look around at the faces staring back at me. Furrowed brows. Confusion.

"Any questions?"

Jimmy Johnstone slowly raises his hand.

"Boss, I hear what you are saying, but they are at home and they are 2-0 down. Surely they will come and attack us?"

"First of all, never fuckin' question me. When I ask a question, it's rhetorical. You think I haven't thought this all through? You think I don't know what European football is all about? Remember, I'm here to talk and you're here to listen. So fuckin' listen. And never interrupt me again.

"You are confusing your own mentality with theirs. If we were 2-0 down and were facing them at Celtic Park, then we would attack. But they are not us. They do not have the players to do what we can do. They will defend. Defend like their fuckin' lives depend on it. I have never been more certain of anything."

I stop speaking. The players look at me. They will scurry back to their rooms and discuss it among themselves. They will question me.

The game ends 3-0 to us. I stand at the edge of the park, meeting every one of my players as they come off. No 'Congratulations.' No 'Well played, lads.' Nothing. Just a firm handshake. And a stare. A stare that says, 'I told you so.' A stare that says, 'Believe in me.' A stare that says, 'Don't ever question my judgement and authority again.' A stare that says, 'This is the start of something. Something special.'

"I'd prefer a Real Madrid or an Inter Milan in the second round. I feel we can beat the big shots," I tell the Press afterwards. They look at me. Disbelievingly. I hold their gaze. Raising the stakes. Demanding respect.

The road to Lisbon.

A season to remember . . .

~~~

I am lying on the couch dreaming of her, sweating into my simmet. I come round to find she is sitting in the lotus position on the floor, fixing me with her deep azure eyes, which are framed by Twiggy-esque lashes, teased outwardly by thick black mascara. She is wearing a chocolate and cream silk headscarf which tones in with her flowing summer dress. Her hair spills out at her crown, soft and gorgeous, catching the light in its myriad of hues.

"Sorry," she says. "I just love watching people sleeping. It makes the finest subject. It's the only time that the human being is truly unaware and unselfconscious. And you are very . . . interesting to look at."

"Thank you."

She flips the pad, which had been resting on her lap, to face me.

"I took the liberty of sketching you. I hope you don't mind."

"Not at all," I say, sitting up awkwardly to view the drawing, trying to disguise my arousal. She smiles, knowingly. The sketch is in black soft pastel. She has expertly approximated my dormant face with minimal strokes and shading.

"Gosh – that's excellent; you have made me look quite respectable!"

"Your tattoo, 'Cumbie forever'. What is this?"

"A gang."

"The artist who is also the street-fighter. How enigmatic!"

I feel a flash of tired irritability, taste the dry sourness in my mouth. An image of us stoating around the Gorbals like urban princes flashes into my mind. We owned the joint, stole what we couldn't afford, but never from anyone who couldn't spare it. We weren't liberty-takers. And no-one ever got a doing who didn't deserve it.

"I'm finished with all that now."

"Ah, but still proletarian experiences you can draw upon, no doubt. For your painting."

Yeah, and maybe at my exhibitions they will feed me fish from a bucket.

She gets up, walks over to the sideboard and lights herself a *Gauloise* from a table lighter.

"Where is everyone?"

"Outside, enjoying the sunshine. They've gone to Primrose Hill to play football."

"The great unifier."

"I told them not to awaken you after all your driving. You looked so peaceful."

She throws the cigarette packet at me. I grab it. She throws the table lighter. I gasp as it lands on my loins. She smiles wryly, amused, walks over and sits beside me. I light up. She smokes like a movie star. I choke and splutter on the thick tobacco. I feel shabby, awkward and inadequate alongside her.

"Barbara seems rather taken with Mark."

"The poor lassie. She's in for a big disappointment."

"What does that mean?"

"Nothing."

She slaps the pad upon my lap.

"Anyway, it's your turn now."

"Sorry?"

"To sketch me."

"I'm not great with pastels."

"Well I have pencils next door."

"An easel?"

"Yes. I shall pose on the chaise longue."

She leads me through to where several works in various states of completion lean against the walls and furniture. The room has a kind of shabby luxury to it. Rubber plants festoon the window sills, matching the rich verdant garden outside. Sunlight streams through alder branches and dapples an ancient sofa and chaise longue. There are brimming book-cases, wicker chairs and shelves crammed with Victoriana. A large table dominates the centre of the room, with gnarled carvings on its stubby fat legs, crouching like a prehistoric reptile. An Afghan bong and oriental rugs lend the room the impression of an opium den.

I don't really know what to make of her art other than I rather like it. Most of all I enjoy an impressive work of abstract expressionism, which is simply a series of quite thin vertical stripes in vivid colours over an 8×4ft landscape canvas. When you step back it is really striking yet when you get closer you realise that every stripe has a different surface texture. I walk back and forth a few times, and the image has a queer effect, almost as though it is alive.

I rack my brains and try to think of something insightful to say, try to classify it within a certain movement, try to discern her influences.

I manage: "That's truly fabulous."

"Merci."

"But, forgive my ignorance, I'm not sure I quite understand it."

"There is nothing to understand."

"It kind of just provokes . . . an emotional response."

"Then it has succeeded. It is my best work so far."

She walks over to the chaise longue, luxuriates upon it.

"Would you mind removing your . . . headscarf." I have to clear my throat to remove a nervous, croaky texture in my voice.

She obeys, casting the scarf to the bare boards, allowing her beautiful hair to tumble free.

"Anything else?" she enquires. "Would you like me to loosen . . . this?" she asks, gently fingering her collar, a demure look upon her face.

"If you . . . please."

Slowly she unfastens the first two buttons of her dress. Then the third. A ray of sunlight glows upon her cleavage. I can detect the suggestion of her left nipple. She places her right hand upon her cheek and gazes coyly at me.

I carefully tear a page from the pad and clip it to the easel, surreptitiously adjusting myself within my trousers so I can stand more comfortably.

I pick up a sharp-looking pencil and begin that activity that is conscious yet unconscious, unleash that ability that is innate yet honed by practice. Where does it come from, this need to create? What inner well of inspiration do we draw from? Why is it so compelling, why is it so satisfying?

As I sketch her I comprehend her beauty more and more intimately, like a lover. The way her hair shapes her perfectly proportioned face; the way the extremities of her hair are gilded amber by the sunlight. This amber reaches through the tumbling waves to auburn, then to lodes of pure chestnut. The freckles that randomly decorate her cute flat nose, that nose which, like her large almond-shaped eyes, fit her oval face. Those eyes, light blue and sparkling as the Aegean, framed by darker, arched eyebrows and pronounced lashes. The intelligence and kindness in those eyes, the knowing in her expression. And her mouth, that light-pink rosebud, yet broad when she smiles, to bring it into even more glorious harmony with the overall subtle wideness of her visage. The slight rouge of her cheeks, the sallow skin of her long neck, the profile of which glides and blends into that of her full bosom.

I think of Debbie, feel a pang of misplaced guilt. Then a spiteful thought flashes through my mind: 'If only she could see me now. *That* would show her!'

We start to converse as I work.

"What do you do?"

"Until recently I was working in a locomotive works. Now I've got a new job in a wee shipyard. I start when I get back."

"What do you do, exactly?"

"Just labouring, mostly. I had a welder's apprenticeship in a yard when I left school, but I chucked it."

"Why?"

I shrug my shoulders.

"Tell me."

"I hated it. The place was so bloody depressing. It was where my old man had previously worked, on account of the fact that they would employ Catholics. It ruined his health. I mean, don't get me wrong, I love my da, and everything he did for us; he slaved for us, but . . ."

"But you don't want to be him."

I make a pained expression with my face in agreement.

"You don't need to be. Did you ever consider going to art school?"

"I had the grades, but I didn't work enough on my portfolio."

"Why not?"

"I didn't see the point. Da's health was deteriorating; he developed this chronic chest complaint and he stopped working. Someone had to bring a wage in. It was my duty. God, how quickly time passes – that was five years ago."

"Well haven't you done your bit now? Have you any siblings?"

"Four older sisters."

"Are they married?"

"Yes."

"And their husbands work?"

"Yes."

"Well maybe it's their turn to help out."

"Oh, they are very attentive, believe me."

"Well then, perhaps it is time to think about yourself. Tell me, what is your masterpiece?"

I muse upon this for a moment then plump for the portrait I did of Jinky, using oils.

"That would be my study of Jimmy Johnstone."

"Who is he?"

"A footballer."

She unconsciously rolls her eyes skywards, just slightly, but enough to make me more intent on continuing.

"I did it in the post-impressionist style – I don't know if you've heard of the Glasgow Boys? Jinky – that's what everyone calls him – Jinky is Celtic's best player, and that's saying something because we have a smashing team. He's incredibly skilful and as nimble as a ballet dancer. His talent is a gift from God. I used this photograph I saw of him in a newspaper, it really captured my imagination. In it he is taking the ball past a Rangers defender, his jersey two sizes too big for him, socks at his ankles, the number '7' on his shorts, his expression totally focused on the ball, yet you know that at the same time he is aware of everything going on around him. Painting him was in one way quite easy, not least because of his distinctive appearance: his diminutive stature – especially when compared to the big Rangers half-back, and the vivid colours of his red hair and the emerald hoops on his top. But in another way painting him was very challenging. Because Jinky is an artist himself, although he probably doesn't realise it. He is a wayward genius and a force of nature; sheer, unconscious expression. In a sense that is the purest and most beautiful form of creativity, that which is utterly spontaneous, in the moment, without form. I had to try and capture that dynamic element to him in a still image, and I think that I succeeded."

"Well, it sounds most interesting."

"So, you study at Saint Martin's?"

"Yes. All of us so."

"What's it like?"

"It is fantastic. And in London we are so graced for inspiration."

To prove it she takes me to a gallery. It was set up by one of that mob of sugar merchants who have the refinery in Greenock. We need to catch the Tube to some place called Pimlico.

The vastness of the underground stations staggers me. All these hundreds of people, all determined, all focused on where they are going. I feel as if I'm the only one in the throng drifting aimlessly, my destination now unclear. But I'm also the only one with a gorgeous redhead holding my hand. She leads, frequently glancing back to smile at me, guiding me through the crowd. We board.

"Your football team is Celtic? That is to do with the Celts, right?"

She has to lean close to me in order to be heard above the racket of the train. I can smell her skin cream and I feel a shiver of excitement as her soft cheek brushes against mine.

"Yes. Except you pronounce it *S*eltic, a soft 'c'. We were founded by Irishmen living in Scotland. Hence Celtic."

"I am a Celt too."

"Yeah?"

"Yeah! Can't you tell from my red hair? I am from Brittany. Although we moved to Paris when I was eight. Then London. My father got a job with the *Ambassade de France*. I stayed on after . . . my family left."

"So that's why your English is so good."

"Thank you. Do you mind my saying . . . the way you speak, it is easier to understand than your friends. Scottish is quite a difficult accent for me."

"I suppose I try and speak that little bit clearer when I'm with people from foreign climes."

"But I am a Celt, remember. Not so foreign."

"Indeed you are. I could tell there was something special about you the first moment I laid eyes on you."

"Et tu aussi!"

"I have, therefore, decided to bestow the title of honorary Celtic supporter upon you, even though you didn't know how to pronounce the club name two minutes ago!"

"Merci!"

"Don't mention it."

We emerge into the sunshine. The bright red pillar boxes and telephone booths contrast with the white-painted Regency facades. The place is tree-lined and peaceful. It's hard to believe we are near the centre of the biggest city in Europe. I'm enjoying my sense of wonder and I think she can sense it.

She smiles at me. Surely it couldn't be that she fancies me? No, she's probably just amused by this peculiar species that has wandered into her ken: *gorbalae vulgarus*.

Inside the Tate one of the paintings in particular catches my eye, *Ophelia*, by John Everett Millais. We got *Hamlet* at school, and it's odd, the artist seems to have painted the exact image of Ophelia's suicide that was inside my head. I kind of lose myself gazing into it. The colours are vivid and gorgeous, the scene tragic yet serene.

I look at Delphine. She looks at me, smiles.

"So you like the gallery?"

"It's fabulous."

"You haven't seen many paintings, no?"

"I suppose not."

"But you could travel. To London, Paris – to see glorious paintings for yourself if you so wished?"

"Maybe, but it's hard to get away, y'know?"

"But after all you are travelling all the way to Lisbon to see a football match."

I sigh dramatically. Stop and look at her. Eye to eye. Try and keep a straight face.

"I'm going to tell you something, something profound and true, something you may have trouble grasping at first yet I want you to remember it for the rest of your life. Now don't thank me for it."

"Okay, okay. Hurry up – don't get me all excited."

"The thing I am going to tell you is this: the feeling, that feeling you get when you regard a beautiful painting . . . you can get that from fitba – football, too."

"No!"

"Honestly. If it is played properly." I am closer to her now – glad I brushed my teeth before we came out. "With skill and imagination. It can be beautiful, expressive . . . it engages you. And my team, Celtic, we have a tradition of playing like that. We can be a bit dour, us Scots – "

" – dour?"

"It means dull, stern. Us Scots can be like that, but at the same time we can be passionate, romantic. We are a strange, schizophrenic race. Especially those of us who have the Irishness in us."

As she walks away, towards the Constables in the next room, she throws a smile back at me. She looks rather like Brigitte Bardot, but with red hair.

"I rather like this strange race of men."

I feel a warm glow. Then I think of Debbie and the glow rapidly fades to nothing.

~~~

"Everyone is talking about Inter Milan," I tell the players. "Everyone is talking about their system. Everyone is talking about how they will suffocate us. Suck the life out of us. Everyone is fuckin' wrong. Put all that talk out of your minds. Put Inter Milan out of your minds. We will come to them later. Today is about us. Celtic. Today is all about what we are capable of. Today is about what we will do to them. Not what they will do to us."

We work on team shapes and movement. The focus on the wide players to create, the full-backs to overlap, the midfielders to commit opponents. Not gentle probing. Not cat and mouse. Not playing into their hands. Instead fast, direct, really getting in behind them. Taking them out of their comfort zones, getting them turned. The players absorb every word and respond instinctively. I walk between them, urging, cajoling, encouraging. I feel like a puppeteer pulling the strings. I look at Sean. Sean smiles.

We are ready.

Another team meeting. As I speak, you could hear a pin drop. I look at them. Their faces gripped in concentration. Some even taking notes. Then a hand goes up.

"Boss, I'm desperate for a pee. I can't hold it in any longer. Can I be excused?"

The spell is broken, the players look at me, then at Jimmy. They wait for the eruption. Not this time. I stay calm.

"Aye Jimmy, you might as well. In fact, I'm surprised you are still awake."

He half-smiles, scurries to the door and closes it gently behind him.

"Wee bastard never listens to me anyway," I add.

The players laugh knowingly, and we return to the job in hand . . .

How to cope with a wayward genius. Lesson No.1.
Willie Hamilton snores like an asthmatic horse. It is Friday night and the walls of the Stein household are shaking. Willie is in the spare room. Dead to the world. The wife nudges me.

"You'll need to go in there and roll him on his side."

But Willie needs his sleep. I need Willie fresh for tomorrow. A well-rested and sober Willie Hamilton . . . what a thought. Willie Hamilton. Compulsive gambler. Excessive drinker. Football genius. Two-footed. Quick. Strong. Lethal.

I have been carefully crafting this Hibs team for six months.
"Stein's side can beat anyone on their day," write the Press men.

But our 'day' always coincides with the presence of Willie Hamilton. We need Willie more than he needs us. All Willie needs are the betting shops and the boozers on Leith Walk. A risk-taker in life. A risk-taker on the football field. One destructive, the other creative. Jekyll and Hyde. Mr Hyde snoring away in our spare room. The only way to keep him sober. I look at the alarm clock. 4.15am. Jean rolls over to face me.

"Is this really necessary John?"

It is going to be a long, sleepless night. But tomorrow, at 3pm, it will all be worthwhile.

I did not expect a fanfare on my return north of the border, that's for sure. *Stein signs for Celtic* read the headlines on the sport pages. Four words. No adjectives required. Four words that represented something unthinkable, unforgivable to many. A Burnbank man switching to the other side. The defection of a Rangers man. Four words that would lead to a lifetime of alienation. But four words that also foretold an association which would bring a lifetime of joy and fulfilment. However nothing comes easy. As I said, I did not expect a fanfare.

I had braced myself for the reaction of one side of the great divide, but the reception from the other did not inspire much confidence either. Celtic were then a club mired in mediocrity, their post-war record dominated by underachievement. In 1951 they won the Scottish Cup, their first major trophy since 1938, and followed it up the same year by lifting the Festival of Britain St Mungo Cup. The following season, they failed to defend the Scottish Cup after losing a replay to Third Lanark. When I arrived in December 1951, their role as closest challengers to Rangers had been taken by Hibs. They sat 12th in a 16-team league and criticism from the supporters was at its height. Celtic were in a sorry state and revolution was in the air. The signing of a 27-year-old centre-half from non-league football was hardly enough to quieten the discontent. I was the cheap option, a spare part plucked from the football scrapheap by chairman Bob Kelly. The supporters were not happy. If I had been in their position, I daresay I would have felt the same. So, the boldest decision of my life was made all the harder by the worst possible timing. But life is about making the best of opportunities. At the end of 1951, one path led to alienation and almost universal disapproval. The other led to the mines. Every time I heard a mutter under the breath from a supporter of either side, I thought of the alternative. Taking the first path placed my destiny in my own hands. The second led to the darkness. The blackness.

I became a Celtic player on December 4th, 1951. I arrived as a Celtic player on May 20th, 1953. At the start, I had been fourth in line for a centre-half slot. But injuries to Jimmy Mallan and Alec

Boden gave me a chance. I seized it with relish and had become a stalwart by May 1953. The Coronation Cup final. Hampden Park. One hundred and seventeen thousand fans. Even the Glasgow weather displayed an impressive sense of occasion with warm spring sunshine bathing the stadium. A tournament we should not have even been in. Another season of underachievement had left the supporters disgruntled but Celtic's ability to pull in large crowds saw us take our place alongside the top teams in Britain for the one-off competition.

It had been a poor season for the club so far, yet it marked a significant point in my career. Stepping into that Celtic dressing room had not all been plain sailing. The look on certain faces said it all: 'Who the fuck are you? Some dud from Llanelli? You don't deserve to be here. Fuckin' prove yourself.'

"I'll have these bastards eating humble pie soon," I vowed. For others, it ran deeper. It wasn't because I was a 27-year-old from non-league football. I could deal with that. In the dressing room after a defeat to Rangers at Ibrox, Charlie Tully said: "There's too many Protestants in this team." Tully. The genius. The entertainer. The folk hero. Something snapped. *Fuck you.*

Next thing I knew I was in Tully's face.

"You fuckin' bastard. Take that back or I'll kill you!"

I had him by the throat before I felt his hands on me. Dragging me off him. I hear his gravelly Irish voice coaxing me, "Leave it Jock. You're bigger than that."

Sean. Where would I have been without Sean, looking out for me, supporting me? Something changed in that moment. Respect soared, attitudes mellowed. 'Don't cross the line with the Big Man.' *Fuckin' right.*

At the start of the season, Sean appointed me vice-captain. When Sean broke his arm against Falkirk on December 20th, it was down to me to take the armband. I revelled in it.

The disappointment of the domestic campaign had turned the Coronation Cup into a resolve to salvage something from the season. I stressed to the boys the need to take it seriously, play every game as if it were a cup final. They responded. Arsenal, the English champions, were dispatched in the first game, then we beat Manchester United to reach the final against Hibs. From the rubble of a dismal season, we had the chance to end it on a high. We also had a new face. Neilly Mochan had joined us just a few weeks earlier from Middlesbrough. A big Celtic fan, Mochan's presence had further inspired optimism going into the final. Hibs were formidable opponents. Harry Swann's team had won three titles since the end of the war and played fast, flowing football. Their seven-goal destruction of Manchester United in a friendly game the previous September was a strong indicator of their pedigree. They had it all. But we had momentum. And we had Neilly Mochan. After half an hour, I passed the ball out of defence to Willie Fernie, who slanted it into the path of Mochan, and his right-foot shot from 25 yards nestled in the net. 1-0. Jimmy Walsh added another near the end and the cup was ours. The Celtic supporters celebrated as if they had won the league and I hoisted my first silverware as Celtic captain. As the trophy glinted in the afternoon sun, I gazed out over the legions of fans with their arms aloft. The same fans who had criticised my arrival so recently. *Let it go, Jock. Let it all go.* I closed my eyes and let their songs wash over me, and I felt the tide of scepticism wash away. May 20th, 1953.

The day I arrived.

The world always looked different on the morning of an Old Firm game. I would wake up an hour before the alarm, get dressed and go out for a walk to clear my mind. *It's just another game, it's only two points.* I never believed that. Not for a second. The Celtic–Rangers rivalry ran deep, but for me it was personal. In the moments before the whistle blew I would look around the crowd. I'd see all of them, the men from the Cross, the 'friends' who shunned me, the family members who sneered at me.

Da. My own da. Before every Rangers game. Never a "good luck, son," or a handshake. Nothing. Couldn't bring himself.

Couldn't even fuckin' look at me. Just a long, lingering, heart-breaking silence. Then, Ma kissing me sympathetically on the cheek as I left, feeling every ounce of the pain and disappointment written all over my face.

So I would take in the Rangers crowd. The contempt and hatred etched all over their thousands of faces.

I met them all with a steady gaze.

Fuck you. Fuck all of you.

Suddenly I would be able to feel the blood coursing through my veins, the hairs on my neck rise and my back straighten. I would gently readjust my socks, turn my collar upwards and prepare for battle.

"LET'S GET FUCKIN' INTAE THEM!"

I played in my first Old Firm game on New Year's Day 1952 and lost 4-1. Against 10 men. I did not even shower. Just grabbed my stuff and raced home where I placed my head in my hands and wept, humiliation crashing over me in waves. But success breeds confidence and victory in the Coronation Cup led to a turning of the tide. The 1-1 draw at Ibrox on September 19th 1953 was a sign of how far the team had come. Then, in the New Year's Day fixture of 1954, Mochan scored with half an hour left for a 1-0 win. The team continued to grow in stature and a superb nine-game winning run left us requiring a draw at Easter Road on April 17th to win the league. Mochan delivered once more with two goals before John Higgins scored a third to secure our first title in 16 years. The significance of it was huge. We were no longer a decent cup team who could produce heroics on their day. We were consistent. We were courageous. We were Celtic. And we were back where we belonged.

~~~

Me and the boys chip in for a fish supper to thank our hosts for their hospitality. Nicky walks me, Mark and Eddie down to Camden High Street where the chippy is. Rocky, curiously, decides to stay behind at the last minute; says he's too tired after all the driving and playing football. As we walk away from the house I feel a sudden dark wave of resentment towards him as I realise he has outmanoeuvred me. It was his bloody idea to get the suppers in. To get rid of me for a bit.

Suddenly the sick feeling in my stomach lifts as I hear a voice behind me.

"Nicky! Tim! Wait for me!"

We turn. She stops, takes off her shoes, and breaks into a run to catch up with us.

We amble onwards together, a merry band on the cusp of a golden age.

"Do you fellas realise that Camden is one of London's auld Irish areas?" enquires Nicky.

"Naw, Nicky, I didn't know that," says Eddie.

"How about we drop into one of these boozers to mark the occasion?" I suggest.

"Sounds good to me!" declares Eddie.

The shop is pure rammed on account of it being a Saturday night. Smoke comes over the top of the snugs. A band jammed into the corner table. Sure enough the lion's share of the punters are Irish, young and old. It's a rare wee community atmosphere in the joint.

"You boys fram Glasgow?" says an old timer whose ears and National Health specs are too big for his face. He is propped upon a bar stool and sips from a pint of stout.

"We are indeed," I declare.

"Are yez Celtic?"

"We're too good-looking to be the other mob!" says Eddie.

"Good lads. Will yez be watchin' da game on da television on T'ursday?"

"Television – we're going to it!"

"Sweet Mother of Mercy! Yez are goin' te Lisbon? Pat! Pat!"

He tries to get the attention of the hard-looking barman who has a map of Eire for a face. "PADDY!"

About a dozen faces turn to him.

"Dese fellas are only goin' te Lisbon – te see the Celtic!"

We are feted like returning sons. Pints of stout, wee whiskies, pats on the shoulder. The band even dedicate a song to us.

As down the glen came McAlpine's men
With their shovels slung behind them
It was in the pub that they drank their sub
Or down in the spike ye'll find them
We sweated blood and we washed down mud
With quarts and pints of beer
But now we're on the road again with McAlpine's Fusiliers.

"This is fucking brilliant!"

"Pure magic!"

"The berries!"

Delphine just looks at me, smiles.

I chat with the old fella. He's a nice old guy.

"Where are you from Barney?"

"County Meat'. What about yersels?"

"The Gorbals."

"The Gorbals! Jeezus and His Holy Mother. Pat! Pat! PADDY!"

Again about a dozen faces turn to him, including that of the barman.

"Dese fellas are only fram da Gorbals! God bless ye Tim. Da Gorbals indeed!"

"It's the holy ground, so it is."

"It is dat right enough. I've been der."

"Have you now?"

My blarney detector rises to full-alert status.

"Aye. Stayed der one winter . . . not long after da war, da first one. I'd fallen foul o' the wrong people in Dublin – those were troubled times in Ireland. I went along te Celtic Park quite a few times. They had a smashin' side then, so they did!"

"What players did you like?"

"Willie McStay, Alec McNair, Joe Cassidy, Jean McFarlane, Adam McLean . . ."

Christ, so much for Barney the Blarney!

"Tommy McInally was a great player, wonderfully gifted. He was fast as greased lightning, and had a fine pair o' balls swingin' between his legs. He hardly ever wasted a chance. He had scored t'irty-nine goals da season before, including a fookin' hat-trick on his debut. But he was a loony. He'd showboat, ye know, show off his skills te da fans. Used to piss the manager off no end, an' his team-mates. Maley couldn't control 'im."

"And last, but by no means least . . ."

"Patsy!"

"Patsy Gallacher."

"Da greatest player who ever pulled on a pair o' boots – and I mean dat son. Da Mighty Atom we called 'im, on account of 'im bein' such a slip o' a lad. The genius of da wing. A fookin' Irish poet – 'cept he used a ball instead o' a pencil."

"Tell me, Blarney – I mean Barney, what was your favourite-ever Celtic match?"

"Oh, let me tink now . . . Rangers 0 Celtic 2, January 1st, 1921. Cassidy scored about five minutes before half-time. Den he scored again midway through da second half. Big Willie Cringan was magnificent at da back. He kept da Huns at bay. And McNair – the Icicle we used te call him, was steady as usual. He played more games for Celtic dan any other player, did Alec. But it was Joe Cassidy who stole da show. We went on te win da title dat season."

He puts his roll-up between his lips and begins rummaging

with both hands in his jacket pockets for something, cursing under his breath. He lets out a little exclamation of triumph then fixes me with his eyes, misty grey and glassy beneath the milk-bottle lenses.

"Der's sometin' here I want ye te have."

He presses a little Saint Anthony medal into my palm.

" 'Twas blessed by da Holy Father himsel'. Not his current Holiness, da prior incumbent, an' one again."

"I can't take this Barney!"

"Yes ye can. Kiss it in Lisbon and offer up a prayer dat Celtic will prevail. Did ye know dat Saint Anthony was born in Lisbon?"

"Thank you Barney."

We head out and get the suppers.

"Delphine, I'm sorry if I neglected you in there."

"Not at all. In fact I was impressed you took the time to talk to that old man. It really made his night."

We watch the others walk ahead, Nicky enjoying the company.

"Nicky seems better. Now he's met Margaret-Mary."

"How do you mean?"

"He was always quite . . . brooding. Melancholic. It kind of runs in our family."

"And you think she's cured him? Cured his melancholy?"

"I don't mean cured exactly. It's just that he seems better, that's all. I reckon he's in love with her."

"Love! Everyone thinks they're in love."

"Well, they're obviously very happy together."

"No they're not, it's all the same, nobody is."

"Why not?" I ask, quite taken aback.

"It's not natural."

I decide to eat a few chips.

~~~

November 25th, 1953. The day the scales fell from my eyes. I peered through the murk and witnessed football in its purest form. The most thrilling expression of the game ever delivered. I was mesmerised, even before the first whistle blew. Ferenc Puskás, standing in the centre circle after the coin toss, casually juggling the ball with feet and knees, then back-heeling it to a team-mate. Who were these men? They were the Magical Magyars and they were about to rout an England team containing Stanley Matthews and Alf Ramsey, 6-3. The trip south had been organised by the chairman. Most of my Celtic team-mates treated it as a jolly. Not me. I stood there, amid the sea of humanity, and felt my life changing. I fished around in my pocket and found a pencil and a scrap of paper. I kept writing down the same word: 'Attack'.

At the end of our victorious 1954 season, the chairman announced that he was sending the entire playing staff to the World Cup finals in Switzerland. My heart leapt. It meant another chance to see Hungary, who had just followed up their Wembley win with a 7-1 victory against England in Budapest. Just about every theory I ever had about football was taken to new extremes by the Magical Magyars. They were unashamedly, gloriously different. Puskás' juggling summed them up: 'We are Hungary and we do things our own way.'

Coached by Gusztav Sebes, they were the first team to take tactics seriously. At Wembley, it had taken me until 10 minutes into the second half to work out their formation. By the time I arrived in Switzerland it was clear in my mind. Three defenders, one sweeper and two full-backs that spent most of their time in the opposition's half but were fit enough to get back and defend. A defensive midfielder added another layer of protection but, otherwise, the whole team was set up to attack. In Jozsef Bozsik they had a talented playmaker. Nandor Hidegkuti played as a deep-lying centre-forward and spent entire matches completely unmarked, wreaking merry havoc. Zoltan Czibor tore up and down the left wing like an Olympic sprinter. Then there were the front two: Sandor Kocsis and the legendary Puskás. Hungary ran over the top of teams, overwhelming them in attacking waves. It was so exhilarating it almost did not seem real. In their group games they destroyed South Korea 9-0 and West Germany 8-3. It was like watching a different sport. Their defeat to West Germany in the final robbed them of their destiny, but they had changed my life forever. Wherever I went in football, the image of the Magical Magyars and their brand of attacking football was my touchstone.

Preparation is not all about tactics. It is not all about training fields and magnetic boards and team-talks. It is about creating a spirit, getting inside the heads of players. Preparation is about being in the moment before it arrives.

We are in a small room at Seamill. The players are sitting on rows of plastic chairs. Usually, we would have a quiz, something light-hearted, but tonight I have chosen something different.

"Gentlemen, watch and marvel," I tell them. "Neilly, stick the lights off," I say to Neil Mochan, club legend and now trainer.

The room plunges into darkness and Neilly turns on the cine projector. Grainy footage flashes up on the white wall where I have been standing. The European Cup final, 1960. Real Madrid v Eintracht Frankfurt. Hampden Park. One of the greatest games ever. One of the greatest displays of attacking football ever witnessed on such a stage. A murmur of approval sweeps the room. The players are sitting upright in their seats now.

Goal after goal. Wave after wave of attack. Thrilling attacking football. Puskás, Gento, Di Stefano. Football raised to an art form. Every goal greeted with a cheer. I look at Sean and wink. Sean smiles.

The game finishes, the footage flickers out, the room goes dark. The players clap and cheer.

I stand up. "Gentlemen, it is not what you achieve, it is how you achieve it. Now, get to your beds you fuckin' miserable bunch."

~~~

We approach Nicky's house, mellowed by the stout and the evening sunshine, the fragrance of fried cod whetting our appetites. I consider how differently I feel about this house now that it has gained some familiarity with me. Now it represents warmth and possibilities.

Inside there is little conversation amid the satisfied chomping and Rocky, to be fair to him, doesn't take long to get over being pissed off at our being delayed by the boozer. Nonetheless I can tell he wants Delphine. But he's not getting her. Not this time, buddy. Christ, he fancies himself. I don't blame him. Got those dark-Irish looks and no shortage of patter. I think back to the only time I got a click he wanted. These recruiters were over from Ireland. One of them was a sexy colleen, Mairead. Very intelligent woman. Very feisty. I reckon my knowledge of international socialist struggle trumped Rocky's Plaza dance-floor chat-up lines and I ended up pulling her. His face the next day! Anyway, it all turned a bit sour when next thing I hear they had got Iggy all set to take the IRA oath. There's me running round the Gorbals like a blue-arsed fly, pulling in every favour I am owed – and quite a few others – to get him off the hook. Mairead wasn't too keen on me after that. Said I didn't have the stomach for the fight. She was probably right. I suggested to her that maybe it would be better if there wasn't a fight.

"Would you like to come to a party? It's quite nearby."

"Sounds good, Albie."

"Shall we get a few bottles of plonk out of the car?" Eddie winks at me when he says this and we get set, armed with some of the worst red wine available to humanity, *Lanliq* and *Eldorado*.

"At lease no-one else will half-inch it," reasons Eddie.

The party is one helluva do. It's in this grand, beautifully furnished house in Swiss Cottage.

We walk in, into another dimension. All of our senses are assaulted. The fug of hashish smoke, the hypnotic throb of psychedelic music. A huge white sheet is suspended from a balcony. Weird, abstract images are being cast onto it by a projector slide filled with coloured oils. Other striking images are being superimposed on top of this: a naked woman, her skin covered in tattoos, a bloom of jellyfish, an Easter Island statue, a close-up of a beehive, a Rothko, an iguana, Fred Astaire in a set piece from *Top Hat*, the Milky Way, Lenin, a mushroom cloud, a hundred shaven-headed Buddhist novices in brilliant orange robes, an orchid blossom, an extreme close-up of a gastropod shell, a scene from *The Wizard of Oz*, a troupe of dancing circus horses.

"Haud the bus!" exclaims Rocky.

"Beats the Blarney Stone," I observe.

The revellers are a sight to behold. Men and women dressed in all manner of strange attire mill around chatting or dance almost imperceptibly to the driving bass-line of the Beatles' *Tomorrow Never Knows*. Nobody – apart from us – seems remotely fazed by the proceedings.

There is a man dressed as a wizard, a woman as Boadicea, a Georgian gentleman – complete with blusher and powdered wig, and several pixies.

"Fucking hell. Nobody telt me we were going out guising!" says Eddie.

Two homosexuals mince by, holding hands.

Eddie turns to Mark. "At least you'll feel right at home, Olive."

My peaked corduroy cap, Paisley shirt and leather coat give me a slight air of bohemianism and I find it mildly amusing that for once it's Rocky and Eddie who don't fit in. They are attired like mods from the planet 1964. They talk sharply to one another, but I can tell they are huddling together for safety. I feel a wave of tender love for them, for this moment, for this trip.

A beautiful mulatto girl approaches me. She is wearing a headdress and face-paint that make her look like Cleopatra, and her naked breasts are incongruously pointed. She is holding a tray of joints out to me and I take one. She kisses me, full on the mouth, then regards me for a moment, quite deadpan.

"It's going to be quite a summer, darling."

I notice Delphine is chatting intensely with an older guy, who is incredibly tall, perhaps six foot five, and has gentle, intelligent features. He's aged about 30 and his black polo-neck jersey lends him an even more elongated impression. Delphine is holding a sheet of paper in front of him, which he is examining carefully. I notice they are glancing over at me.

They walk over and Delphine introduces him as Peter, one of her tutors at St Martin's. He comes across as a pleasant fellow with a proletarian Lancashire accent.

"Delphine tells me you have school qualifications. Do you have a portfolio?"

"I reckon all the stuff I've done since I left school would be enough for five portfolios."

"Why don't you apply – for St Martin's?"

"Next year?"

"No, this year."

"Surely I'm too late?"

"Are you over 21?"

"Yes."

"We keep a number of places for mature students. We've had at least one cancellation, I believe. And this year there's no waiting list."

"I'll think about it."

Delphine takes my hand and we dance. We have to shout to be heard above the music.

"So. What do you think about that?"

"Very interesting."

"You think you could see yourself living in London, studying art . . . visiting your little French friend Delphine?" She winks at this last part.

"Jeez. Give me a chance to catch my breath!"

"Come on, seize the day!" she says, grabbing my arms. "These are hallowed times!"

I smile at her. For a moment it all seems so easy. To reach out and grab this exciting, multicoloured world of London. This strange music and mind-expansion. Hot birds like Delphine and cool cats like Peter. Art. No more shitey jobs. Just painting all the time, and getting proper tuition, and getting better and better at it.

Then I think about Da and Ma and Debbie and home and going to see the Celtic, and I come back to Earth.

"I hope you don't mind my showing Peter your sketch of me. It's just that I think it's amazing. You have real talent."

"Not at all, I'm grateful. Just one thing."

"What's that?"

"Do you mind if I keep it? To remind me of . . . London and all."

"Of course," she says, smiling as she restores the drawing to my possession. "Are you enjoying yourself?"

"It's quite an experience."

"Tell me honestly."

"Part of me is fascinated by it, but part of me . . ."

"Doesn't want to give in to it?"

"Perhaps. But I'm not sure that part of me is wrong."

She puffs from our joint, then places it between my lips. We are illuminated by purple and red lights. The dope hits me now. Christ she looks beautiful.

"What do you think of it, Swinging London and everything?" I ask.

She raises her eyes to the ceiling, a little smile formed on her lips.

"It's a gas. Maybe it's even important. And if it's not, then so what? At least we'll have had some fun!"

An inconceivably thin hippie fellow who has posh hair and is wearing a luridly patterned silk shirt is gyrating rhythmically to the music. His eyes are gone, he looks utterly fucked. She notices me looking at him.

"You realise he is tripping? On LSD."

"No, I didn't know that. You ever tried it?"

"Once."

"What was it like?"

"It was a very profound experience. And quite a joyful one at times. But disturbing also. Like visiting the realm of insanity for a day. It was a bit too . . . real. I wouldn't want to go there again."

I feel a tap on my shoulder. It's Rocky.

"Eddie needs a word with you."

I go to find Eddie, leaving Rocky blethering into Delphine's earhole. I can't find him. I bump into Nicky and Albie. I stop to share my joint with them.

"Enjoying yourself?"

"To be honest with you big cousin, I've never seen anything like it."

"Aye, it's good craic."

"Is this like your regular Saturday night?"

"It has been recently. Ever since we discovered . . ."

"LSD?"

"Aye. Keep it to yourself, but."

"Aye. No bother."

"I wish I was coming with yous. To see the Bhoys."

"Why don't you?"

"I can't. I've no breid. And besides, I need to babysit these freakoids. You think they'd survive without me?"

He says it like he means it. He takes a draw from the joint then passes it back to me. We both watch as Rocky begins to swing Delphine round and round the dance floor, totally inappropriate for the vibe.

"You seem to be getting on grand with Delphine."

"I was," I say ruefully, as I watch them scatter two pixies and a bearded giant wearing a kaftan and a top hat. Not that Delphine seems to be caring. Rocky certainly isn't.

"She's a great lassie."

"She's a madwoman!" interjects Albie.

"What Albie means is that she's a cracking laugh."

"I didn't mean it in a bad way."

"I know, Albie," says Nicky, soothingly. He turns back to me. "He just means that she can be a wee bit erratic. She needs a little settling down. Maybe the right man in her life."

"I've gottae find Eddie."

I try upstairs. Various stoners lounge around chatting. I chew the fat with Austin, Margaret-Mary and some of their pals for a minute. At the end of the passageway is Mark, sprawled on a couch, a glass of wine in his hand, with Barbara hanging on his every word. Thinks he's a bloody sophisticate. He looks up and gazes at me, kind of as though he's checking me out. Maybe it's just the hashish making me imagine it.

"Here, Tim."

It's Eddie. I hadn't noticed him sitting with his back propped against the wall, all by himself.

"What's up?"

"Nothing."

"Rocky said you wanted a word with me."

"No I didn't."

"The sly fucker."

"Here, you want some Lanny?"

"Aye, alright."

I take a long draught of the foul fluid.

"Fuck me, that stuff's like pishwater."

I notice another opened bottle lying on a nearby surface. Only a glassful out of it. I read the label.

"*Chateau Margaux*, 1953."

I take a slug.

"Sweet Jesus and his Holy Mother, it's the berries!"

"Best of the century, dear boy," interjects a passing hipster.

I hand it to Eddie.

"Doesn't taste any better tae me. I'll stick with the auld commotion lotion if it's all the same to you."

I peer over the balcony at the party in full swing. I gaze at her from afar. She has donned a pair of Jackie O sunglasses and seems to be getting closer to Rocky on the dance floor. I feel a pang of jealously. I compare her with Debbie. Pretty Debbie: sweet and cute and doe-like. Delphine: gorgeous, clued-up, spontaneous; a woman. Yet there is also something gentle, even vulnerable about her. And I want her. But she's found herself another little boy now. I feel like a tool for thinking I could pull her.

I turn back to Eddie.

"Here. Have the end of this joint."

I leave him collapsed on the floor, chasing oblivion. Maybe I'll go back to the flat.

Outside the rain is falling quite steadily, hissing noisily on the lush canopy. Standing close to the trunk of a mature tree I keep the worst of it at bay. The songbirds are already in full chorus, whistling and chirruping into the late spring London dawn. I can smell privet pollen, damp grass cuttings and the deep spicy fragrance of leylandii. The gloomy, overgrown gardens, heavy, ornate palings and neo-gothic townhouses remind me of the mansion areas in Glasgow's West End. I light a cigarette, torn between my fascination with this place and a wistfulness for home, for Debbie. Christ, all this gloom. I have to remind myself why I am here, en route to seeing Celtic playing Inter Milan in the biggest match of all time. Things start to make sense again. I take a long drag on my cigarette and begin to enjoy the prospect of a new day – May 21st, 1967.

"Mr Stein. How are the preparations going?"

"Fine, son. Fine. Got the boys down by the seaside now. Where they can be together, no distractions. Where I can keep an eye on them."

"I suppose it gives them a chance to bond?"

"The bonding was done a long time ago, now it's just about letting them relax while keeping their fitness sharp."

"Think we'll do it, Mr Stein?"

"I know that we can do it. But there are other factors."

"Such as?"

"The referee for instance. A ref cost Liverpool a place in the final two years ago. They were playing Inter. Bill Shankly reckons they got at him. But he doesn't need to be bent. Just incompetent."

"What else?"

"The heat. The Italians are used to playing in it. My peely wally players aren't. Then there's other factors, the less tangible things. A break of the baw here, a mistake there. What mood your main men happen to wake up in on that particular morning."

"But Mr Stein . . . putting all that aside, do you believe

that we will do it? I mean, deep down, in your heart. Do you think we're . . . meant to win it?"

"Aye son. I do."

"My auld man, he's a bit of a romantic. He thinks that Celtic are – how does he put it . . . anointed. That's it."

"I do believe that there are other forces at work in this world. Forces that we can't see or understand. You've just got to give them a helping hand."

"So you're saying the big man upstairs loves a trier, eh Mr Stein?"

"That's about the size of it, son."

"Wish He'd give my auld fella a break of the baw. He doesn't keep well, Mr Stein."

"You think very highly of him, don't you?"

"Aye. I do. If you could make this good thing happen – the European Cup . . . well, what's the point in saying it. You know it anyway."

"It would mean the world to your auld da?"

"It would mean everything to him, Mr Stein. Everything to a whole load of folk. You realise that everyone loves you Mr Stein? All the Celtic support. They think you're a god."

"Ach, I'm no wanting to hear that."

"But how do you take it all, the pressure? How can you cope?"

"I soak it up. But I'm like everyone else, son. I have my moments. We all of us have things about us that bring us down to ourselves."

There is a sound beside me. It is Delphine. My heart leaps into my mouth.

"Leaving us already?"

I reply with a smile and instantly start angling my next move. I offer her a fag and she accepts. I light it for her in one go.

"Who were you talking to?"

"Just the voices inside my head. You and Rocky seemed to be getting along nicely."

"He is perfectly charming. But a little too much of a . . . man's man for me."

An image of myself in the midst of a gang battle, brandishing a pickaxe handle and breaking heads flashes into my mind. I wonder what Delphine would make of it.

"I love the rain."

"Me too," she replies as she demurely exhales a slither of blue smoke. "Although sometimes it gives me the blues."

"Glasgow is a city of rains and the folk who live there complain about it all the time, but I kind of like it. I mean, when it's raining at least something is *happening*."

She smiles, amused by my theory. Facing me, she steps backwards out of the relative shelter of the tree. Her dress instantly spots with raindrops. She reaches her hands forward for mine.

"Delphine. I . . . have a girl. Back home."

"I know. Rocky told me."

"I bet he did."

"But all is not well between you, no? Mark told me that part. You are loyal to the idea of her but in your heart you know you are moving on. Who knows . . . perhaps even you are going to come to St Martin's!"

She hauls me into the street. Her warm breath smells of red wine. We dance and splash around for a little while, then I draw her towards me. I stroke her red hair back from her forehead and gaze into her eyes.

Then I kiss her, as the first rain of summer sings in the gutters and soaks us to the skin.

Day Three

Sunday, May 21st, 1967

I awake with a start, a knock at the door. I heave my legs out from under the covers and test my ankle on the floor. I pull myself up, grab my dressing gown and shuffle to the door. I open it and am dazzled by a bright light. In front of me is an Italian camera crew.

"Ah, Mr Stein, we have come from Milan to interview you?" At least they knocked.

"Right, first of all, turn off the fuckin' camera. I'm not addressing your fine nation in my pyjamas. Give me an hour and I'll meet you in the lobby. Now get that thing out of my face." So much for the tranquil seaside retreat . . .

An hour later, I stride into the lobby. The reception is going like a fair. Boom microphones are being brandished everywhere. Camera crews are pushing and shoving, trying to get the best shot. In the middle of it all, I spot a tuft of ginger hair sticking up. I might have guessed. Half the Italian media corps has descended on the west coast of Scotland and there is only one player they want to speak to. Jimmy has found a captive audience.

"Right, boys, the party is over. I'll be doing all interviews from now on." Jimmy grins impishly and disappears back to his room, but not before I land a size nine on his arse.

"I'll see you later."

The interrogation starts. "Mr Stein, Mr Herrera has been on TV in Italy to demand that the Portuguese, as fellow Latins, support his team. Are you worried about this at all?"

My mind drifts to the Celtic fans, snaking across mainland

Europe in a noisy cavalcade. I think of the ferries crammed full of them, singing loudly. I think of small French villages taken over by the green-and-white hordes. I think of the choruses of *The Celtic Song* that will fill the streets of Lisbon and charm the locals. Then, I think of Herrera. Po-faced Herrera, with those features that look as though they have been carved from granite. I think of him on Italian TV sternly stating that it is the duty of the locals to get behind his team. He's fuckin' deluded. Off the pitch, there's only one winner. He is in for the shock of his life. I turn to the camera.

"Being part of Celtic Football Club means so much to so many people. If you took your camera crews out into the streets of Glasgow on Thursday evening, it will be like a ghost town. Why? Because everyone will be glued to television sets watching the game. And those people will be the unlucky ones. Because for every person watching TV in Glasgow there will be another who has made the trip to Lisbon to watch the game. All I'm saying is that Lisbon had better be prepared for the biggest and friendliest invasion the city has ever seen. The Celtic supporters will take it over and every local who even ventures out to do their shopping will be enlisted as a Celtic fan for the week. So, to answer your question . . . no, I'm not worried. Any more questions?"

"Mr Stein, Mr Herrera has said that he has arranged for Inter to have the 'lucky' dressing room. What do you think of that comment?"

I smile, can't help myself.

"I think that football is played on a pitch not in a pavilion. And I think that luck is something that you earn through hard work. We have won every competition we have entered so far this season. You might call us the luckiest team in Europe!"

The journalists laugh. I smile contentedly.

"Watch out for the mind games, the gamesmanship," Shanks had told me. In truth, I knew what to expect. The business of winning can be ugly. Where do you stop in your pursuit of success? It is a question that cuts to the core of being a football manager. For some,

there are lines that they will not cross. For others, those lines are mere blips on the horizon. Each to their own. The important thing is to be prepared, have your wits about you, make sure that you are never compromised in your own pursuit of excellence.

Bravely, the Italian press bowl one more googly.

"Mr Herrera also claims he has acquired two of the footballs to be used in the match . . ."

"Only two?" I reply. "We have been training with three for the last week. Jimmy Johnstone sleeps with one under his bed every night. Big Billy McNeill takes his into the shower with him every morning. I always bring mine to breakfast with me and sit it on the seat beside me."

The place is in an uproar by now.

"Thank you for your time, Mr Stein."

"No problem, I'm always available to chat to good gentlemen like yourselves. Just stay away from the wee man with the red hair or you will have me to answer to."

Show over, I drift back to my room. Match balls? Lucky dressing room? Come on tae fuck Herrera, surely you can do better than that. I chuckle as I slip back under the covers.

~~~

The road to Lisbon. Albany Street. Sometimes the sun shines on the bitumen. Regents Park looks beautiful.

Rocky got four hours in his scratcher and assured us he's okay to drive. I, meanwhile, had sat bolt upright in my bed, sleep an improbable scenario as thoughts flickered through my brain like midgies dancing in a lozenge of sunlight. Last night's booze and the sleep deprivation mean I have a dry nausea sitting in my stomach, and it feels like someone has screwed a wood-vice to the lower rear of my skull.

Eddie didn't bother with bed. He seems disoriented as he blinks in the daylight.

"How you keeping Eddie boy?" I ask him.

He responds with an abstract sound that rises from a guttural noise deep in his larynx up into a cheerful exclamation:

"Haaaaaaaaaaaaaaay-yap!"

I feel a bit sorry for Barbara. She seemed gutted to see Mark go. I also felt kind of sad saying goodbye to Nicky and the others. Life's like that, I suppose. Mistrustful introductions followed by melancholy goodbyes.

"Keep it slow – there's coppers about," I complain irritably.

I had anticipated Rocky being jealous when he saw Delphine and me holding hands earlier on but instead he was disarmingly pleasant.

"How's it going, big fella?" he had simply asked with a wink as he chewed some gum.

That made me suspicious. Does he have Debbie waiting for him back home? Did he only flirt with Delphine in order to stoke up my desire for her, hence motivating me to pull her, hence driving a further distance between myself and Debbie?

Shite, I've done it again. Underestimated people. Paranoia. Guilt. This hangover has new complexities to work through.

"Haud the bus – I'm only doing 30 for Christ's sake!"

There is a pause. He smiles. It never takes Rocky long to regain his good humour.

"Ya bloody woman driver you!" he adds.

"Aye, loosen up ya tube," slurs Eddie, passing forward the bottle. He's moved onto *Emva Cream Sherry*. He's evidently on a bender, and I don't doubt he could keep it up until Lisbon. I take a draught and the spiders scuttle back into their nests, for now.

But there *are* cops around, and one of them, on a motor-cycle, has taken a particular interest in our heavily-laden, green-and-white decorated Imp. He motors alongside and

signals to Rocky to pull over. We stop. The cop dismounts
and approaches the driver's window.

"Bit early in the morning for festivities, isn't it sir?" he
says, clocking Eddie's bottle.

"I've not touched a drop. Honestly officer."

It's true. Rocky was about to touch a drop, but hadn't yet.

"Where you all off to?"

"Dover . . . then Lisbon."

"For the final?"

"Yes."

"I'm a Fulham man myself."

"That Johnny Haynes is some player."

"He certainly is."

"Is Tommy Trinder still your chairman?"

"Yes. He's bloody marvellous is Tommy."

"My mother loves him." Good old Rocky. Always quick
with the flannel.

Another police motorcycle splutters to a halt. The second
copper dismounts, starts fiddling with his radio.

"What's that?" asks the first cop.

"What?"

"What they're sitting on, in the back."

"Oh, it's a railway sleeper."

"A railway sleeper – you're joking!"

"No, gen up. Someone swiped our back seat in Glasgow
last Sunday. Fu-God knows why. On the Lord's day as well,
officer. We couldn't lay our hands on a new one in time so we
had to chop up a railway sleeper."

I'm waiting for the cop to get his book out, charge us under
some by-law like the bastards back home, but instead his
officious expression gives way to one of profound amusement.

" 'Ere, Pete," he shouts over to his colleague, "come 'ere
and get an eyeful of this! They've only got a railway sleeper
as their back seat!"

His pal comes over. He finds it equally hilarious. The two almost slap each other on the back with mirth.

"You boys Celt-ic?" asks the second cop.

"Yes officer."

The first copper surveys the rest of the vehicle, the amused expression still on his face. He comes back round to address Rocky.

"Now, no drink-driving lad, alright?"

"Understood."

He checks the tyre, kicks it gently.

"Anyway, I hope you win, lads. Come on. You deserve the royal treatment after giving me such a laugh."

"Pardon?"

"We'll escort you, far as Whitechapel. Railway sleeper! That's a new one. I ask you!"

The cops mount their bikes and wave us off, then accelerate beyond us, taking the lead. Inside the Imp there is a shocked silence. I glance behind me; Mark and Eddie are wearing identical expressions, their eyes wide open and their jaws hanging low.

"So this is how it happened," I observe. "This is how four Gorbals chancers in a Hillman Imp were given a polis escort through central London!"

"And one French girl!"

I glance in the mirror at Delphine, perched happily between Eddie and Mark in the rear, having insisted that I take the passenger seat. Her hair is up. She looks cool and demure in her kinky boots, brown skirt and red roll-neck sweater.

"And one French girl," I add, smiling, feeling so glad that she asked if she could get a lift to the south of France.

"They will talk of this for years to come in the Gorbals," says Eddie, almost in a reverential whisper, as he solemnly shakes his head from side to side. "*Years.*"

"If anyone believes us!" says Mark.

"They'll believe us alright," says Rocky. "This makes us legends, boys, legends. DO YOU HEAR ME? THIS MAKES US FUCKING LEGENDS!"

"They've even turned on their blue lights now!" I splutter.

"Look, they're holding up the traffic for us!" adds Delphine. "People are waving at us!"

Sweet Jesus, what a feeling.

"What about it my china?" I ask Rocky.

"The best, my friend. This is the best of times."

"W-W-WOOOO-HOOOO!" hoots Mark.

"LISBON HERE WE COME!" shouts Eddie.

~~~

What is a manager's job? It was a question I had never thought too much about until one day in April 1955. We had narrowly lost out on retaining the league title, but the situation was made worse by the events of the Scottish Cup final against Clyde. It may have been the first final to be televised live, but it was not one that any followers of Celtic would have wanted to see again. We should have had the game wrapped up inside the first half hour, with Bobby Collins to the fore, but it took until the 38th minute for Jimmy Walsh to open the scoring. We should have built on our lead, driven home our superiority. We didn't, and we paid. With two minutes left, a corner from Clyde's Archie Robertson caught in the swirling Hampden breeze and went into the net. Instead of hoisting the trophy, we steeled ourselves for a replay.

Nothing could have prepared me for the team-sheet for that second game. Collins: dropped. Mochan: dropped. Walsh: switched from his usual inside-left to right wing. McPhail: moved from centre to inside-left. Fallon: brought in to lead the line after a lengthy injury absence. Not so much a team-sheet as a suicide note. I watched the manager, Jimmy McGrory, read out the names, his head bowed, desperately trying to avoid eye contact.

Spirit fuckin' crushed. It was not his team. How much it ever was, was a source of debate, but this selection had nothing to do with him. The dropping of Collins was the biggest shock. Some of the lads speculated that the chairman had not taken kindly to his physical approach in the first game. Either way, it was never clearer that the boss had been completely undermined by the chairman. It came as no surprise that the replay, on a foul evening at Hampden, ended in a 1–0 defeat. As we trudged off disconsolately at the end, I looked over at the boss, a hunched, broken man. I vowed then that if I ever managed a team, no-one would pull my strings. It would be Jock Stein, master of his own destiny.

~~~

The police escort was a wonderful turn-up, yet nothing would have prepared us for Dover.

We pull into the ferry terminal.

"Holy Jesus!" exclaims Mark.

"Have you ever seen such a thing of pure beauty," whispers Eddie. We look out to sea.

Beneath a perfect sky, upon a sparkling Channel, the Townsend ferry *Free Enterprise II* is sailing into harbour, her green-and-white livery complementing a massive sign on her portside, 'GOOD LUCK CELTIC'. Rocky pulls in and we all step outside to gaze in awe at the glorious sight. Then we realise that there are dozens of other Celtic cars in the queues, and we salute each other enthusiastically.

All the crew wear green-and-white rosettes, and hand us a sprig of lucky white heather as we climb up from the car deck. We assemble with around two hundred other fans in the bar and start to make merry. Half the Gorbals is here. There are Tongs too, but nobody is giving a fuck, everyone's just shaking hands and passing round pints and striking up sing-songs. Delphine is feted by the company and catches my eye, smiles over at me. Then the captain makes a Tannoy announcement that he will fly a Celtic flag from the mast and myself and a dozen others instantly dash back down to the cars. I detach our Eire flag, race back upstairs and present it triumphantly at the bridge entrance.

"Well done Tim!" says Rocky as he slaps my back.

"You're a legend my boy," adds Eddie.

"You d-d-d-dancing bear!" says Mark.

We watch the flag flutter up the pole into the gorgeous azure heavens, I glance at Delphine who looks fantastic as she unfastens her red hair to let it billow gloriously in the wind and I consider that if life can't get any better than at this precise moment then I don't care.

I sit on a bench and she settles on my lap.

"Tim."

"Yep."

"You realise that you are beautiful." Her face is rested upon my shoulder as she gazes into my face, stroking my hair. "You are the most beautiful man I have ever seen."

"I have a lovely personality as well."

"Sure. But physically . . . you are literally and utterly beautiful. Your hazel eyes and hair, your delicate, noble features. Your slim, lithe build. You must sit for me. Properly this time."

"That's very flattering . . . if only we had time. Delphine, when you are in France, are you going to visit your family?"

"My sister is in Switzerland for the summer. And my father . . . it is very difficult. We don't get along."

"And your mother?"

"My mother is dead."

"I'm sorry."

"It's okay."

She takes my cigarette from me, draws from it, places it back in my mouth.

"I've never met a man such as you. A man who straddles two strata with such ease. You capture the zeitgeist."

"The what?"

"You capture the moment in that you are a man for our changing times of social deconstruction. You reflect the lower classes finding their means of expression. I find it very attractive."

I make to get up.

"Excuse me."

She slides off my lap, her expression a little puzzled. I stand up and walk over to the rail and gaze at the French coast.

"What is wrong?"

"Nothing."

"No, not nothing."

I turn to her.

"It's just that . . . Delphine, I'm just Tim Lynch from the Gorbals. Lynchy. I'm just bobbing and weaving, trying to get by like everyone else."

"So you wish to spend your life in some menial existence just to comply with some class stereotype?"

"No."

"Well come to London, go to art school – follow your heart." She winks. "And besides . . . I'll be there too." She walks down the stairs.

If someone had suggested this idea a week ago I'd have burst out laughing.

None of us boys have visited the continent before, so the crossing would have been a real treat anyway. We are as excited as a bunch of weans on their way 'doon the watter' for their summer holidays. We eagerly pore over the little roadmap the AA dished out for free. We are constantly going upstairs – 'up top' as we call it, for a fag, and to watch the white cliffs retreating and the coastline of the Pas de Calais getting nearer.

Then, before we know it, it's back to the car deck. Rocky, who is as high as a kite with excitement, jumps into the driver's seat.

"Tim, I'll take another shift at the wheel, okay? Okay?"

"Aye. If you want."

I'm shattered so I am secretly grateful for the offer.

We cheer loudly as the Imp bumps noisily onto French soil.

"M-mind and drive on the right!" says Mark.

~~~

European football is not all glamour. The Marcel Saupin Stadium could be mistaken for Gayfield on a storm-tossed evening. Shipbuilding is the main occupation in the town of Nantes. Football fever set in an industrial heartland. Home from home for us, you could say. I have watched our second-round opponents and am confident.

"How will you approach the tie?" ask the Press men.

"We will play the same team that led us to victory against Hearts at the weekend," I tell them simply. A statement of intent. The Frenchmen are a decent, technically accomplished side, but they have lost their previous four matches. They are no match for a team of our attacking abilities. I believe that. Not everyone does.

"Do you feel your team are good enough for this level?" ask the Press men, their voices betraying doubt. I look at them closely, huddled round the table, scribbling into their notepads. Professional sceptics. Professional critics. The power to shape public opinion, but who is holding them to account? I feel the anger rising.

"What the fuck would yous know about it?" I reply. "The stuff this club has had to put up with over the years. Incredible. I think about yous lot every time I feel like sitting down and watching the 7-1 game from 10 years ago. Only I can't do that because some fucker conveniently forgot to take the lens cap off for the second half of the game. No footage. Beyond a fuckin' joke.

"Every week you fill your columns with shite about my players. What do you really know about it? What do you know about trying to perform in front of 100,000 people? What do you know about pressure? You can fuck off with your deadlines. That's not real pressure. You're no fuckin' fit to write about football. What do you even know about kicking a ball in a straight line?"

"Come on now, Jock, we're entitled to our opinions . . ."

"Yes, you are, but I am saying, 'what are they really fuckin' worth?' "

I am on a roll now. "Right. Let's see what you can do. Follow me."

They follow me out of the Press room to the muddy training pitch. Neilly obliges with a bag of balls. I place one on the penalty box.

"Right, let's see you hit the target."

By this point, the players have congregated at the side of the pitch. The first Press man steps up in his brogues. He takes a long run-up but, as he prepares to strike the ball, his left foot slides on the turf and he lands on his arse. The players erupt, even his fellow hacks are laughing. The next plucky contender skies the ball 10 feet over.

"You're a danger to low-flying aircraft with a shot like that. Pathetic."

Ten minutes later I call time.

"That was an embarrassment. You should all be ashamed of yourselves. Remember, next time you pick up your acid pen to slaughter one of my players I'll be poring over every fuckin' miserable word of it. And if you're out of line, I'll be kicking down your office door. And remember this as well — I've watched every one of you fail to hit the target from 12 yards."

Stein 1 Press 0.

The players sense the opportunity to make an early impression but the line between attacking and being cavalier is a fine one. In 16 minutes, Nantes take the lead and the stadium erupts. Fireworks light up the night air, raining down onto the pitch, and thousands of Nantes supporters suddenly find their voice. I look at the players for their reaction. Ronnie Simpson grabs the ball out of the net and punts it to the halfway line. The Nantes players are still celebrating as the ball is re-spotted in the centre circle. My men are impatient, eager to atone. None of them look to the bench for direction. They know what they need to do. We have set ourselves up to attack and we will continue to attack. Not only that, but we will attack with more determination. Why? Because that is what we do . . . better than anyone. Ten minutes later Joe McBride equalises and the noise level abates. The band of travelling Celtic supporters bounce up and down. As the home side, the pressure is on Nantes to continue to take the game to us, but as they push forward we pick them off. At the start of the second half, Bobby Murdoch springs Bobby Lennox who sprints clear and dispatches the ball into the net.

"It's all over," says Sean. And so it is.

We knock the ball around with ease for the rest of the game. Stevie Chalmers scores a third. Jimmy Johnstone turns on his tricks, bamboozling Jean-Claude Suaudeau in a manner that must surely qualify as a cruelty sport.

Then, an extraordinary thing happens. The French crowd start to cheer Jimmy. Every twist and turn meets with roars. Sean laughs.

"Even the French love him, Jock."

"The French know their football."

The final whistle blows. We are clapped off the pitch. The quarter-final of the European Cup within our grasp.

A straightforward 3-1 home win in the second leg deposits us in the last eight of the European Cup. As the players relax in the bath afterwards, word filters through that Liverpool have lost 5-1 to Ajax. Everyone is delighted. Liverpool put us out of the Cup Winners' Cup last season and were considered one of our biggest threats. The shock of Liverpool's exit is matched by the excitement over the emergence of Ajax, particularly their young protégé, Johan Cruyff. Everyone is talking about them. Hugely gifted ... but young and inexperienced. Can they bear the burden of expectation? That is a question for another time. For now, they serve as the perfect diversionary tactic. Outside the dressing room I keep the lid on the significance of our progress to the last eight. Inside, I remind the players that, while the Dutch are blazing a trail, we are continuing to make impressive progress.

"Forget Liverpool and Ajax," I tell the players as they prepare to drift off into the night. "We have now won all four of our matches, home and away. That is an impressive achievement at this level of football. We are now a force to be reckoned with. Fuck the rest of them. This is about us."

~~~

The road to Lisbon. Sometimes Rocky drives like a clown.

He's aye showing off and playing the tough guy. Despite the fact that the Imp is fully laden he insists on overtaking lorries, at an agonisingly gradual rate.

Up ahead the bank of cypress trees that lines the highway swoops westwards; we are approaching a bend.

"The thing about the Hillman Imp is that they tend to oversteer," says Rocky.

"What's that?"

"When you are cornering the rear wheels don't follow the front ones; it can cause a spin, if you don't know what you're doing."

"Well drive a bit more slowly then ya bloody madman!" I demand.

Rocky responds to this by turning to me and grinning. He then stares dead ahead, raises his bottle of *Eldorado* to his lips and takes a long draught. Then he slams the gear lever down

into third and floors it. Full throttle. I look at the speedo. The
needle crawls pathetically up to 65mph. He turns to grin at
me again. Smart arse. Best not say anything else – that will
just encourage him. The curve in the road is approaching.
He's not slowing. I glance at him. He has a maniacal
expression on his face. The needle reaches 70 and falters
there. Back into fourth gear. The engine complains as we go
in, but the Imp is holding the road. It's not until we are
coming out of the bend that I start to feel the rear wheels go.
I glance at Rocky; I can tell by the look on his face that he
is losing control. In an attempt to hold the road he has
straddled the left-hand lane. In the middle distance a lorry is
approaching, its horn already moaning. The rear of the car
suddenly lurches forward.

"H-h-holy Mother of G-G-God," exclaims Mark.

The car starts to spin. It is horrible, sickening. In a panic,
Rocky slams on the brakes, which only makes things worse.
There are a series of sharp collisions as the car leaves the road
and is punched upwards by the uneven ground. I hear the oil
pan fracture violently. The lorry roars by, its horn a long
descending blast. The flat French landscape whirls around us
as the screech of asbestos against steel ebbs and flows from
the brakes. Had we met a tree or a drop or a bank or even a
ditch at the side of that road I believe we would all have been
killed. Instead we come to rest relatively unharmed amid a
cloud of dust. All of us have banged our heads on the roof;
Eddie, Mark and Delphine have caught the worst of it in the
rear and blood is already trickling down their faces. I feel a
wave of sickness for Delphine. She's my guest, I'm responsible. A protective instinct kicks in.

"Delphine, are you alright? Christ Jesus tell me you're
okay!"

"I'm fine, I'm fine," she says, wiping blood from her face.
She is sheet white.

We clamber out to survey the damage. All of the tyres have blown and both the driver's side wheels are at a funny angle. The windscreen has spider-webbed, much of the lower body-work is crumpled and the boot has sprung.

The shocked silence is broken by a *whumpf* as the engine catches fire.

"FUCKING RUN FOR IT!"

But Rocky leaps over to the open boot and begins flinging our luggage as far as he can into the brush. Then he dashes round and scoops all the precious items from the glove compartment.

"FUCKING LEAVE IT ROCKY!"

"I CANNY – THE MATCH TICKETS!"

He races away, spilling the odd wallet or passport as the petrol tank explodes in a long, rapidly loudening *whoosh*, like someone turning up the heat on a giant primus stove.

We stand aghast, watching the funeral pyre of our Lisbon dream burn away.

"Fellas, I'm really sorry. I just misjudged it."

Hush, now. There will be time for words, recriminations, later. Let the fire burn. Let the dream be reduced to ashes. Let the windows pop, let the tyres melt, let the acrid poison rise from what were once the seats into the forget-me-not-blue sky. Listen as the camping gear crackles on the roof-rack barbecue and wonder where you will sleep tonight. Breathe in the carbon and petroleum as the glorious sun shines down mockingly and muse upon what might have been.

And most of all, try not to scream at the top of your voice: "ROCKY! YOU ARE A BLOODY EEJIT!"

A bit of the Celticade jolts us back into reality. It is the Murphy brothers from Eglinton Street.

"You boys alright?"

"Just about, Dessie."

"What the fuck happened?"

"I think a tyre must have gone or something. I - "

"Don't fucking do it, Rocky."

For once Rocky shuts up. The Murphy brothers sense the tension abroad.

"Could yous shuttle us into the next village lads?"

"Aye, if you like. Or you could just wait for your pal."

"What pal?"

"Daft Iggy. He's about two minutes behind us."

"What are you talking about? Iggy's in jai - "

At that moment - that precise instant - there is the blast of a car horn from the highway. We turn, *en masse*, to witness a 1966 Mark III Ford Zodiac cruise to a halt. Its metallic sonic-blue paintjob and gleaming chrome radiator grille sparkle in the sunshine as *Nowhere to Run* by Martha & the Vandellas stomps from a French radio station. It is a truly beautiful sight. The driver emerges. Four jaws drop. Iggy. The man himself. The unlikely messiah.

As if the situation couldn't become any more incongruous, the passenger door and one of the rear doors open and two stunning young French women emerge. Then a car pulls up behind - a 2CV, and two other French beauties get out. The four lovelies mob the bold Iggy with a barrage of questions and French exclamations.

"*Mon Dieu!* Iggy - what is all this - are these your friends? - Are they alright?"

Iggy removes his green-tinted sunglasses, the expression of concern on his face giving way to a smile once he counts us all as present and correct. I notice a peace symbol is pinned to his collar. The Murphy brothers leave.

"I take it that's . . . that was the Imp?" he asks, in his rather squeaky, raspy voice which is reminiscent of Private Doberman's from *The Phil Silvers Show*.

"Aye."

"What happened?"

Rocky goes to open his mouth, then thinks the better of it.

"Rocky decided to see how long it would stay airborne."

Iggy gazes sombrely at the burning wreck.

"I'll tell you one thing Rocky, it's gonnae take something to get it through its MOT."

"Your car, on the other hand, will come through with flying colours," I say accusingly. "Did you win the Pools?"

"I borrowed it . . . from a bloke in Dover. Just as well for you lot."

"And your court case?"

"The guy whose motor the cops pinched me in . . . he came forward and said he had lent me it."

"Why did he do that?"

"Big Vinnie made it worth his while."

"I bet he did. Come on, let's get the wagon loaded," I order. My tone is scolding, but in fact I've never been so delighted to set eyes upon anyone in my life.

Eddie and Rocky playfully assault Iggy. It's their indirect way of expressing their pleasure at seeing him. Rocky looks doubly delighted, having been delivered in the most extraordinary fashion. As usual he has come up with the proverbial salmon in his mouth.

"Looks like we've swapped one Imp for another imp!" muses Eddie.

"But this is a Zephyr Eddie, no an Imp."

"I didn't mean the car ya tube, I mean you. One Imp for another imp. And it's a Zodiac, by the way."

"So it is."

Mark is crouched sulkily on his haunches away from the group, dabbing the blood from his face.

"I don't give a fiddler's if it's an E-Type J-J-Jag. I'm no going in it," he shouts over.

I walk over to speak with him.

"What's up?"

"I-I-I'll hitch a lift from here on in."

"How?"

"I-I-I made myself a vow. I'm having nothing more to do with Iggy's th-th-thieving."

"What are you on about? We're in France – we'll no get stopped."

"It doesn't m-m-matter. It's the principle. It wasn't Iggy's car to t-t-take."

"Come on to grips. This is our big chance, our only chance."

"No Tim. He thinks he can just help h-h-himself, and damn the consequences for other folk. I'm no h-h-having it."

I sigh and study the horizon for an answer.

"Mark, usually I'd agree with you, but can you no make an exception? Look, you're against this because you're a religious man – right?"

"R-r-right."

"Well don't ye see what this is ya madman? It's Providence! It must be – for Rocky to scud the Imp and for Iggy just to happen along right away, by sheer chance – it's too much of a coincidence. All five of us were *meant* to see this gemme!"

"B-b-but it's wrong."

"It's the lesser of two evils. The bloke will get over us borrowing his motor. We'll no get over missing the final."

He folds his arms.

"An evil means can n-n-never justify the end. I'm telling you now Tim, there's no way I'm getting into that s-s-stolen motor."

I glare at him, my patience wearing thin. He chooses *now*, he chooses *this* instance to make a stand.

"Alright. Suit yourself." I turn to bark out orders to the others. "Rocky! Eddie! Iggy! Delphine! Let's get a move on – Mark's staying here."

"What for?" asks Eddie.

"Fuck knows. So he can act like Ben Gunn and beg for a bit of cheese."

"It's because that's a hooky m-m-motor," shouts Mark.

"Aye, that's right, it's because that's a hooky motor," I confirm. "And it's gonnae remain a hooky motor. So let's follow our individual consciences and say no more about it."

"But Tim – "

"What Iggy? If Mark wants to make a stand then fuck him."

"Haud the bus Tim!"

"And you can shut your face too Rocky, don't fucking start me after your performance today. Look, I'm no missing this gemme because of any stubborn holier-than-thou bastard and I'm fucked if I'm gonnae feel guilty for it. Now get in the fucking car."

They obey, and the four French girls board the 2CV after a brief, hushed conference with Iggy. Delphine seems taken aback by my aggressiveness but I can't do anything about that right now. Mark starts to look uncomfortable, rising slightly as we tumble into the Zodiac. Even Rocky goes quietly. No wisecracks or threats and he has the good grace to leave the front passenger seat for me. Just as well. I am in command for now.

The interior is plush and cool compared with the Imp. Iggy starts the engine. Then he waits, reluctant to leave his pal.

"What are you waiting for? Drive!"

We move off slowly, in awkward silence, Rocky and Eddie gazing behind them at the retreating figure of Mark, set black and featureless against the sunlight, forlorn and probably already half-filled with regret. The 2CV follows us. A mile down the road I am confident we are out of sight.

"Pull in."

"What?"

"Pull in. Here. In this lay-by."

Iggy obeys and the French girls pull in behind us. I light myself a cigarette. I close my eyes and slump down in my seat with a sigh.

"What are we doing Tim?"

"We're gonnae wait here for a wee bit."

"What?"

"Mark painted himself into a corner. Let's give him some time to swallow his pride."

I feel Delphine's hand on my shoulder. She gives it a little squeeze.

A quarter of an hour later. I can imagine Mark's thoughts.

He sees a car emerge at the brow of the incline, its outline distorted as the chrome flickers with light. Is it the Zodiac? Yes. I think so. Is it? Yes, yes it is!

It nears, passes him, then slows down and swings round 180 degrees. It draws up alongside him. The rear door opens. No further invitation is offered but he rises, shouldering his haversack. He walks to the car and gets in.

~~~

Tring Tring. The Jimmy Johnstone hotline. That's what the wife calls it. Any hour of the night. I usually catch it by the second or third ring, in an attempt not to wake the family. Sometimes I make it, sometimes I don't. Many a peaceful slumber broken by the little red-haired terror. "He's up to his tricks again," they tell me . . . my spies. I have spies everywhere. Every pub he has ever supped in. And even ones he hasn't got to yet. An army of informants. Sometimes I go straight round. Overcoat pulled over the pyjamas, driving to some backstreet boozer in my slippers. Sometimes I wait till morning. Wait till I see him traipsing in. Still fou' o the drink. "Work the wee man's arse off," I tell Neilly. And

Neilly does. Neilly cracks the whip like never before. I watch him closely. The deathly pallor. Then the pinkish hue returning to the cheeks. Then the ruddy glow. Jimmy never shirks. Never cuts corners. Jimmy works like a beast. The excesses of the previous night oozing from every pore. I watch as he ducks behind an advertising hoarding and empties the contents of his stomach onto the cinder. Then, he is back into it, barely missing a beat. By the end of the session he is the same old Jimmy. I watch as he impishly nutmegs Bertie Auld. "You're dead, wee man," Bertie shouts, as Jimmy skips away from him with the grace of a ballet dancer and the deftness of a pickpocket. But Bertie has more chance of catching the bubonic plague than he does of snaring Jimmy. No-one catches Jimmy. Not until after dark. Not until the drinks start to flow and my phone starts to ring. Tring Tring. "Hello, Jimmy Johnstone hotline."

~~~

Forty miles on we pull in at a rest spot, which has parking spaces and some picnic tables.

Outside I am hit by a sensation of déjà vu as I survey the surroundings. We get the tanner ball out and start kicking it around. Rocky encourages a few French lads to join in, then dazzles them with his skill, reminds me why he had trials for Clyde and St Mirren. Me – I couldn't kick my own arse.

"Check it out," he boasts as he skips past two tackles and chips the ball into the imaginary net. "Worthy of Boaby Murdoch himself!"

I notice Delphine ambling away. I decide to join her.

The grassland we stand on is threadbare and dusty. A farmer is burning a wood fire nearby. The land is flat, then rising slightly towards a bank of tall pines with ragged foliage which stand majestic against the electric-blue sky. In the middle distance are golden crops. A chalk wagon path lined with cypress trees leads to a thicket of conifers on the horizon. We stroll for a little while.

"I've seen this place before."

"You have been to France?"

"No."

"It could be a van Gogh . . ."

"No."

"Somewhere like it? Back home?"

"No. I think it was in my dreams. I had a vision of it. I knew I was going to come here."

I breathe in deep satisfaction.

"That smell of wood smoke. It's wonderful. It takes me back to a lost time. Childhood holidays down the west coast. Fairlie, Rothesay, Millport. Happy days. Da would always bring a kettle and a frying pan and we'd cook sausages on the beach."

I sigh unconsciously.

She smiles sympathetically. "You are close to him?"

"He's the finest man I know. Although God knows I've put him through the wringer often enough, what with my running with the gangs and all."

I wipe a tear; the wood smoke has got in my eye.

"You know, he fought at Passchendaele. In 1917. He was shot twice and then, when he went back to the front line he was almost killed by a shell. The shrapnel has troubled him ever since. I think he was haunted by all that, the hell of the place, the guys he saw killed. Yet he came back, made a life for himself, a family. Never complained. Now he's laid low by . . . I don't even know what."

"Are you in mourning for your father?"

"How can I mourn him if he isn't dead? He's ill, but not terminal. He'll be with us for years yet, God willing."

"Well that's good to hear. But what I mean is that deep down the idea of his permanence is dead. So you mourn for him now, hoping to prepare yourself, hoping to soften the blow when the day comes. I know; I did it with my mother."

"Did it work?"

"Actually it did a little bit. But my mother was a wonderful woman, so in a way it would ill befit her to ever stop mourning."

"Tell me about her."

"She had beautiful hair. She was very kind. She loved flowers. She was a terrible cook. She was extremely gentle. There was a lot to love, even though she had a lot of . . . problems. She was a fine person. And your father is a fine person too. I can tell because he has such a fine son."

I want to change the subject.

"I find that so fascinating, how a perfume can do that, transport you back in time, so vividly. Like that wood smoke."

"Have you read any of Marcel Proust? France's greatest writer – *a mon avis.*"

"He was the guy that wrote the longest-ever novel?"

"Yes - *À la recherche du temps perdu.* In it he describes what happened to him after drinking a little tea in which he had soaked a piece of cake. Immediately he experienced something akin to time travel, as he revisited a childhood scene. Not just the way it smelled, but the sounds and sights of the place too, and the way he felt. Proust was interested in the involuntary memory, and how it was like a window to the past. He said that things long since past live on like souls, until one day they are resurrected by a tiny droplet of their essence as smell or taste, provoking your unconscious memory."

"That's fascinating. It's just good to know that someone else has had such thoughts. That's what art and literature are about: connecting with other people, making abstract ideas tangible. That's what I want to achieve."

"Who inspires you?"

"Mostly just plates I've seen in books," I murmur in reply.

"Who?"

"Rembrandt, Rubens, Caravaggio, El Greco, Ribera . . . all I need to do now is see a few of their paintings in the flesh!"

Suddenly she reaches over and kisses me.

"What was that for?"

"You deserve to be inspired. I find you a most fascinating person."

Gently, I stroke her face. We kiss for a long time.

~~~

The end, when it came, crept over me like a lengthening shadow. The darkness began to descend on August 31st 1955, when I injured my ankle in a tackle with Rangers forward Billy Simpson. The pain cut through me like a knife. The dampness of the sponge seeped through my socks and onto my skin. The pain only got worse. I hobbled around for a bit, before limping off. I knew it was bad. Months passed, winter arrived. I sat in the stand, huddled inside my coat. 'Keep the joint moving' they said. So I did, gently rotating my ankle. The pain gradually lessened, though never left me completely. Would it ever be the same again? It was not a question I was prepared to entertain. I had to get back, feel the jersey on my skin once again. I made my return against Partick Thistle on December 17th. It felt great. We won 5-1 and I was back where I belonged. The adrenalin coursed through me as I left the pitch but, in the dressing room, a brutal truth awaited. I peeled off my sock to reveal a swollen ankle. Fuck. As I stepped into the shower, I felt a sharp pain that chilled me. Would it ever be the same again? As the months passed, I settled into a familiar pattern: play one game, miss three or four. Even when I did play, I felt the difference. To spectators it was barely noticeable, but to me, it was spirit-crushing – tackles that I previously would have won I arrived moments too late, players I would have swatted aside suddenly stole a half-yard on me. I clung on.

Then the end came. We travelled to Northern Ireland to play Coleraine in a friendly in 1956. A ball was launched towards the penalty box and I rose to meet it. As I landed, my leg gave way and I crumpled to the turf. The pain took my breath away, tears welled up in my eyes, random thoughts flashed through my mind. Jean. The kids. The mines. The blackness. The darkness. As I hobbled off, I looked back at the spot where I had landed. It had been a long journey. Now, on a humble patch of grass in Northern Ireland, it was all over.

From adversity springs hope.

"Jock, we want you to take charge of the reserve side," said Bob Kelly. I did not hesitate.

"You have a deal."

I felt the excitement rising. I knew that I would never kick another ball competitively again, but this was the next best thing. This was my first foot on the coaching ladder. This was what I had been preparing for my entire career, even if I didn't fully realise it. For years, I had scrutinised coaches and managers, noting down everything, coaching drills, man-management techniques, tactics. My jottings became a bulging scrapbook. I soon had to buy another. Diagrams, random thoughts, anything that entered my head made its way into the scrapbook. I kept it in the drawer of the bedside table. Every night, before I switched the light off, I would scribble down my thoughts for the day. Some people collect stamps. I became a football obsessive, soaking in every detail like a sponge. But what were they but words on a page? Just big ideas . . .

Occasionally, I would flick through my jottings and wonder why I bothered. Where was it all leading? As I gripped Bob Kelly's hand that summer's day in 1957, my mind drifted to those scrapbooks, nestled in the drawer. Words on a page. Not any more. Suddenly, they were my coaching bible. The words could be made flesh.

The reserves. The second string. The stiffs. An elephant's graveyard. Not on my watch. This was competitive football and I wanted to win every match. I wanted young, enthusiastic, talented players who I could mould, who would listen intently to everything I told them . . . who wanted to win as much as I did. I looked around the dressing room with growing excitement. Billy McNeill, a tall, fresh-faced centre-half who was simply unbeatable in the air. Paddy Crerand, a tigerish midfield general whose authority disguised his tender years. Bobby Murdoch, a young midfielder with the ability to pass any opposition to death. John Clark, who I made my first-ever signing, a quick, aggressive, thoughtful player with a great reading of the game. I could do something with these boys. I could make them mine. As a recently retired senior player, they looked on me with a mixture of awe and respect. I got in amongst them, got the tracksuit on, tried out new training drills, taught them positional play, got to know their characters. I wanted to work on specifics, build on players' strengths, work tirelessly on their weaknesses. I set up low benches around the park and got Crerand and Murdoch to hit long passes and get the ball underneath them.

"Shite Paddy, again, again."

But those boys were quick learners, open-minded too, and I watched them getting better and better. We would fire streams of crosses into the box for Billy, who would rise, higher and higher, bulleting headers into the net.

Every evening, after training, we would walk to Parkhead Cross to get the bus home. "Mind Clarky and Billy, you two are going fuckin' nowhere till my bus arrives, doesnae matter if yours turns up first. I'm the boss."

Then, when I got a car, I would drop them all off, telling stories on the way, them hanging on my every word.

I would look at them sometimes, their young faces flushed with enthusiasm, excited by the challenges they were being given, buzzing at their ability to rise to them. Then I would glance over at the first team, trudging round the pitch like mourners in a funeral procession. I was doing something right. The results provided further proof. In the Reserve Cup final of 1958 we thrashed Rangers 8-2 over two legs. Kelly's Kids, some called them. Good boys, talented boys. They would go far . . .

~~~

The campsite we plump for that night is rough and ready, which is happily reflected in the price and the fact that the farmer is unconcerned by our recent deprivation of camping equipment. He even lends us a tarpaulin which, by utilising the overhead boughs of two splendid lime trees and some lengths of tow rope, gives us an effective shelter. We buy some old French Army blankets from the farmer. We still have the stove and borrow some pans from the French lassies, who set up their tents nearby.

Mark is rummaging around in the car.

"Here, has anybody seen my g-g-guide book?" he shouts over.

"Aye," says Eddie. He winks over at me, grinning his alcoholic smile.

"W-w-where is it?"

"I used it to wipe my arse with earlier."

"You are *j-j-joking,* right?"

"Naw. And I hope that the one you have for Spain is more absorbent – that French one was fucking glossy!"

The air is heavy with the smell of grass and clover pollen. The gorgeous, golden, sunny, confectionary smell of the lime blossom drifts downwards as our excited chatter floats up into the branches and the songbirds begin their evening debate.

Mark, who is an experienced camper, is in his element

organising all of this. Eddie is tickled by Mark's rustic mode.

"Mark - you're the camping expert, right enough," observes Rocky.

"He's the expert at being camp, more like!" says Eddie.

Mark gets a fire going, and we lounge around it, bevvying. Iggy canoodles with Céleste, a rather fetching little brunette with short hair like Joan of Arc, while in the river Rocky shows off to Delphine and the other French lassies, swinging from a tyre swing and landing in the depths with an almighty splash.

Eddie is already half-jaked, topping up his day's intake with some revolting homemade wine the farmer's wife gave us. He is the only one who is able to stomach it.

For all Iggy isn't, shall we say, classically handsome, a lot of birds seem to go for him, I think partly because he doesn't chase after them too much. Maybe they like to mother him, maybe they find his vulnerable quality irresistible. Céleste plays with his hair as he lies on the grass. Then she gets up and walks over to join her pals for a swim in the river.

Eddie is perplexed, ogling the frolicking females from afar.

"Christ help me, I can't get that Josephine bird's diddies out of my mind. I just can't get over them. They are . . . perfection! What a size, as well - like ripe melons!" He turns to face Iggy. "And that Céleste's no bad neither. How come a wee monkey like you gets to pull a lovely big bird like that?"

Eddie's monkey accusation is somewhat hypocritical. His own squat, strong body is ill-proportioned; the legs too short, the arms too long. His big chin adds to the simian impression.

"I have a magnetic personality."

"You're a spawny wee bastard more like."

"Did I ever tell you how I got to be so wee?"

"Was your coal man a small fellow?"

"It was the Luftwaffe's fault."

"Shite."

"Are you serious, Iggy?" I ask, intrigued.

"Gen up! They had a big air raid, when my family was staying in the Calton. Quite a few people were killed that night; my auld man had to pull bodies out of the rubble. Anyway, a bomb hit our tenement – the same block Saint Alphonsus chapel is on, and brought on my mother's labour six weeks early."

"And that meant you turned out to be a short-arse?" asks Eddie, incredulously.

"Aye! Ever since I've been small but perfectly formed."

"Is th-th-that true, Iggy? Did an air raid really bring on your b-b-birth?" asks Mark.

"Aye. I emerged kicking and screaming into a world of explosions and fumes."

"And it's been full of explosions and fumes ever since," grins Rocky, who has returned from the river.

"Honest to Christ, Iggy, you don't half come out with some shite," says Eddie.

I steal a look at him, try to gauge how bad his drinker face is. Then I look at Iggy, his expression totally benign. He's like that, is Iggy. Never gets that pissed off with folk. Always sees the best in them. A real mellow fellow. Wish I could be a bit more like that.

"Iggy. Your favourite-ever gemme," I interject.

Iggy ponders this for a moment.

"Can I have three – no, four!"

"Away you go!" says Eddie. "You only get one ya tube."

"Aye, Iggy. Just the one."

"To be honest I'd have to say the quarter-final against Vojvodina, in March."

"Are you joking? That was the worst experience of my entire life!" says Eddie. "The *tension*."

"I know, I know. I know it was tense. But I just had this wee feeling."

"You *always* say that!"

"No, really Eddie, I did! And all that tension was worth it, for the way it ended. They were a great side, big and strong, and of course we were a goal down from the away leg. After nearly an hour, we finally scored."

"Stevie Chalmers!" chips in Eddie.

"One singer one song," chides Rocky.

"Aye, Stevie Chalmers, after their keeper Pantelic had flapped at the cross," continued Iggy. "Then, attack after attack after attack. But Vojvodina were well-organised, hard to break down." Iggy's voice has lowered to little more than a whisper. He has captivated his audience, even though we all know the ending. "Then, in a last-gasp attempt, we force a corner. Charlie Gallagher sends over a peach and big Billy is there to banjo it into the net with his head. Oh what *joy!* That was worth it. That was worth all the tension. In fact, that made all the shite we've had to put up with over the years worthwhile."

"Well telt Iggy," says Rocky. "What a night."

"What a bevvy afterwards!" recalls Eddie.

"It was th-th-then, after that match, that we knew we'd make L-L-Lisbon," says Mark. "Dukla in the semi were tough, we knew they had M-M-Masopust, but once we had beaten V-V-V-Vojvodina I knew we'd be okay."

"You know what boys," I say. "That was another glimpse of the genius of Big Jock. He organised a friendly with Dinamo Zagreb, just so that we could get a feel for Yugoslavian football. We lost it 1-0 but that didn't matter. Big Jock had gained knowledge and insight."

"Mind Real v Eintracht?" says Iggy.

"Mind it!" exclaims Eddie. "It was the greatest game ever played on British soil."

We Glaswegians have revered the European Cup ever since Real Madrid came to town in 1960. Me and the boys – all of us – were there. It was truly an honour to watch Alfredo di Stefano, Ferenc Puskás and José Santamaria destroy Eintracht Frankfurt 7-3, and lift the trophy for the fifth time in succession.

"To emulate that mighty Real," says Iggy. "Just think!"

We all nod in sombre agreement. It feels great being together. The five of us.

I watch Delphine come out of the river, dry herself, head into one of the tents and emerge a minute later, wearing a dress now. The other boys can't see her from where they are seated. Barefooted she walks across the meadow, never so much as glancing over at me but I can feel the signal, like telepathy. I drain my can of heavy and make a show of being casual.

" 'Scuse me lads, I can feel the call of nature."

The evening sun has bathed a thicket of pine trees in gorgeous amber. Every fragment of bark, every needle is exulted by the weird light. The trees cast fantastic shadows into a secluded glade, where I sit down on a soft bed of moss. I can smell the sweet hint of wild strawberries, the cool odour of mint and the freshness of nettles.

I reach up for her, as a kite whirls above in the thermals. She takes my hand.

~~~

"Do you ever wonder about life, Sean?"

"What do you mean, Jock?"

"I mean what it's all about? Do you ever wonder about the world and your place within it? When you question if where you are is where you are meant to be? I do. I wonder about all those things. I wonder if it is right to be so obsessed with one thing. I went out for dinner with Jean last week. We went to a lovely restaurant, just the two of us. God knows we don't spend enough time together. I sat there looking into her eyes. Into the eyes of the woman I loved, the mother of my children, and you know what I was thinking, Sean?"

"No, Jock, what were you thinking?"

"I was thinking about Jimmy Johnstone and what the wee bastard was up to at that precise moment. Then I wondered how Bobby Lennox's hamstring was doing and if big Billy was in his bed yet. I mean, that's not right, Sean, to be that consumed by something. I spend more time with my players than I do with my own children. I see more of your ugly mug than I do my wife. That bothers me. Football is my life, but surely there's more?"

"Aye, there is more to life, but do you not sometimes think that your choice has been made for you?"

"Aye, Sean, I know what you are saying. I'm not a religious man, but I feel, somehow, that what I am doing is like a calling. There's the parable in the Bible about the three servants who are given talents by their master. Two of them invest their talents wisely and multiply them. The other one buries his talent in a hole in the ground. When the master returns, he looks favourably on the ones who have invested them, and punishes the servant who buried his. That story always stuck with me. Everybody has their own unique talents. Some men build bridges, some build ships. Me, I build football teams. Then there is the realisation that I build them better than most. So what do you do? I've asked myself that question at every point in my career. I could have stayed at Dunfermline. I had turned the club around, taken them to new heights, even had some success in Europe. The club was buzzing again. I had a cosy life. I could have picked the kids up from school every day and spent lots of time with the wife. But what about the talent? So I went to Hibs and I was successful again. Bigger club, better players, more fans, more pressure. I handled it all. I flourished, and so the same question comes round again. Is this enough for me, or should I be taking it to another level? Am I burying my talent in that hole in the ground? So I take it even further, push the boundaries again. I join Celtic and it's the same again, a bigger stage and more success. Then, Europe, and I have the chance to really make a mark, to write my name into football history, to do something that no British team has ever done before. And so here I am, sitting in a hotel on the west coast of Scotland, on the edge of something memorable, something truly historic. And I'm sitting here thinking that this is my destiny, everything which has gone before has led to this moment. And I love that feeling, I cherish it, I let it fill my senses and course through my veins. Then I think of Jean, and the kids. I think of the birthdays I've missed, the thousands of moments that I will never get back. I look in the mirror sometimes and I see an absent father, a neglectful husband . . . then I wonder, 'Has it all been worth it?' It's a fuckin' terrible price to pay, Sean."

"Aye, Jock, but remember, this is not all about you. There's more to it than that."

"That's the one thing that consoles me, Sean. Football is my life, but it is also my passion. Not many men are privileged enough to find their passion in life. And mine's is not a private passion. It is the most public of passions. My actions impact on people's lives. Don't get me wrong, I enjoy basking in the glory. The old ego likes a stroke from time to time. People see you as a god-like figure. They worship you, but that's not why I do it. I do it because I know what football means to people. I appreciate its place in society. Football is the centre of people's lives. It gives it meaning. Life is hard, particularly for the working classes, and football is their game, it is a light in their lives. To play a part in that is something special."

"And it's about Celtic, too, Jock . . ."

"Aye, Sean, it is. It's about Celtic, too. More than anything, maybe, it is about Celtic. Life is strange. You find acceptance in the strangest of places. I never thought it was possible that a Burnbank man like me could have ended up on this journey. But here I am. It teaches you a lot about life, about what acceptance really means. It is easy to accept someone who is the same colour or religion as yourself. That's not real acceptance. It's when you are forced to deal with difference, asked to think different thoughts, that's when the process of acceptance starts. I fuckin' love beating the Rangers. That feeling will never leave me, but it's about more than that now. I don't feel the need to prove points any more. Those days are gone. That's why it all comes back to this moment in time. This is us, taking on the cream of Europe. You think anyone in France, or Yugoslavia or Italy cares about religious differences in the West of Scotland? They would laugh in our faces. This journey is bigger than all of that. It is not about 'them' and 'us'. It is only about us. Maybe one day there will be no 'them' and 'us'. That's some thought, eh, Sean?"

"Aye, Jock, it's some thought right enough. But let's not hold our breaths."

"Don't worry, Sean, I'm a realist. I know the score, but I also know something else. We have a football match to win and it is high time we got to our scratchers."

~~~

She leans her head upon my chest, my breathing slowing now. I sigh inwardly with contentment, rid of my mind, savouring the moment. In the distance I can hear the others party round the fire, singing approximate lyrics to *A Whiter Shade of Pale* which crackles from the Zodiac's wireless.

"I feel like I understand you. I feel like we've . . . got a connection." She raises her head for a moment and looks directly at me. "Do you feel that? Like we have a connection?"

"Sure."

"I feel as though I want to look after you," she says.

"Why?"

"Because it's as though . . . somewhere inside you, you don't think you are . . . worthy."

"Worthy of what?"

"Of happiness. Of me."

She turns away, fumbles in her bag. She is silhouetted, downing something.

"What's that?"

"Nembutal. To help keep the demons at bay."

She leans her head on my chest again.

"Perhaps I also need looking after," she adds.

She traces her fingers along the scar tissue on my neck, a thoughtful expression upon her face.

"Did somebody hurt you?"

"The Tongs – a rival gang – put the chase on me. I fell through a skylight."

"When did you decide to . . . get out?"

"Not that long ago."

I close my eyes and remember that Indian summer's day, eight months past . . .

. . . The street ahead is deserted. Silent except for the low rumble of our boots. We pass the Four Crowns for courage. Suddenly an empty ginger tin sails through the sunshine and clatters across the bitumen. A nervous flutter in my belly, I have to clench as my bowel threatens to turn to water.

Out of the depths I cry to Thee, O Lord. Lord hear my voice! O let Thy ears be attentive to the voice of my supplication.

Thank God Iggy isn't here, it's enough just worrying about myself. We all instinctively look up the side street but it's just fleeing wee kids playing at being tough guys. I glance around me, at a hundred of my Cumbie comrades and I feel better. Proud. Then a wee bit embarrassed at having felt scared. No-one else seems scared, or at least they're not showing it. Two hundred yards ahead a shopkeeper nervously pulls down the shutters before scuttling inside, dragging a Lyon's Maid sign with him. No-one speaks, which heightens the tension hanging in the air. Is this real? Are we imagining this danger? What is all of this *for*?

The sense of unreality is shattered by the ambush. Our scouts have failed us; we had no warning of the imminent attack. A fusillade of bottles shatter on the ground, then their infantry charges. Score upon score of them emerge from close mouths and they are not short of front. "COME AHEAD YA FENIAN BASTARDS!" Another team has boldly marched into their bit – bad enough. But even worse – 100 times worse – we are Tims on our way to Celtic Park; and for an Old Firm game, no less. And this the bluest, Orangeist of Hun areas, with the fiercest Prod gang in the entire city. They knew we were coming. We knew they would know we were coming. There was no danger we would take the roundabout route, no danger we would go a half mile out of our way to the Gallowgate when we could simply march directly up over the bridge and up Main Street towards the holy ground, towards Paradise.

"CUMBIE YA BAS!"

If you, O Lord, should mark our guilt, Lord, who would survive?

But with you is found forgiveness:

For this I revere you.

We meet like opposing armies. Us versus them. Wallace versus the English. Jacobites versus Redcoats. The sounds of combat would make a hard case lose sleep. Whacks and smashes and thumps and clangs and sighs and moans and shouts and yells.

My soul is waiting for the Lord more than a watchman for daybreak

I choose my man. He's smaller than me but he's gemme and he's tooled up good – a hatchet. But so am I. Out comes the pickaxe handle from under the Crombie. I've got a long reach and this is a long weapon. Means you can keep anything sharp from getting too close. Don't want to end up looking like one of those stitched-together guys. Coupons like roadmaps. I swing and swing and swing. I miss but it unnerves the wee cunt. He's not so brave now. The next swing disarms him. The next one glances off his back as he beats a retreat. I get my bearings. More and more Derry are pouring into the medieval mix. Where are they all coming from? I have to clench again. Then I remember. We are Cumbie. Pure mad mental. We never lose. We never run away. I won't let my pals down.

Let the watchman count on daybreak and Israel on the Lord

So I face the foe, my blood up now, a battle cry on my lips as I step forward, swing, step forward, swing. All that nervous energy has transformed into adrenalin and I'm driving the bastards away, swatting them like flies. In the midst of battle champions are born and I am already a heid-the-baw, a man to be reckoned with. *Whoosh, clunk* as I break heads.

We are winning.

Israel indeed will He redeem from all its iniquity.

Thrash, bonk. Your fathers helped break the General Strike, then swelled the ranks of the Blackshirts in the 30s. *Swish, thunk.* Four generations of Irishmen despised and oppressed. *Swoosh, crack.*

They are starting to do a runner. They are defeated. And on their own turf as well.

Glory be to the Father, to the Son and to the Holy Spirit.

The Red Van has already emptied of coppers before I even realise its arrival. The shout had gone up but I was in a different dimension. I'm coming to now, rushing back into consciousness. My enemies lie stricken at my feet, cradling their bloodied heads, and as I look upon this scene the adrenalin rapidly ebbs and the familiar sickness floods the pit of my stomach. The darkness. Self-righteousness gives way to self-disgust. At this precise moment I know: I can't do this again – ever. I don't care who's in the right any more, I can't do *this*. The polis want the main men; they want me. No fucking way. I am off like a bullet, hurdling walls and tip-toeing along dykes and tearing through closes and dodging motors and leaping fences. Almost spent, I stagger by a tenement midden and am halted by a voice.

"Tim!"

It is Rocky. Unselfconsciously we embrace, panting for oxygen. Our breathing gradually slows. I am shivering with spent exhilaration and the relief that follows trauma. Rocky lights me a cigarette. Hands it to me. We are like comrades in arms back in the trench after a patrol. I take a long draw from the fag and we smoke in silence.

We team up with most of the boys at our usual spot at the back of the Jungle. But Eddie and big Vinnie and Coco all got lifted, and a wheen of others. Eddie could get sent down, what with his record. The atmosphere is terrific, the tension almost unbearable and I'm drained of emotional energy. The special hatred that is the Old Firm. Eighty-thousand voices screaming for victory. The noise, the communal one-upman-ship, the tribal formalities, the bravado. But underneath it lurks the horror at the very idea of losing to them, and everything spiteful and rotten that they stand for. I look upon their ranks massed in the away end, tinged with royal blue, and feel a pang of repulsion. A club that refuses to employ a Catholic in any capacity *as a mark of honour*. Nonetheless I can't help but secretly wonder: what makes them tick? They are still people, after all. What makes them be like *that*?

Thank fuck we got in on time. It's all over within four minutes. Bertie and Boaby. Only the second fixture of the league campaign but already we can sense it: this season is going to be something special. Stein has got them motoring. They aren't just cavalier and entertaining; at last they have become so dynamic, so incisive. I can't stop thinking of a certain date: May 15th, 1963. Scottish Cup final replay. Celtic 0 Rangers 3. We melted away before the whistle. Celtic supporters. We melted away. Skulked off. But enough was enough. To be so utterly and completely defeated yet again, to feel that now familiar feeling of total dejection, to have to endure even more of their triumphalist bile; it was just unbearable. It all seemed so permanent, so never-ending. The Huns were so strong. Nil-three. How do we come back from this? Year upon year of pish, the club utterly rudderless, the fucking chairman still picking the team!

Then the Big Man arrived. Stein. And everything would change. Everything. Starting with the '65 cup final against Dunfermline. It was the opposite of the '61 final, when Stein managed the Pars and they did us over. Take heed. Stein did us. Welcome him back into the fold. He's a Prod but the fans don't give a fuck. They've cheered plenty of Prods since day one. Leave the bigotry to the Huns. Stein is a Celtic man through and through. Loves the club. Cut him and he bleeds green. But more than that, he knows what to do. He's a leader, a reader of the game, a tactical genius, a motivator. Sign him up and be done with it.

Outside Celtic Park I make a bold statement but one that I instinctively believe to be true: "This is the best side Rangers have ever fielded and they are gonnae have to get used to second place. Fucking enjoy it, chaps."

The euphoria of the goals helps me forget the violence for now. However, deep down I know that it will come back to haunt me in the dead of night. Deep down I know that I can't do that stuff any more. But how does a fella get out? Seems like everyone I know is part of the deal . . .

. . . Delphine gently places a lit cigarette to my lips. She lights one for herself. We smoke silently. Then we get up and wander through the shadows back to the camp.

Day Four

Monday, May 22nd, 1967

I am awoken by the fine smell of the last of our Gorbals hamper – square sausage and white pudding – frying merrily alongside eggs and bread bought from the farmer.

Mark has taken charge.

"M-m-morning darling!" he says cheerfully as he hands me a mug of strong tea.

"Thanks Mark. Good night?"

"M-m-magic. What a laugh we had round the fire. Some of us went skinny-dipping in the m-m-moonlight."

Eddie comes to life with a series of hacks and returns our greetings with a grunt. He looks upon the coming day with mild dejection, then lights a cigarette and immediately coughs violently. His hair looks as though it has been fashioned from steel wool and his face is florid with bad living.

"Then Rocky got off with that J-J-Josephine bird," adds Mark, glancing over at Eddie.

"Harry Hoofter," murmurs Eddie, half under his breath.

"W-w-what was that?" asks Mark.

Eddie doesn't respond except with a familiar *spark* sound as he opens his first beer of the day.

"Where's Iggy?" I ask.

"He went away for a w-w-walk by the river last time I saw him," replies Mark. "He wasn't looking too c-c-clever."

I wolf down my fry-up, pull on my trousers and jersey, and

survey the morning. The girls are all bathing in the river, their squeals testament to the temperature of the water. I light up my first fag, usually the best one of the day, but this morning I have a vague sense of unease. The sun moodily refuses to dispel the haar. Something doesn't augur well.

"I'll go and see if Iggy's okay."

I find him spewing his ringer into a little irrigation ditch. He looks deathly pale and utterly wrung out.

"What have I telt you about bevvying too much?"

"I know," he manages, between *baarfs*. "God forgive me, I'd commit murder for a drink of Bru."

"You can't handle it ya dumpling. There's no shame in that. You just need to accept your limits."

"I know. I just got carried away. I was enjoying myself too much. *Baaaaarf.*" He looks up at me and smiles thinly, his eyes moist. "You'd think I'd be old enough in the tooth to have learned by now, eh big fella?"

He leans over again. I look at his bent-double profile. Poor wee bastard. The vomiting subsides.

"Here, I brought you some water."

I coax the bottle towards his mouth. He takes a few sips, then sits on the edge of the ditch.

"You'll be alright in a minute. And don't worry, I'll drive. Now when you feel a wee bit better get Mark to make you a cup of strong, sweet tea. And see if you can hold down some dry breid or something."

He nods his head at me, his big brown eyes full of gratitude.

I use some of the water to brush my teeth, then I leave him and head further down the river, out of sight of the others. A slight breeze brings the cooler air, which has been sitting above the water, gently towards me. It smells refreshing. I undress and roughly lather myself in carbolic. Then I tentatively tiptoe into the water, and immerse myself fully beneath the surface. I keep my head submerged for a while. The coldness shocks the darkness from my consciousness; I find stillness within the roaring moving water. As I dry myself on the bank I feel invigorated. A pair of songbirds chatter to each other in the adjacent meadow. I think warmly upon last night and wonder if today isn't going to be so bad after all.

"You'll be arrested if you're no careful."

It is Rocky. He is perched upon the exposed roots of a willow tree a little further along the bank, languidly smoking a cigarette. His eyes are obscured by his Wayfarers so I can't read his expression.

"At least I'll be nice and clean for court!"

There is a lull, an unnatural awkwardness between two people who are so familiar to each other. The silence is loaded with portent, with anticipation. I feel a flutter of butterflies as I pull on my underpants and trousers. He takes off his sunglasses. I can see his eyes now.

"Delphine told me you're thinking about going to London, for art school?"

"It's just a daft idea. It'll likely come to nothing."

"This 'cause you split with Debbie?" he asks, squashing the fag butt into the earth with his shoe.

"We haven't split . . . or at least, I'm gonnae win her back."

"Maybe you think you're too good to work for a living."

"Naw."

"Well what then? You think we're all chumps, graftin'? Think we get a buzz out of it? Do we fuck. But we get on with it. And you know what – there's something good, something *noble* in sweating for your living." He clasps his fingers together and stretches his inverted palms outwards. Then he continues: "I work piecemeal, and I work like a bastard – twice as fast as any other Joe. So I earn more, and I get to buy whatever threads that I want. And before the summer's out

I'll have bought a new car. Think I might plump for a Cortina, the 1600 one. And one day I'll earn enough for a good hoose for me and my wife. What the fuck have you got to offer her? Eh?"

"Offer who, exactly?"

He realises he has become animated, so he pauses and coolly lights another cigarette – always in one motion from a match, then begins again: "Look, let's get this straight. You went with Delphine last night. And you and Debbie. It's ending, isn't it?"

"Naw!"

He doesn't reply.

"I mean . . . aye. Prob'ly."

He clears his throat as he stubs out his cigarette. Inhales. Here it comes.

"One time you asked me if it was alright for you to go out with her. Do you mind?"

"Aye," I reply, straightening myself up to face him.

Tell me this is not happening.

"Well one day, no today, no tomorrow. Prob'ly no for at least a whole year. But one day, I'm gonnae ask you the same question."

There is a long pause as the enormity of what he has said sinks in.

"Rocky, you and Debbie went out together ages ago. When yous were just kids. It was years before I took up with her. You can't compare it."

"I can."

"You can't. I'm crazy about her. She's the best thing in my life. What did you have – puppy love?"

"Haud the bus. You think the feelings you have at 16 don't matter? That they can't stay with you? Have you had any idea how hard it has been for me, with yous two going out?"

"But yous split up." My voice sounds thinner, more

whining than I expected. "You chucked her I seem to recall. You were chasing that wee bird from Anderston."

"That's all true. But I was just a daft boy back then. Now I know what I want. And yous are breaking up. And there's no point in all three of us continuing to be unhappy."

"But you're supposed to be my best pal, Rocky. Does that no count for anything?"

"Of course it does. That's why I'm being up-front with you. And I've no touched her, that's the honest truth. I'm no a liberty-taker."

I walk over to him. He won't rise to it, won't get to his feet. So I do it anyway.

He gets up, water in his eye where I have punched him.

"I'll no fight you Tim."

I hit him again. Same place. A guy of Rocky's rep just standing there and taking it. It's unnerving.

"Deep down you knew this was coming."

I go to hit him again but this time he leans back and avoids it. He steps back and adopts the pugilist's poise. We exchange blows, I connect with his face three times, he with mine twice, more to repel me than anything more. Then we end up on the deck, wrestling and writhing in the dust. Rocky is strong and down here my slight height advantage means nothing. He rolls us over and I am in the shallows, the water gushing over my face, throwing me into a panic. He drags me up and pins me to the dry ground, sitting on my chest. I struggle. He yells into my face from point-blank range.

"THAT'S ENOUGH! THAT'S ENOUGH! THAT'S ENOUGH!"

I let my body go limp. He gets up. I sit up.

"Your nose," he says.

Blood is streaming down onto my naked chest. I take out my handkerchief and apply it. He puts his hand on my shoulder.

"Tim – "

"Get your haun off of me!" I yell as I get to my feet. "Get your fucking haun off of me!"

He relents, sits by the willow tree and regards me.

"Tim, I'm sorry . . ."

"You'll just have to find someone else," I state.

"I'll no meet someone else. You will."

"Me? No *you* will. You always do."

"You're the one who will likely move onto art school. Meet someone on your level. You always think I'm the big hit with the birds. But I'll never meet anyone as good as Debbie."

"She's my girl."

"She's no. She never was."

"What are you talking about? We've been going out for near-on two year!"

"But she belongs to the Gorbals. You don't."

"What?"

"You're getting out of this life. And that's brilliant. But the Gorbals, it won't forgive you. And Debbie – you can't take her with you."

"Naw. Because I've got her, you want her."

"Naw. Don't you understand? She doesn't even prefer me; it's just that . . . she knows where she is with me."

"You just can't stand me having someone you can't have. You had to end up on top, be the boss man as usual."

"You're wrong," he says, his voice trembling with emotion. "You always think the worst of me. I can't help the way I feel. Neither can she."

The last three words are like being kicked – physically kicked – in the stomach. I have to sit down. I have my back to him as I watch the river flow by for a moment.

"Listen Rocky, here it is, plain as you like. You go with Debbie if you want. But you and me are done. Comprende?"

Silence. Then he does something extraordinary. He weeps. He puts his face in his hands and cries and cries. A sickness creeps into my stomach. Eventually I walk over. I look down at him. The hard man of the Cumbie. Indestructible, unruffable, beautiful, untouchable – greeting like a wean. His perfect slacks and sky-blue polo shirt now soiled by earth and blood. The sobbing subsides. He looks up at me.

"I'm sorry Tim. I'll tell Debbie to forget it."

He stands up and says: "Will you forgive me?" and offers me his hand. Instead of accepting it I embrace him.

We get ourselves cleaned up as best we can and then walk back to the camp.

"Christ, Celtic are playing in the European Cup final and here's us scrapping like a couple of bams," I complain.

"We should be ashamed of ourselves," agrees Rocky.

But it will take time, not words, to wash away the violence that has passed between us.

~~~

The boots are on. The pit boots, that is; boots that could tell a thousand stories, of friendship and camaraderie, humour and warmth. Other stories, too, of pain – physical and mental – of loneliness, and of death. I raise my foot onto the top of the car wheel and tug at the laces. I place my foot back on the ground and watch a puff of black dust rise up. Thin strips of blackness are left streaked across my hands. Reminders of another time and place.

I stand at the bottom and gaze up at the black mound rising into the milky late-afternoon sky. I start to climb. I feel the crunch of the coal slag beneath my boots. It feels good. I climb higher and higher, fixing my gaze on that peak. The climb gets steeper. I have to use my hands now, scrabbling on all fours, palms stained with the blackness, beads of sweat trickling down my neck.

Then, finally, I reach the top. I slowly clamber to my feet and look around. And there it is. The West of Scotland spread across the horizon. I look to the east and see the Lanarkshire coalfields, where it all began. I think of the men who spend their days in darkness, risking their lives to gouge out more of the black stuff from the bowels of the Earth . . . united by the ever-present threat of death.

I remember the roll-call of deceased: *three killed in explosion, seven killed in roof fall, 11 killed in fire.* Some more specific: *James Clancy, 37, struck by hutch; Tom Gardner, 17, death by methane gas poisoning; George McMillan, 24, crushed by stone.* Names in the local newspaper but to us not just names: friends, comrades. Dead. Men snatched before their prime. We would watch their young, lifeless bodies being carried out and into mortuary trucks. My own father, a roadsman in the pits, survived a haemorrhage and several gassing accidents. I think of the lessons that should have been learned and the conditions miners are still forced to put up with, the negligent attitudes of the fuckin' colliery owners, the ignorance of the politicians. I think of the unions – the great unifier – McGahey and the rest, fighting for the rights of men who are more deserving of respect than those who claim to represent them in the Houses of Parliament.

I look closer and try to pick out the location of Earnock Pit, where I started; then, across the river to Bothwell Castle where I moved in 1943; finally, the Priory Pit. Thirteen years in the darkness.

I look at my watch, nearly 5pm. Soon, the shift will finish and the pubs will fill up. Every night I watched as men fell out of these places, staggering home with brew in their bellies and fire in their eyes. "If you want to break my heart, go to the pub with your father." My mother's words. Enough to inspire a lifetime of abstinence.

I think about the petty religious differences that bubble back to the surface whenever these fine, courageous men emerge blinking into the daylight; the scourge of sectarianism, dividing the working classes and distracting them from identifying the real enemy. How the fuck did we end up with this form of religion which is expressed in tribal loyalties to football teams?

I gaze westward over the cityscape and pick out the black lines of the church spires stretching into the darkening sky. Religion. Karl Marx called it the opium of the people. He was wrong. In its purest form, it is uplifting and civilising. I can see and appreciate its influence on others, even if I can't experience it fully in my own heart. I think of Matt Busby, a true man of faith, whose dignity shines out of him. A man who combines his love for God with his love of the game; a man who has built his club around a strong moral framework. I admire that, but religious belief does not burn in me. What do I believe in? A Higher Power – I suppose so. But most of all I believe in football. And in football's ability to bring joy, to inspire people and make their hearts sing. That is no cliché. That is my reality every time I walk out of the tunnel on a Saturday or scan the faces in the crowd after we score a goal. Every time we win a trophy or I shake hands with a well-wisher in the street, I look into their eyes and I see it. I see it burning within. Faith and hope. What do I believe in? I believe in Celtic Football Club and I believe in football. Football is my religion.

A stone's throw from here lies Ormiston, the Lanarkshire mining village which produced Matt; to the west, Glenbuck, where Shanks was born and bred. This is the cradle of Scottish football. What is it about this little corner of the world that produces leaders of men? "When a manager gets his players to do what he wants them to do, when he merges them all together, it's a form of socialism," said Shankly, spoken like a former miner. 'How do Busby and Shanks build such great teams? Where do they get their understanding of teamwork?' people ask. The answer lies underground, in the deep bond on which each other's survival depends.

It is about courage, a quality that cannot be given to someone, but must exist already. In football, talent is nothing without courage. Courage is being able to control a ball in a tight situation and to not be afraid of the opposition; to be able to absorb the anxiety of 100,000 fans and still keep your focus and do what the situation requires. Miners can spot men who have courage. They are the ones whose spirits shine in the blackness. The darkness.

Then there are a chosen few who find a way out, who are able to raise themselves from the bowels of the Earth and do something exceptional. They are the ones who spot light in the darkness and do not stop until they have reached it; the ability to see beyond the black walls, to peer over the smoking chimneys and the smog, to look upon distant horizons and resolve to change the natural order of things — those are the qualities that make good men great. For some of us, like myself, Shanks and Busby, football was that brilliant, dazzling light. It continues to illuminate our lives and others around us. But we will never forget the darkness.

I pick out the floodlights of Celtic Park, jutting into the skyline, lighting up lives. I look down at my blackened hands. Hands that once emptied hutches and filled them up again for eight hours a day, but now direct professional footballers . . .

Tomorrow I will board a plane to Lisbon and the grey smog of Glasgow will be replaced by heavenly blue skies. There, under an Atlantic sun, I will place my destiny in the hands of 11 young men whose ability to kick a bag of leather around a patch of grass holds more importance than they could possibly comprehend. I picture it now, in my mind's eye . . . the aftermath of victory . . . the clouds parting, the smog lifting and heavenly rays pouring down on this little grey corner of the planet . . .

~~~

Delphine tends to the swelling round my left eye.

"You know a person has no right whatsoever to strike another person? I thought you had rejected violence?"

"The gangs, aye."

"And what of this? You think this is a way to settle a dispute? It is . . . barbaric. It is beneath you. It diminishes you."

She continues dabbing. I try not to wince.

"I have already tended to Rocky. You want to smash your friend's face up like that? You ought to be ashamed."

I recall the image of my fist landing on his face as he just sat there. I remember him weeping. I feel a wave of nausea, a sense of self-disgust that almost overwhelms me.

"This is about your girl, isn't it?"

"How did you know?"

"Women's intuition."

I watch her as she selflessly concentrates on my wounds. Her expression is resigned, defeated. I feel sorry for her.

After a while she says: "You do realise you will not stay with them?"

"Who?"

She gestures with her head in the general direction of where the boys are situated.

"What are you talking about? These are my friends. My brothers."

"You will leave them behind."

"Never. If I am not loyal to them then I am nothing."

"It isn't a question of loyalty. Although in a sense it is – loyalty to oneself. You do not belong with them. You will move on."

"I didn't realise you were such a snob."

"I'm not a snob, I'm a realist. I'm merely identifying what will happen."

She looks at her shoes, then says: "And you can fall in love again."

"I know. It's just hard, at the moment, to get my head round that."

"Why? You think you can't recover in a few days? A few hours?"

"Delphine, that's . . . heartless."

"I don't mean to be heartless. I'm just trying to open your eyes to how society has been conditioning you . . . and everyone else. This thing called 'love', it is an illusion of higher feelings, a trick of nature to disguise a merely animal need to procreate. A misnomer for hormonal processes."

"I'm sorry, Delphine. I'm not sure I understand what you are on about. And I'm not sure I want to."

I get up and walk away.

The rest of the morning is awkward to say the least. The weather becomes overcast and drizzly. As well as my eye my lower lip is swollen, my nose encrusted with dried blood, and the skin of my left forearm has been serrated by gravel. Rocky's left cheekbone and eye socket are starting to bruise. Eddie, Iggy and Mark are all noticeably astonished by our appearances but know better than to say anything for now. We pack the Zodiac. Iggy's hangover persists such that he is installed in the passenger seat while I take the wheel for the next stretch of the N10. Rocky, Eddie, Mark and Delphine squeeze into the rear.

"What's that smell?" asks Eddie.

"Iggy's got his shoes off, they are pure l-l-louting," says Mark.

"Christ Iggy," says Eddie, "you are fucking Abraham Linkin'!"

The French girls accompany us southwards for a few miles before they must leave us, and we wave off their 2CV as it splutters towards Paris. Rocky and I spend the rest of the morning being self-consciously courteous to one other, laughing loudly at each other's jokes, ensuring to offer the other a fag.

Somewhere in the pit of my stomach lurks a terrible feeling that I've done him a great injustice. Him and Debbie.

We stop at a village – more a handful of buildings than a village – just outside Poitiers. Mark walks over to a little shop to buy lemonade and cigarettes.

"Here, Mark," Iggy shouts after him. "If you're going to that wee dairy gonnae get us an *Evening Citizen*."

"They'll no have a *Citizen* here ya tube," says Eddie. "We're in fucking *France*!"

"Oh," says Iggy. "Alright well. Here, Mark, gonnae get us an *Evening Times* instead."

"Give us peace!" exclaims Eddie.

Delphine excuses herself to make a call from a payphone. I watch her for a while as she walks away from me.

We enter a *Relais-Routier* to escape the light rain and sit down. We are the only patrons. It is a small, modest establishment, brown interior, gleaming chrome *Gaggia* coffee machine, clean plastic tablecloths.

"I'll be getting this fellas, my treat," says Iggy.

The boys murmur protests and gratitude.

"How come you're so flush?" I ask him quietly.

He surreptitiously produces something from his inside pocket and shows it to me under the table. It is a wad of banknotes. He strokes it between his index finger and thumb and grins inanely.

"Big Vinnie owed me for a wee job."

I frown at him disapprovingly.

The waiter, a boy in his late teens, approaches, and Iggy begins babbling in broad Glaswegian.

"Alright there my china, I'll have square sausage, and black pudden, and a tottie scone, and fried breid, and egg. And have you got any chips on?"

The waiter just stares at Iggy, bemused.

"He's *French* ya tube," says Eddie. "Doesn't know English. I'll show you how it's done."

Eddie proceeds to speak with a strange French lilt.

"Have yeez got any squerre sauseege?"

Blank stare.

"Squerre sauseege?" he repeats, making a little square with his fingers on the table. "Have yeez any?"

Blank stare. Eddie turns to us.

"It's no use lads," he says in a lowered tone. "The boy's half-daft."

"Haud the bus – you're just speaking English with a French accent," says Rocky. "Let me try."

He turns to the waiter.

"Havez vous de sausage de square?"

Blank stare.

"Alright, how about la pudden de noir? Havez vous la pudden de noir?"

Twenty minutes later and we have finally ordered thanks to Delphine's arrival and intervention. The starters – radishes, bread, butter and salt – have largely remained untouched. My pals' faces are bemused as they survey the main course, a rather exotic-smelling stew.

"What in the name of Jesus is this?"

"Can they no do normal food? Aw, no offence Delphine."

"It's alright. Look, just try a little. I promise you will like it."

I poke at mine with a fork. Try a little. Then a little bit more.

"You know what, fellas? This is no half-bad."

Mark tries a little.

"You're r-right!" he agrees.

"Quite tasty!" says Rocky.

"I like it!" says Iggy.

"You see!" beams Delphine.

We munch away happily. All except Eddie.

"It's pure rancid more like. Gives me the boke." He clatters down his cutlery. "Me with my delicate stomach. I'm away to see if there's any of that corned beef left in the car."

There is a pause, then we all burst out laughing, and I divide Eddie's portion up between us.

"Eddie doesn't know what he's missing," declares Iggy as he wolfs down the last of his stew. "What was that anyway, Delphine?"

"Horsemeat," she replies, with a wry curl of her lip. "Iggy – what is wrong? You have gone a little pale!"

Once on the road again Iggy – who was dying an hour and a half ago – has joined Eddie in swilling cheap wine. I catch his eye disapprovingly.

By the time we stop again in the late afternoon the rain is off and the humidity is high again. We pull in by some nice wooded countryside and we all stretch out and stroll around. Delphine and the boys get the stove on for some tea. I take my fags and wander into a nearby glade. I sit beneath a tree to ponder the day's momentous events.

"H-H-Hi."

"Christ Mark, you gave me a fright."

"S-sorry."

He sighs, sits down. Silence.

Then he asks: "H-how are you?"

"I'm fine. Why shouldn't I be?"

"It's just that, you and R-R-Rocky."

"We had a scrap, so what?"

"W-w-what was is all about?"

"I'd rather not talk about it."

"Was it about D-D-Debbie?"

"Why the fuck would it be about Debbie?"

"No r-r-r-reason."

He gets up and wanders into the glade, closer to me. Makes a play of examining the surroundings.

"Tim, do you ever think that you and m-m-m-me are . . . s-s-s-s-similar?"

"No really, no." My voice betrays my irritation.

Eddie arrives.

"Christ, can a man no get some peace? It's like Sauchiehall Street round here!"

"Here, Olive, away and bugger off and put your pinny on so I can have a word with Tim."

It's barely 4pm and already he has his bad-drinker face on. Mark leaves.

"Why do you always have to do that?"

"What?"

"Put him down."

"I just take the piss out of him a wee bit 'cause he's a fairy."

"Naw he's no. We can't all be tough guys like you."

"Ach, he's as bent as an Arab's sword. And anyway, I'm only kidding around."

He offers me his bottle, I shake my head. He takes a long draught.

"What happened with you and Rocky well?"

"Nothing. It's all sorted now."

"Was it about the Cumbie?"

"Naw. Like I say, it's all sorted now. And what about the Cumbie?"

He looks away, takes another swig.

"It's just that back home . . . folk were saying you don't give a fuck about the Cumbie no more. Saying you are a shitebag. Saying that you think you're a cut above."

"Let them say what they like, see if I give a fuck. The Cumbie is a load of auld garbage anyway."

"Keep your voice down ya tube!"

"THE GANGS ARE A PILE OF PISH – THE CUMBIE IS A PILE OF SHITE!"

"That's right, let Rocky hear you; see how interested he's gonnae be in your views."

"He won't give a fuck."

"Aye, right."

"He won't. You don't get it, do you Eddie? One day Rocky's gonnae team up with a right nice wee lassie, and you'll see a different side to him. He will toe the line – guaranteed. And top of the list will be no running with the team anymore. And he'll be right no to."

"Shite. Just 'cause you've let the side down don't go dragging in Rock. He knows what it's all about."

"And what exactly is it all about? Could you explain that to me?"

He has to think about this for a moment.

"It's about survival. Comradeship. Identity."

"Is it fuck. The gangs are about parochialism."

"Para-whit-now?"

"Parochialism. A narrow prejudice against folk from other bits." I stub out the cigarette I had been smoking. "Fucking ants do that."

"Do what?"

"Knock fuck out of each other just 'cause they come from a different anthill. You think just 'cause some guy is born a mile away across the river in the Calton that makes him a bam?"

"Of course no. But you can't stand by and let the other mob take top spot – because they will. That's a fact of life. That's Glesga."

"But it doesn't have to be like that. I mean, it's no even about religion; the Tongs are our biggest enemy and they're mostly Tims too for Christ's sake!"

"So you think you are just gonnae sail off into the sunset? Leave us to fight off the interlopers? To deal with the polis?"

"I've already done it. And anyway, these guys are my brothers. They will understand."

He snorts, takes out a fag, lights it, then continues.

"Two years I did in the Bar-L for that mob, for serious assault. And you're just gonnae abandon us."

"I'm glad you mentioned that. Wee Peachy got killed so you and Rocky take over a team to Bridgeton to sort the guy out. But who gets done for it? Was it Rocky? Was it fuck. It was *you* Eddie. You. It's guys like you who do the porridge. Guys like Rocky, they come up smelling of roses every time."

"I already told you – Rocky's solid."

"Ach, turn it up," I say, rising to leave.

"Don't walk away from me Tim! You can't just leave us! They are tearing the Gorbals down brick by brick, without the Cumbie, what are we?"

I spin round to face him.

"We have our pals, our faith, our families." Damn, shouldn't have said that last one.

Then it occurs to me. Of course. It's so obvious.

"And we have Celtic. No matter what changes that will always be there for us. The club. Our identity."

He sits down on a mound of baked earth. Takes a draught from his bottle. A drag from his fag. Sighs out blue smoke.

"You're fucking kidding yourself on. It's all a dream."

"What is?"

"All of it. You getting out. Celtic winning the European Cup. It's no gonnae happen."

"It might. You gottae have a dream, Eddie. The whole existence of our club was based on a dream, and a hope for something better."

"We're up against the best team in the world. We're gonnae get fucked."

The dull light exposes his ugly, scarred features. Face like a Hallowe'en cake. His cheap suit is crumpled. He wears it in honour of the big occasion; the only big occasion of his life. I feel so sorry for him. Where is he going to end up? All that boozing's got to take its toll.

"My auld man came to see me."

The statement crackles into the dry heat. I can hardly believe he has said it. Breached the unacknowledged veil of silence that surrounds his father.

"When?"

"Christmas. He'd been living in America."

"How was it?"

"Okay."

Another draw from his fag.

"Naw, better than okay. It was great."

"That's . . . great."

"No it isn't. He fucked off again. Said not a word. Tapped me a right few quid as well, the auld bastard."

It occurs to me how other families operate in different, less functional ways from mine. I think of Delphine, too. I feel sad for them both.

"I'm real sorry. Was that why you . . . went off the rails?"

"Aye. Went down to stay with my auntie in Ayrshire. But mostly I just slept rough. Bevvied a lot."

"But you're alright . . . now?"

He smiles thinly.

"If the Celts win on Thursday, I'll be alright."

"Eddie, the Cumbie . . . it's just that – "

"I know, I know, you said."

"We're getting too auld, Eddie."

He gazes abstractly into the distance, takes a last draw from his fag.

"Let's go and get a cup of tea," I suggest.

The road to Lisbon. Several thousand Celtic supporters strung along it in clusters like beads on a rosary.

As I walk back to the Zodiac my attention is drawn by a growing growl of motor engines. It is a strand of the Celticade. We all rush over to the roadside to salute them. Iggy is waving a green-and-white scarf to identify us as fellow pilgrims. Suddenly my mood soars as the convoy thunders by; what a joyous sight it is to behold! They are waving, and shouting greetings and slogans to us. One phrase is repeated several times. It sounds like '*swear-us-a-suit*'. I hear it again and again. '*Swear-us-a-suit, swear-us-a-suit, swear-us-a-suit.*'

Then I decipher it: 'Suárez is oot.'

Luis Suárez Miramontes of Spain. Inter's classy, intelligent midfielder. Unfit for duty. Undoubtedly a boost for our chances.

"The Celtic fans!" Rocky exclaims simply, once only a cloud of dust and fumes remains. The Celtic fans, indeed. The greatest supporters in the world. The salt of the earth.

In towns and villages in France and Spain, curious locals in white-painted squares are coming out to stare as every conceivable type and age of vehicle passes by, festooned in green and white. Some of these motors look as though they would struggle to make it to the end of London Road, let alone to London, let alone to Lisbon. Most of these travellers haven't been abroad before and for them a road adventure such as this is a true one-off. Boulogne, Rouen, Chartres, Tours, Angoulême, Bordeaux, Biarritz, San Sebastian, Burgos, Valladolid, Salamanca. Horns are sounded festively, cheers exchanged, songs sung.

We'll be running round Lisbon when we come,
We'll be running round Lisbon when we come,
We'll be running round Lisbon,
Running round Lisbon,
Running round Lisbon when we come!

Lisbon. A word so often used that it has already passed into folklore. Now less a place, more a concept, a state of being; a new mutual state of heightened being that has existed since the Dukla match in Prague.

Or a fictional, mythical place. Tir Na Nog, Narnia, Fairyland, Lisbon.

On and on they drive, that single destination in mind, and a single goal: *to be there*. To witness history. To witness the culmination of everything good about Celtic. They sense that this is the hour, that this is the time. And afterwards – in ways not yet fully revealed or comprehended – nothing will ever be the same again. A victory will draw a dividing line in the collective consciousness between everything that has occurred before and everything that will occur afterwards. For an entire community Celtic has always been about pride, about defiance. But to become the first club from northern Europe to win the ultimate prize in the game; that would make their sneers ring hollow for evermore.

~~~

"It's a poisoned chalice, Jock." So they all told me. Dunfermline, third bottom of the First Division with two months of the 1959-60 season remaining, relegation a very real prospect . . .

"Bide your time. Something better will come along."

I went to the interview anyway, one of three candidates. They started the interrogation. But I had some questions for them, too. Soon, I was interviewing them. "What is the financial situation at the club? Who would I deal with about signing players? Would I have complete control of team matters? What were *their* ambitions for the club?"

I liked their answers. They knew where they wanted to be. The structures were in place. They just needed to sort out the football side, get the team motoring again. It made sense.

'We'll be in touch, Jock,' they told me.

I phoned Jean immediately afterwards. "I've got it."

Poisoned chalice, or the opportunity to make my name? I needed no convincing. My experiences with the Celtic reserves had stood me in good stead, but I needed a new test. I wanted to work with first-team players. I thumbed through my scrapbooks every night and wondered if anyone else thought about football as much as I did. I had ideas that no-one had even thought of, but I needed to know they worked. Now I was about to find out.

It was a curious twist of fate that my first game was against Celtic. Twenty minutes before kick-off and the dressing room resembled Sauchiehall Street on a Saturday afternoon. Directors, injured men, youth coaches; all hanging about, distracting the players.

"Right, everyone who is not in my first-team pool get the fuck out . . ."

They thought it was a joke at first. One look at my face told them how serious I was.

"I mean it. OUT. FUCKIN' OUT. Every single one of you. And don't come back. This is a place of work, not a social club."

If the players didn't know I meant business before, they knew then. I had given them their place, made them feel important. This was about them and their ability to perform. I wanted focus. I did not bombard them with tactics. I put it to them simply.

"I want you all to think about how it feels to lose, that feeling of trudging up the tunnel after another defeat. Think about the Saturday nights this season that have been ruined by a bad break, a late goal, an individual mistake, whatever. Think about the guilt and the disappointment. Think about those feelings and hold them for a moment . . . then banish them from your minds. Forget everything that has gone before. Think only about this moment. Think about your team-mates. Think about that patch of grass out there and think about what you are going to do on it, how you are going to express yourself. Think about how you will feel walking up that tunnel after beating one of the big boys.

Think about telling your friends and family how you got one over on the great Glasgow Celtic. Hold that feeling. Let it enter through your feet and rise up through your whole body. Feel your spine tingle, the hairs on your neck rise. Now, stand up, get out there and win this fuckin' match!"

Inside the first minute, we were one up courtesy of Charlie Dickson. The game finished 3-2, the first victory in four months. I looked around the dressing room afterwards and saw players who had been reborn, flushed with confidence. After that, we inflicted Kilmarnock's first league defeat in 21 games and went on to record wins in all our remaining games. No Dunfermline team had ever managed to win six consecutive First Division matches. We avoided relegation. Poisoned chalice, eh?

The summer brought with it a chance to strengthen the squad. Willie Cunningham and Tommy McDonald arrived from Leicester, and I started to build a spine to my team. By the end of season 1960-61 we were up to fourth in the league. We also reached the club's first Scottish Cup final, against Celtic. I started the mind games immediately by booking Seamill Hydro, Celtic's traditional pre-big match retreat. The game ended goalless and went to a replay in midweek. In the 67th minute, Davie Thomson scored and, two minutes from the end, Charlie Dickson added a second after a mistake from Frank Haffey, the Celtic goalkeeper. Bob Kelly, by now president of the SFA, was in the presentation area. "Well done, Jock. You're fairly making a name for yourself," he said, with a warm handshake.

Silverware has a habit of attracting attention and Newcastle United came in for me soon after the Scottish Cup final triumph. The Magpies offered me a £4,000 a year salary — double my annual wage at Dunfermline — but there was more work to be done at East End Park. Harry Swan, the Hibs chairman, offered me the vacant post at Easter Road but, again, the challenge of European football at Dunfermline was an attractive one.

We negotiated the first couple of rounds of the Cup Winners'

Cup by beating St Patrick's Athletic and then Yugoslavian side
Vardar 5-2 on aggregate. That set up a meeting with Újpesti
Dózsa, of Hungary. The quarter-final tie took us to Budapest, the
home of the Magical Magyars, whose style of play had excited me
all those years before. Alex Smith scored after 40 seconds and
Tommy McDonald added another in the eighth minute. Ujpest
came roaring back and made it 2-2 by the half hour, but still I
urged my team forward. The game ended 4-3 to the home side,
but we had proved a point. We had shown that a Scottish team
could go away from home in Europe and have success through
playing attacking football. Despite losing the return leg 1-0 at
East End Park, the experience had been successful. "If there is any
glory in defeat I think we earned it tonight," I told the Press. "We
are learning all the time at this game and for a first attempt at a
continental tournament Dunfermline have done very well. There
will be a next time."

I did not have to wait long. The following season we were given
a slot in the Fairs Cup after a Greek team withdrew. I knew we had
the quality to cope. Our fourth-placed finish the previous season
was an indication of how far we had come in a short space of
time. But we had our work cut out when we drew Everton in the
first round. The Merseyside club was nicknamed the 'Bank of
England', having lavished huge amounts of money on assembling
a squad of big names, including Scottish internationals like Alex
Young and George Thomson. A couple of days before the first leg
I pinned up an interview with an Everton player from the *Evening
Times* with the headline: *Who are these Country Cousins?* I
watched from my office as the players gathered round to look
at it. "Look what these fuckin' bastards have said about us." The
disrespect cut them deep. They were like rabid dogs. All I needed
to do was let them off the leash.

The first leg was at Goodison and it crackled from start to
finish. They scored a disputed goal. Stevens' header from Billy
Bingham's corner was goal-bound but Willie Cunningham got his

head to it on the line. The ball then bounced off the underside of the crossbar. My players were adamant that it had not crossed the line but the referee controversially awarded the goal. The match degenerated into a war of attrition, and the savagery continued after the game when we were showered with objects thrown from the home fans and then the team bus was attacked as we left the ground. We had lost 1-0 but the game had represented a minor tactical triumph for me. I had asked Cunningham to play as a floating defender, dropping in behind the centre-halves, picking up loose balls and offering us an extra layer of protection. He had argued against me, but I had been insistent. Against quality opposition away from home we had to be extra vigilant and the tactic proved a masterstroke. Apart from the controversial goal, Everton had barely laid a glove on us. Something I had noted in my tactics book some years before had come to pass on the European stage. It was little surprise that, in spite of everything, I left Goodison with a spring in my step. A week later, in front of 25,000 at East End Park, we beat them 2-0 to progress to the next round. After the game, I told the Press that we could not lose against Rangers at Ibrox that Saturday. I looked at their faces: 'Who the fuck does he think he is?' But sometimes, when you know you are good, you need to say you are good. And we were a good team. After our 1-1 draw against Rangers, I spoke to the Press men with more than a touch of defiance.

The element of surprise is a powerful weapon in football. I used it to my advantage in the next round of the Fairs Cup against the holders, Valencia. After losing the first leg 4-0 in Spain, I had nothing to lose. "As long as we give a good account of ourselves tonight, eh Jock?" said the chairman before our home leg. I bristled. I was not prepared to accept it was over. The pitch was rock-hard, and I had to make sure the game went ahead. "The pitch is going to be okay," I told the officials on their arrival at the ground, "the groundsmen have been working day and night to make it playable. We haven't had a game called off in six years."

I saw them tapping the frosty turf with their shoes. "You'll see that it's a bit hard, but it's a man's game," I told them, "nothing deserving of a call-off." Valencia were not happy, not fuckin' happy at all, but my charm offensive had convinced the officials to push ahead with the game and they overruled the Spaniards' protests. My team-sheet raised a few more eyebrows. I brought in Alex Edwards, a 16-year-old, and Jackie Sinclair, three years his senior, for their debuts. The response was awesome. Within 17 minutes we were 3-0 up. The game finished 6-2 to set up a play-off in Lisbon. In February 1963, we lost 1-0 to Valencia in the Portuguese capital and exited the tournament. It was a disappointment, but when I saw Valencia go on to win the trophy I started to think about what was possible, about how far I could take it.

~~~

The humidity builds upon itself, layer after layer. Please Lord, grant us rain.

It is Biblical when it comes. Such is the deluge that at one point we have to pull over; the wipers can't cope. But it clears the air and cleanses the land, and afterwards I can smell ozone rapidly giving way to the delicate sweet pollen of wild flowers and the aroma of damp leaves. The soil gives off a marvellously satisfying fragrance as it slakes its thirst.

"T-T-Tim. We're ahead of s-s-s-schedule, aren't we?" enquires Mark, looking up from his Spanish guidebook.

"Aye," I reply contentedly, feeling pleasantly relaxed by the driving.

"Well then, after the S-S-Spanish border the morra, could we follow the coast road for a wee while? Then we could come down into B-Bilbao and onto B-B-Burgos from there."

"Sounds fine."

"Can we no just push on to Lisbon? Contingency and all that," complains Eddie, slurring his words slightly.

"It says here that B-Burgos is on the P-Pilgrims' Road," says Mark, ignoring him. "For Santiago de C-Compostela."

"Compost-whit?" asks Eddie.

"It's the Way of St J-J-James. Where pilgrims used to travel in m-medieval times from all over Europe. To visit the relics of the apostle James. Which r-reminds me, I want to get to M-Mass soon."

"Aye, I wouldn't mind sending one up myself," agrees Iggy.

"Here, Mark. How come you're so interested in going to Mass and Jesus and all that?" enquires Eddie.

"Because I had a r-r-religious experience."

"Don't mumble."

"Because I had a r-r-r-r-r-religious experience."

"Pah! When?"

"When I was f-f-f-fourteen."

"Where?"

"At P-P-P-Pluscarden Abbey. I'm sure I've t-telt you this before."

"So you had a religious experience. What happened – did you realise all the other monks had willies?"

Eddie somehow appears physically uglier in this mood. His skin greasier, his hair wirier, his features blunter.

"Get to f-f-fuck."

"I will n-n-no," mimics Eddie cruelly. "Here Rock, did ye hear the one about the fella with the terrible stutter? He goes up to the dancing looking for a lumber. He's jigging with this bird, who as it happens has also got a stutter, and he goes, 'M-m-m-my name's P-P-P-Peter, but I'm no a s-s-s-saint.' And the lassie goes, 'M-m-m-my name's M-m-m-Mary. But I'm no a v-v-v-v-very good dancer!'"

"I should c-c-congratulate you Eddie," says Mark.

"On what?"

"T-t-twenty years of d-dedication and you've achieved it."

"Achieved what?"

"Being a complete p-p-prick."

Silence in the car. Delphine looks awkward.

"Mark. Your favourite-ever match," I say.

"I can't be f-fucked."

"Go on."

"You t-tell it. May 20th, 1953. You were there t-too."

"I certainly was. I was one of the 117,000 there. The Coronation Cup final. Celtic 2 Hibernian 0. Sure Hampden was covered in banners of green. What a day. We had beaten the English champions Arsenal, then Manchester United, to get there, but now we were up against the greatest forward line in the world; and probably the best Scottish football had ever produced: the Famous Five. Smith, Johnstone, Reilly, Turnbull and Ormond."

"Away!" interjects Rocky. "The Celtic forward line that won the 1938 league title was the greatest ever. Delaney, McDonald, Crum, Divers and Murphy."

I smile, thinking of Dad. That's his favourite team.

"Jimmy Delaney was some player right enough," muses Iggy. "The classic Celtic winger. So flamboyant. So skilful."

"Well for the sake of my and Mark's story, and considering that none of us were alive in 1938, can we just pretend to agree that the Famous Five were the best ever? Anyway, nobody gave Celtic much of a chance, not least 'cause Charlie Tully was injured. Hibs had beaten Spurs and humped Newcastle to get to the final and were in great shape and determined to win. But Neilly Mochan was on fire and scored with a thunderbolt on the half hour. In the second half Hibs battered us, the Famous Five doing their stuff. But Johnny Bonnar was magnificent that day. Some of the saves – you should have seen them! It was as though the spirit of Johnny Thomson had come back to wander the Earth. Jock Stein was tremendous. I always admired the Big Man for his honest and committed play; he truly arrived that day. Served notice that things were gonnae be different at the club from now on; that we were gonnae start winning things. Willie Fernie was also on fine form. And with just three minutes left Jimmy Walsh sealed it. Amazing. We went on to win the double the following season. No the most dominant Celtic performance ever, but a famous and vital victory nonetheless."

Iggy turns to Mark.

"How is it your favourite gemme, Mark?"

Mark looks thoughtful.

"It was my f-first-ever match. My d-d-da took me, God rest his s-s-soul. He put me on his sh-sh-shoulders so that I could see Big Jock lift up the c-cup ... it was just so s-s-special."

There is respectful silence in the car as we ponder the premature demise of Mark's dad. He was a lovely, devout Irish gentleman. Mark worshipped the ground he walked on. The only sound is the hypnotic throb of the Zodiac's pistons and the *whirr* of rubber on damp asphalt. I steal a glance at Eddie. His face looks grim. He takes another draught of cheap wine. He speaks.

"Stop the car."

"What?"

"Stop the fucking car."

I pull over. Eddie leaps from the rear before the Zodiac has come to a halt. He strides up a bank and over the other side.

"Where the fuck is he away to?"

"I'll see to it."

I follow him up. He has stopped over the brow of the bank, out of view of the car. He aggressively withdraws his fags and lighter, lights up, drags from the cigarette as though his life depends on it. I approach tentatively. The earth is baked as hard as ceramic.

"Gonnae be some party if we win this."

No response. He scans the horizon as though searching for something. Need to make him feel better.

"Mark can take a joke, you know."

Silence.

"Come on ya maniac, come back to the car."

He turns to me. His eyes are glassy. He holds it together. Just stares at me, his eyes pleading, desperate.

So we sit for a while under a juniper tree, smoking our fags as the sun casts a gilded splendour over the pastures of Aquitaine. Soon it will begin its exeunt from the stage and we will reach the ocean.

~~~

I watch for him out of the window of my new office. Look at my watch. Five minutes late. Ten minutes. Then I spy a figure in the rain, sneaking through the side entrance. Looks like something the cat dragged in. My blood boils. Wee bastard. I bolt downstairs, taking three at a time. I can feel the anger rising, like a fuckin' volcano ready to erupt. I'll kill him. I'll fuckin' kill him. No-one fucks with me like this. No-one fucks with Big Jock.

I burst into the dressing room. The players are all in their training kits. I scan the room manically. Jimmy is there, too, with his training kit on. Looking like butter wouldn't melt.

"How the fuck did you get changed so fast?" I ask.

"What do you mean boss?"

I look at the pile of clothes lying beside him. Then I look right through him. He looks away, like a frightened puppy.

"You're at it son. I just watched you come through the fuckin' side entrance less than two minutes ago. You were late. And no for the fuckin' first time."

"No me boss. Must have a lookalike . . ."

I look him up and down. My fists are clenched. I'm shaking with rage. Scared of what I might do next. Then, my gaze returns to his feet.

"Are you going to fuckin' train in those," I scream, pointing at the pair of brown brogues he has forgotten to remove during his lightning-fast change routine.

His face turns scarlet. The players laugh uproariously. I glare. I could murder him. I could fuckin' murder the disrespectful little bastard. But something holds me back. Something kicks in, tells me this is not the time or the place. I unclench my fists. Then, I turn and walk deliberately away.

I walk back upstairs. Slowly, this time. One by one. Rage has passed. It's something else now. An eerie calmness. I can't explain it. I start to think of the job I have ahead of me. I have just taken over a club that has been underachieving. No silverware for seven years. It is my job to restore them to their former glory. Hundreds of thousands of hopes and dreams rest upon my shoulders. What a fucking burden to carry. I need men I can trust, rely upon.

Does Jimmy Johnstone fit? Sheets of rain sweep in from the Atlantic and the wind whips viciously around the training field. Strands of ginger hair are plastered to his skull. His socks are rolled down to his ankles. The cuffs of his sleeves are pulled over his hands. He grips them tightly as he hugs the touchline like a life-raft. He looks like a drowned rat. Then, the ball comes to him, landing with an almighty splosh, like a big steam pudden. Suddenly, his back straightens. He is on his toes now, tap-tap-tapping the ball with his right foot, searching for a potential victim. They all back off, but he seeks them out, bobbing and weaving, the pride o' Parkhead, the Benny Lynch of the Calton.

I turn to Sean.

"I'm thinking of selling Jimmy."

"Hmmm . . ."

"You don't sound surprised."

"I'm not. He's everything you love and everything you hate rolled into one."

"Exactly. Look at him now," I say, gesturing to the training field. "That kind of talent is God-given. But what the fuck is he doing with it? He could be one of the greats, but he is always up to something, cutting corners here, taking liberties there. He's cheating himself, he's cheating us and he's cheating the fans. I fuckin' hate him for it. For wasting that talent. I used to want to murder the little fucker. Now, I think I just want him off my hands."

"Let's see how it goes, Jock," says Sean. "It is early days. He might respond."

Sean is right. No rash decisions or knee-jerk reactions. But his card is marked. More than marked. This job and this club are bigger than one player. I can't let him run rings round me, like he does every day to his team-mates in training. I've got to lay down a marker, send out a message that no-one messes with Jock Stein. I'm the man at this club. Not the fuckin' chairman or the rest of the board. Big Jock. No-one fucks with Big Jock.

What more powerful statement of intent than selling Jimmy Johnstone?

I think on this as I trudge through the glaur, back to the pavilion. Then, a roar goes up. I look back and see him skipping back to the halfway line having dumped Gemmell on his arse and stuck it past the goalkeeper.

Jimmy Johnstone. Jimmy fuckin' Johnstone. This kid could make me or break me.

~~~

The road to Lisbon. A stretch of it kisses the Atlantic.

The evening sun, which has turned the water a gorgeous ultramarine colour, embroiders everyone and everything with a golden light that is so liquid it is almost tangible; you imagine you could reach out and hold a little pool of it in the palm of your hand. We follow the N10 southwards for a few miles before I spin the wheel and we drive down towards the last sands of France.

We happen across the accident almost casually, as though it is a random item of scenery, a banal piece of street furniture. It doesn't announce itself with any drama; we just round a curvature in the narrow road and it is *there*.

I pull over and there is a moment of shocked inaction before we all get out.

It is surprisingly peaceful; the only unnatural sound is the low hiss of steam escaping from one of the two mangled vehicles' radiators.

The driver of the truck is pinned by the steering wheel. Rocky approaches, turns away, is immediately sick.

Eddie approaches, clapping Rocky on the shoulder consolingly as he does so, examines the scene inside the cab, and turns to face us.

"Iggy – there's a house back up the road. Drive Delphine there so she can call for an ambulance and the gendarmes. Mark – see to the guy in the car. Tim – help me here."

He has taken command. Sobered up. Clear-thinking, level-headed, practical. A different man.

I walk towards the truck, my stomach filled with dread.

Several tools and parts are scattered inside by the impact. A short shaft has impaled itself into the driver's abdomen. He is conscious and in a great deal of pain. He is bleeding profusely.

"Can you smell that? Petrol. We need to get him out," Eddie says. "Here, help me move the dash."

The dashboard has disengaged from the chassis and is sitting on the driver's lap.

"Come on, it'll be okay," he urges me. Presumably my face has gone chalk-white. I certainly feel very peculiar.

As I prop up the dashboard with a jemmy Eddie manages

to haul the driver out while holding the shaft steady where it has entered the poor man's body. Once he is clear I grab his ankles and we lift him away, and lay him gently on the grass.

"Give me your shirt," Eddie says. "And your simmet."

I obey, and he wraps the items round the wound and holds them there.

"Are you no gonnae pull it out?" I ask, the words almost sticking in my throat.

"Best to leave it in. Hopefully we'll no be far from a hospital. Nip over and see how Mark is doing."

I leave him and go over to the wrecked car. I walk by Rocky, who is crouched down on his haunches, his head bowed.

Mark is perched at the driver's opened door, holding his hand, murmuring softly as he reads from a missal. The ground is covered in little cubes of glass. It is a silver sports coupé, its once sleek, tapered, bug-eyed front end now crumpled beyond recognition. I look inside.

The man, a young man, handsome and dapperly dressed, is terribly injured. He is dying. Yet Mark holds fast, speaking softly into his ear. I notice the man's left hand is not only clutching Mark's hand but also a rosary. Deep-red blood is flowing from under the man's cuff and onto his and Mark's hands. It then gushes down the beads and patters upon the road.

I listen in to Mark's words. His stutter has evaporated.

". . . May St. Joseph, the most sweet Patron of the dying, comfort you with a great hope. May Mary, the holy Mother of God, lovingly cast upon you her eyes of mercy . . ."

I look on in awe, because the man is smiling. There is actual joy - pure joy - on his face, as he gazes across the fields, into the Bay of Biscay, into the distance; yet beyond the distance. Beyond it at something else.

After a while the Zodiac returns and soon I hear the four-note phrase of sirens getting nearer. I notice that the man's eyes have glazed over. He has passed away, yet he looks so peaceful and happy. Mark releases his hand, takes the rosary, which is drenched with gore, kisses it, and places it upon the man's breast. He then closes the man's eyes and makes the sign of the cross.

Two gendarmerie motorcycles roar into the scene, quickly followed by an ambulance. The motorcycles halt and splutter to inertia. The gendarmes are strikingly impressive in their leather jerkins and boots. They flip up their goggles, the lenses of which are smoked dirty yellow, onto their white half helmets, peel off their gauntlets, and dismount. Immediately they take charge of the situation and we are ushered aside.

The truck driver is lifted onto a stretcher by the ambulancemen and swathed in blankets. As he is carried past us he reaches out and clutches Eddie's hand.

"Merci mon ami. Tout va bien."

Delphine relates our brief story to the gendarmes. She then comes over and buries her head on my shoulder. I notice that Eddie and Mark are both blotted with blood. It is on their faces, their clothes; their hands are soaked with it. Both of their expressions bear strain, but at the same time they look heroic in the gloaming light. Eddie turns to Mark and looks at him for a wee while. He places his hands upon Mark's shoulders and embraces him momentarily.

As Mark moves to step by me I grab his lapel and eye him desperately.

"Say something Mark," I beg.

"What like?"

"That bit from John about light and darkness."

"What b-bit?"

"They say it at Christmas. From John chapter 1. Say it, for Christ's *sake*."

Mark emits a little self-conscious cough.

"In Him was life, and the life was the light of m-men. And the light shines on in the d-d-darkness, and the d-darkness has never put it out."

"Say that again," I request, "the last bit."

"And the light shines on in the darkness, and the darkness has never put it out."

Everyone walks over to the car, oblivious to the tears rolling down my cheeks.

~~~

"That's two rounds we have had in the European Cup and the challenges are different, Sean. We're no getting the same space to create as we do in Scotland. Teams are fitter, stronger, better at denying space. Don't get me wrong, we have enough threat to overcome it, but it's only going to get more difficult from now on. Those bloody defensive Tallies are influencing other teams, too. Teams are happier to sit behind the ball, try to hit you on the counter. You saw that at times against Zurich and Nantes. Bloody catenaccio. It'll be taking over the world, soon, but no if I have my way."

"So what's your thoughts, Jock? How do we cope with these bloody defences?"

"I can't stop thinking about the full-backs, Sean. Defensive teams want you to attack the way teams have always attacked; play right into their hands. They want to smother the strikers and shadow the runs from midfield areas. They're good at stopping those sort of attacks. But what if we get our full-backs right up there, too? That'll blow their bastard minds. Big Gemmell has a shot like a cannonball. Look at that thunderbolt against Zurich in the first round at Celtic Park! Let's free him up to get more shots in. And what if we switch him wings, so he plays on the left . . . that way, he can cut inside onto that right foot of his and get shots on target."

"I like it, Jock. Their heads will be spinning. But who will play on the right if you switch Tommy to the left? You thinkin' about switching Willie O'Neill, too, or bringing in Ian Young?"

"I'm thinking about Jim Craig. He slotted in well when we moved Tommy into centre-half for the St Mirren game in early November. He's an athlete, loves getting up and down that line. Loves hitting the byeline and getting crosses in; he could give us another dimension in Europe. I'm thinking of bedding him in the New Year and taking it from there."

I sit at my desk and listen to the rain lash persistently against the frosted window pane. A stormy night in the east end of Glasgow. The calm before the real storm. Tomorrow night we face Vojvodina in the quarter-final of the European Cup. 1-0 down from the first leg. Problems not hard to find.

It has been a difficult few months. The 3-2 loss to Dundee United on New Year's Eve was our first of the season and represented a setback, if not a fatal one. A run of six straight league victories restored momentum but the state of the pitches caused us to lose some fluency. The Saturday before the first leg we could only manage a 1-1 with Stirling Albion – hardly the most confidence-inspiring result to take into the first leg.

The first leg against Vojvodina in Yugoslavia showed their quality. We had to defend for much of the match and conceded after a mishit back-pass by Tommy Gemmell saw us breached midway through the second half. The result was a fair reflection of the match.

Have we met our match? Twice in previous years we have lost first-leg matches and twice been eliminated. Why should it change now against this quality of opposition? Why should we succeed against a strong, powerful team with great technique? Vojvodina are the champions of Yugoslavia, winning the league ahead of Partizan Belgrade, who lost the European Cup final narrowly to Real Madrid last year.

I glance at the newspapers on the desk. Their tone is downbeat.

The Yugoslavs are many people's outsiders to win the tournament and Celtic Park will hold no fears for Vujadin Boskov's impressive side.

The Press think we will lose. I heard it in the tone of their questions today.

'Tough task ahead,' they said, arching their eyebrows. Bastards. Fuckin' doubting, snidey bastards.

"It is only half-time in the tie," I told them. "With 70,000 fans behind us at Celtic Park, we will have the opportunity to express ourselves."

But, beneath the measured comments, nagging doubts remain. They were compounded by the blow of losing Joe McBride a few days ago. It all started back in November, when he came back from a Scotland trip with a stiff knee. He struggled on, while continuing to score goals, but all was not well. Against Aberdeen on Christmas Eve, his knee finally gave way. The specialists had their say. A flaking bone behind the kneecap was the verdict. An operation loomed but I was desperate to get our 35-goal striker back in the frame for tomorrow night's second leg. We stepped up his training ahead of Saturday's game with St Mirren but my heart sank when he crumpled to the turf on the eve of the game. He remains defiant, desperate to get back fit in time for the final. I had a quiet word with the consultant.

"Any chance of Joe being fit for late May?"

He laughed quietly and shook his head.

I have reinforcements. Willie Wallace's arrival in December now looks increasingly important. He took McBride's place against St Mirren and scored twice in our 5-0 win. But it was bittersweet as he is ineligible for tomorrow night. Stevie Chalmers will have to play instead but he is not fully fit. Plus, they have key men returning. Pusibric and Trivic have served their suspensions and will come back into the side. We are facing a team who know their own quality. Before the first leg, Boskov said as much. "I think we will win by at least two goals," he stated.

Stanic's solitary goal failed to fulfil Boskov's pre-match prediction. They were worth their win but I took heart from the fact that they had very few chances and their goal came from a mistake.

Boskov stated after the first leg that he hadn't been too impressed with us and he was confident they would get the job done in Glasgow.

The Yugoslav Press had the scent of a story when they confronted me after, informing me of Mr Boskov's rather ungracious words about us.

"Vojvodina are a very good team but we are better and we will win in Glasgow," I told them.

I head for the car. As I pass Barrowfield, I slow down to crawling pace and look over at our illustrious visitors training. Earlier in the day I refused them permission to train at Celtic Park.

"The pitch is too soft," I told Boskov. "There's been too much rain and I can't take the chance of it cutting up ahead of tomorrow night."

I thought he was going to spontaneously combust.

"I'll take this up with your chairman," he shouted.

"That's up to you, Mr Boskov. But my main concern is this pitch and your boys are not putting a foot on it tonight. You're welcome to use Barrowfield, five minutes down the road. I'll make sure the floodlights are switched on for you. Hell, I'll even drive you there myself!"

"Let's see how they react walking out there for the first time tomorrow night," I said to Sean. A psychological blow? We will see. I move through the gears and carry on down London Road. Out there, in the stormy Glasgow night, fears linger. Have we met our match?

Half-time and the signs are not good. Pusibric should have scored after five minutes but missed from six yards. They are holding firm. The previous month I had arranged a friendly against

Yugoslav side Dinamo Zagreb. We took the game to them in our usual manner. I wanted to see how Yugoslav teams cope with our all-out attack. Very well, was the answer. We failed to score. It suggested to me that we would need to be prepared to adapt, change the focus and momentum, when the real test came.

This match was going the same way. Vojvodina were comfortable to play it out. I had witnessed them see out victory in their third play-off match against Atletico Madrid in the last round. They had character. We have to change the flow of the match, break their composure.

"Tommy, Bobby and Cairney, I want you further up the park. Let's force them onto the back foot more, drive them out of their comfort zones. Jimmy and John Hughes, I want you to switch wings. Let's confuse them a bit."

After the interval, the balance begins to swing in our favour. We start to break their rhythm and the aggregate equaliser comes when Gemmell's cross is forced home by Chalmers.

But the pressure is intense, the crowd's anxiety almost overwhelming.

I hear everything. Every expectant murmur from the watching thousands. Every barbed comment, every fuckin' damning verdict tossed like a sharpened spear from the heaving terraces. Sometimes I look around and take in the gargoyled faces, twisted with rage. They hate me. They fuckin' hate me and they love me. All in the space of 90 minutes. I feel their beery breath on the back of my neck. I feel the burden. Any manager who says otherwise is lying. People look and judge. They see the confidence, the self-assured marshalling of troops from the sidelines, the calmness in the eye of the storm. But they do not fully comprehend the responsibility on my shoulders. The heaving weight of expectation that sometimes brings me close to buckling under the strain. It is a form of torture.

The flip-side is the joy, the excitement, the ability of 11 men under my charge to make people's lives better. It resonates through me, straightening my back when the pressure feels like it will cripple me. My burden is also my lifeblood. Ultimately, it is not about me. I am a representative of the people, a custodian of their hopes and dreams. The Keir Hardie of the dugout.

Managers are often the first to take credit for success, but it is about the players, always the players . . . their ability to absorb information and then to use it amid the cauldron of match-day, when all around they are being willed, urged and abused. The presence of mind to occupy the moment, and then to seize it, that is what makes a good player great.

There are just moments left now. A replay seems a certainty.

"Looks like Rotterdam," says Sean. Then we win a corner. "It's not over yet," I say. "Get a fuckin' move on," I gesture to Billy McNeill, who quickens his pace as he crosses the halfway line. One last, mighty effort . . . the forwards do their job, dragging their markers away from the goalmouth, leaving the way clear. Charlie Gallagher swings it into the middle and then time seems to stand still. The ball hangs in the air. There is a momentary vacuum of sound as Celtic Park holds its breath. I feel Sean gripping my shoulder. Then, he arrives. Big Billy. Like a steam train crashing through the bollards at the end of the track. As the ball leaves his forehead, my arms are in the air. As it arcs into the net, I am already hugging Sean. The ball nestles in the net. We are through. We have come from behind, survived even more pressure on our home ground and have found a way to win. We are through! Somehow.

"There is something happening here," says Sean as we walk up the tunnel. I nod. "This could be a season to remember."

~~~

The street ends in obscurity; a pool of water and a glade of salt grass. In the rapidly diminishing light we dig a little pit in the sand and gather driftwood that has been bleached and dried by the sun. Mark gets a fine blaze going which envelopes us in a bubble of light and warmth amid a darkness that creeps around us like silence. The *White Horse* bottle is passed from person to person like a peace pipe, sealing the bond that has been set between us today.

"What a day," says a downcast Iggy.

"That poor, poor man," says Delphine.

"So young. It's awful. Just awful," says Eddie.

"Certainly puts things into perspective," says Rocky.

Delphine begins to sob. Iggy comforts her.

"What do you say, Mark?" I ask.

"Yous m-m-maybe don't want to know."

"Go on. Nobody will judge you."

He looks around the assembled fire-lit faces.

"I think it was his t-t-t-t-time."

"Away!" exclaims Rocky.

"He was our age for Christ's sake, younger even!" protests Iggy.

"I know, I know. Maybe I haven't expressed myself r-r-right. It's just that . . . I believe certain things happen for a r-r-reason. Even t-terrible things sometimes. Ach, I haven't even worked it out properly in my heid so maybe I shouldn't be b-b-blethering like this, but I do believe that the ways of G-G-G-God are m-mysterious. There's more to life than m-meets the eye. It's no all random bad l-l-luck. And even if today was only that – just a random, tragic event, I believe we can still take m-meaning from things, 'cause at the end of the day good will triumph. That boy – he was p-p-p-peaceful at the end. Naw, more than that, he was full of j-j-j-j-joy."

"Never!" says Iggy.

"Aye!" insists Mark. "You saw it T-Tim. He was j-j-j-j-joyful at the end, was he n-no?"

"Well . . ." I begin.

Suddenly I feel self-conscious with five pairs of eyes on me.

"Aye, he was," I say.

Delphine rises and walks towards the road. After a moment I get up and follow her.

She is standing at the edge of the continent, gazing inland. I place my jersey over her shoulders. She turns and smiles at me.

"Debbie is the love of your life, and you aren't over her. That's why you won't commit to London, isn't it?"

"It's just too sudden . . . my head's all mixed up."

She gazes into the distance again.

"What are you thinking of?"

"What to do now; this is as far as I go. I might stay here, by the ocean. Or I might visit my father. He stays up that road somewhere. About 100 kilometres or so."

"You said you don't get along . . ."

"He is a difficult man, but today . . . that poor man in the car . . . it has got me to thinking. And I don't blame father entirely. He could never come to terms with mother. He moved here, to the south, after she . . . died. He couldn't bear to return to Carnac. Did I tell you that my mother had red hair, like me?"

"She took her own life, didn't she?"

She continues to gaze up the road, into France, her homeland. Then, barely perceptible, a nod.

~~~

I sit alone with my thoughts. The wife and kids are in bed. The television flickers in the corner. A reporter, standing in front of a fountain in a square in Lisbon, is speaking in posh BBC.

"Tomorrow, Celtic will leave Glasgow for their much anticipated meeting with Inter Milan in the European Cup final. Many of their fans are, as you can see, here already, regaling locals with

their songs. Helenio Herrera, the Inter manager, has encouraged the Portuguese, as fellow Latins, to support his team, but it seems that the charm of the Celtic supporters has won them over instead. It all adds up to a carnival atmosphere, but it will be nothing compared to the party if Jock Stein's team can overcome the might of Inter Milan on Thursday."

I turn off the television and sit quietly in the darkness.

The road to Lisbon. The final stretch. The most important part. The most exciting part. The most terrifying part.

~~~

The pension is spartan but clean and welcoming. A hall lamp casts fantastic shadows on the staircase walls. I bunk up with Rocky. The sweet warm aroma of wood and dust greets me. Part of me is already tired of the open road and longs for permanence. And this day has taken its toll. In an effort to help myself feel at home I booze and smoke as I place my few things in one of the dresser's musty drawers, which are lined with glossy patterned paper and contain the odd worthless coin or redundant key. But this night brings a feeling of sorrow that neither whisky nor cigarettes can dispel. The darkness. Everything is altered; everything sits at a slightly different angle or has a peculiar hue to it.

"Mr Stein, did that poor fella die before his time?"

"Perhaps. Certainly it happens. I knew a lad of 16 who died in a pit accident. Suffocated, the poor sowel. All for the price of decent safety standards. Yet death is a part of life, and sometimes folk dying young is a part of life."

"Seems to me the older you get the more of your dreams about how life was meant to turn out get stripped away. And it's the darkness – I mean your darker premonitions – that come true instead."

"Maybe. But it's how we deal with that – the bad things,

*the defeats, the disappointments – that's what makes us men.
It's easy to be strong when things are looking up. When things
are tough you still have to retain some belief, in yourself, but
also in life. Good things can happen too. Your pal, Mark –
you should pay heed to his words. He knows how to give it
up."*

"Give what up?"

*"Uncertainty. Contradictions. He knows to give them up to
God. Us humans, we're no supposed to comprehend everything in this life. Aye, our brains are remarkable for solving
problems, for making things better for humanity. But there's a
whole realm of mystery out there that we can only wonder at.
We can write songs and poems about it but no much else. If we
think on it too much it will drive us mad."*

Day Five

Tuesday, May 23rd, 1967

Jimmy Johnstone hates flying, detests it more than anything. The non-flying winger, that's what we call him.

"Can I no get a boat to Lisbon, boss?" he says, only half-joking.

"Don't worry Jimmy, if we hit the water you'll be first in the lifeboat," I reply. "Then big Billy . . . the rest of yous are good swimmers, so I'll see you in Lisbon. Kick-off is at half-five. And if you're late, I'll fuckin' fine you."

They all laugh. The tension broken. We walk across the tarmac to the waiting plane. I look back over my shoulder.

We'll be running round Lisbon when we come,
We'll be running round Lisbon when we come,
We'll be running round Lisbon,
Running round Lisbon,
Running round Lisbon when we come!

Hundreds of fans, singing loudly, their banners draped over the front of the terminal building, have come to bid us farewell.

"I feel like one of the Beatles," I say to Sean.

"The Beatles aren't as popular as us, Jock. Not this week, anyway."

Cabin crew in aeroplanes have seen it all – sick children, petrified adults . . . but they haven't seen Jimmy Johnstone. We are all sitting on the plane ready for take-off when I feel a splash on my head. I swing round. It is Jimmy, spraying holy water from a small plastic container in the shape of the Virgin Mary. I stand up, the water trickling down my face.

"Sorry boss, but you can't take any chances," he says, flashing a nervous smile.

"Jimmy, if you don't sit down I'll fuckin' sling you off this plane."

"That might no be such a bad thing. I could still catch that boat," he replies.

I frogmarch him back to his seat and the cabin crew breathe a sigh of relief. Another Jimmy drama over.

~~~

My father comes to me when I am asleep. I am amid a throng of people, then he appears, suddenly, briefly, only long enough to say: "Follow your dreams," then he is gone, disappeared into the crowd.

I awake, clammy with sweat in the muggy night.

Rocky is snoring. I take a slug of lemonade. Spark up a fag. The tobacco crackles as the flame jets from the lighter. It illuminates something, a piece of paper slotted into the dresser mirror.

Dear Tim,

I've decided to go. I'm sorry for leaving without a word but I couldn't bear a long goodbye.

I've only known you for a few days but I feel so strongly drawn to you, yet you are breaking your heart over Debbie.

I couldn't sleep so I'm sitting by the beach at dawn. I can hear the terns calling on the shore, enjoying the first warmth of the day as the sun creeps over the horizon. The water looks so gorgeous, framed by the sky and the pale dunes – I wish I could waken you and share this glorious sight; I wish I had time to paint it! The sound of the ocean is so soothing. I feel sadness, but at the same time a strong sense of ardour for being alive and young in these heady days. I feel that the world is brimming with possibilities today and that although we are to be parted now, perhaps forever, that Fate has wonderful things in store for both of us in our lives.

I told you that true love was a fallacy. I lied. You have loved and lost, and I feel for you. I hope Celtic can bring you some consolation in Lisbon. You said that they are the underdogs, the artists; well I have a feeling that Thursday is to be their day. Tell the boys that my love goes with them. They will have a special place in my memory.

I am off to visit my father now. Pray that when he sees me coming up his path he will recognise his daughter and not the shadow of the woman he so loved and lost.

I ask only one thing of you, and it is this: fill out an application for St Martin's. My tutor Peter will expedite it. Come September, if you still wish to remain in Glasgow, then so be it. But at least leave yourself that option.

Know that a little part of my heart will forever keep alive the hope that one day there will be a knock at my studio door. It will be you, Tim, arrived to sit for me.

Au revoir,

Yours,

Delphine Marie Robin

I finish my cigarette and sit there for a few minutes, re-reading the letter. An initial wave of sorrow and guilt gives way to conflicting emotions and desires.

"She was crazy about you."

Rocky's voice gives me a start. He has woken and seen me reading the letter, put two and two together.

"Eh?"

"Delphine. She loved you."

"Garbage. I only knew her for five minutes!"

"She telt me it was love at first sight. A once-in-a-lifetime experience."

I read the letter for a last time. Then I purposefully fold it and put it away.

"You okay?"

"Aye. Go back to sleep, Rocky."

I am okay. From somewhere in the desolate night comes a knowledge that things will work out for the best. I lie back and wait for exhaustion and the comfort of a real bed to coax me back to sleep.

~~~

It is easy to tell when footballers are confident. They swagger, talk the talk. Start to think they are somebody. That's when they start getting ideas.

It starts as a few whispers. Rumblings. When you walk into a dressing room and the conversation dies, that's when you know something is afoot. And there's only one thing that players talk in hushed tones about. Money.

"Must think I'm fuckin stupid, Sean. I know they're plotting. Fuckin' cheek. Don't know they were born, these boys. They need to spend a day down the mines." I am sitting at my desk. I can hear the rumble of voices from the dressing room. When I passed earlier, the door was shut.

"Oh aye," I thought.

I am waiting for the knock. When it finally arrives, it is a timid one, almost apologetic. I ignore it. Another knock.

"What?"

Billy McNeill pops his head in. I don't even look up.

"Boss?"

I carry on writing my imaginary note. I finish it. Look up.

"What?"

"Boss, it's just that the boys have elected me to come and chat to you about our European bonuses."

I stare at him. Fuckin' glare at him.

"So, er, can I have a word?"

"Here's two for you. FUCK OFF."

He turns on his heels. The boys will be waiting for him to come back with some news. But Billy can't go back. Not yet.

I put my head round the door 15 minutes later. Down the corridor, I see the toilet door opening and Billy skulking out. He's been killing time. Kidding on he's been fighting their case for the last quarter of an hour and not sitting in the lavvy counting the bits of toilet paper.

I chuckle heartily, maybe even loud enough for the players to hear . . .

. . . The Palacio Hotel, Estoril, Portugal. Marble tiles, gleaming paintwork. Tropical gardens, Mercs and Rollers parked at the entrance, the crystal-blue ocean a stone's throw away. Luxury. Opulence. Nothing but the best, and what are this team and these players, if not the best?

The Palacio Hotel. A playground for the wealthy, but also an important statement. The players troop off the bus.

"Boss, I think we've stopped at the wrong place. The youth hostel is down the road," quips Bertie.

"The Kings of Europe do not live like beggars," I fire back. "Bags in the rooms and then meet me in the lobby in 20 minutes."

The first battle lines must be drawn. Limits set, rules laid down. I have identified the first enemy in the camp – that burning sphere in the sky. Stein versus the sun. There is only going to be one winner. The players return to the lobby and gather round.

"Gentlemen, you stand on the brink of greatness. Everything you ever dreamed of is now within touching distance. Nothing can be allowed to compromise that. So I will tell you once and I will not tell you again. Stay out of the fuckin' sun. You know what happened in America last summer. A certain little red-haired gentleman came down with sun-stroke. Twice. If I see so much as a freckle on those peely wally faces of yours, I'll fuckin' kill you. Then I'll drop you and send you on the first plane back to Scotland. In that order. Every moment spent in the sun saps your energy, affects your ability to fulfil your destiny. This is not a holiday. This is not about sunbathing. This is not about sight-seeing. This is about making history."

~~~

The road to Lisbon. Spain suggests herself from behind the curtain of the Pyrenees.

We are entranced by the vista of the mountains sweeping down towards the Côte Basque. We plunge into a pleasantly wooded gorge before crossing the border. After we have stopped in San Sebastian to change our money and stock up on cartons of fags and a crate of Rioja, I notice that our conversation has become distracted. We share jokes and stories but now that we are in Spain there's a tense rattle in our voices. We all know that we are ignoring the elephant in the room: two days until the match.

The Basque countryside is beautiful. Naturally terraced hills wooded with pines give way to a dramatic coastline. I close my eyes to commit the scene to memory; I will try to sketch it later.

Eddie shatters the idyll and we all join in on the second line.

Hail! Hail! The Celts are here,
What the hell do we care, what the hell do we care,
Hail! Hail! The Celts are here,
What the hell do we care now.
For it's a grand old team to play for,

It's a grand old team to see,
And if, you know, your history,
It's enough to make your heart go: o-o-o
We don't care if we win, lose or draw,
What the hell do we care,
For we only know that there's gonnae be a show,
And the Glasgow Celtic will be there!

As the song goes into its final flourish our singing startles a peasant farmer, who we overtake as he chugs along on an ancient tractor. He looks at us as though we have just arrived from Mars. We all laugh. The song has cleared the air, relieved the tension, refocused us from yesterday's trials to our love for Celtic, the entire purpose of our trip. Plus we are all glad to have enjoyed the comforts of the pension – we are well slept and fed, washed and shaved; bright as new pins.

"Bar's open!" announces Iggy cheerfully, passing the bottle. I get tore in. Man, that's the gemme; makes you feel alive. Makes yesterday's anguish drain away. Unravel it later. Now there is only the road. The road to Lisbon.

It is nice taking the byways for a while, and apart from the tractor we don't see a single other vehicle. We are off the Celticade's beaten track, off on our own thrilling, private, comradely adventure.

But a little further on I notice Rocky's brow has furrowed. I can feel the power drain from the Zodiac. Rocky is pumping the accelerator but we are slowing.

"What are you slowing down for Rocky?" asks Iggy.

"The car . . . it's losing power."

He glides us to a halt at the side of the road. We all get out. A staccato *phut phut phut phut* rises in pitch and then falls away as the tractor passes by.

"Hauw, auld yin!" says Iggy. "Gonnae give us a ride on your tractor?"

The rubbernecked farmer simply regards us with the same astonished expression, as though we belong to a different species.

I head into the brush and pee against a bank of honeysuckle, enjoying the foreignness of this secluded, sun-dappled place. I take care not to hit a little lizard who is enjoying the morning warmth. I go back to the car. The lads are all helping out so I just sit right down, spark up a ciggy and draw in the smooth blue smoke.

"Okay Iggy – give her some gas."

On Rocky's command Iggy guns the engine. It barks and roars with complaint, then reaches a deafening, whining crescendo. The din sets my nerves on end; will the engine explode, shearing my pals to pieces with ragged shards of shrapnel? Or will it simply surrender, and rupture itself beyond repair in order to stop the agony? Yet Rocky is unfazed, his hand calmly continuing to circle in indication.

I watch him. He is utterly absorbed in the engine, in complete control of it. I wonder if I ever lose myself like that in my painting. Hard to know, I suppose, but I doubt it. Too many subtexts, too much shite spinning around inside my head. I seem to lack a quality of certainty about myself that people like Rocky effortlessly possess. I feel a pang of envy as I consider how much Debbie would doubtlessly be drawn to this man of action, this uncomplicated breadwinner. I think back to when they were both 16 and went out together.

Then I think about the first night she and I spent together. Her modesty, despite her profound beauty. I had watched her silhouette as she undressed carefully, seriously. I treasured that moment as the most precious in my life. I knew this didn't come cheap to a girl like her. I loved her for a lot of reasons but at that moment the main one was that she had chosen me.

Rocky looks up from under the bonnet. Flushed and greasy. Signals to Iggy to kill the engine.

"We need a new throttle cable. Fuck."

~~~

I look out. At the rows of eyes fixed upon me. Scottish Press men, English, Portuguese, Italian. The world's media . . .

I am the centre of attention. They are ready to hang on my every word. They are waiting, hoping, longing for a story. I am not going to disappoint them.

"Thanks for coming along gentlemen. I won't keep you long. I know you all have deadlines, and I, frankly, have more important things to do."

A ripple of laughter.

"I'll take questions in a minute, but first . . . here's my team."

A dramatic pause. They all look at me as if I have lost my mind.

Forty-eight hours before the biggest match of his life and the Big Man is going to name his team . . . he has fuckin' lost it, the pressure has finally got to him.

But I have my reasons. Eleven of them. Eleven names that have been inscribed on my brain for the past month; names that are the most powerful statement of intent I can deliver at this moment. No secrecy, no hidden agendas, no mind games. Just the names of the men I trust to win in the style I want. I may be revealing my hand, but I am showing Herrera that I believe I have a winning hand.

I'm showing that I know my best team, how we are going to play, how my players are going to rise to the challenge and that they can be relied upon on the greatest stage of all. Eleven names that spell out belief and courage. I know my team. Do you know yours, Helenio? And, if you do, do you have the balls to tell the whole fuckin' world? Those names will be the sound of a gauntlet being thrown down. The men who now know they are in the team can relax and focus properly on the biggest challenge of their lives. They know that I believe in them. Their backs will straighten. They will now feel they can conquer the world.

I reel through the names once more in my mind, the names that have become like a mantra. I do not need a sheet. They are tattooed on my brain. I stare straight ahead and out they come, tripping off the tongue.

"Simpson . . . Craig . . . Gemmell . . . Murdoch . . . McNeill . . . Clark . . . Johnstone . . . Wallace . . . Chalmers . . . Auld . . . Lennox."

I reach the end and wait for the scribbling to stop. They put their pencils down and look at me.

"Any questions?"

Silence.

"Well, I think that means you have got your story! And that means I can get back to the real stuff. Thanks boys."

I walk out. I stand for a moment and listen.

Still silence.

~~~

Eddie, Iggy and me volunteer to walk westwards to find help at the next village.

"It'll be okay lads," I say as we amble along. "Even if we miss today we've got all of the morra to get to Lisbon . . . and even Thursday morning and afternoon if needs be."

The road curves slightly and we happen across a middle-aged, olive-coloured SEAT 600 which is parked up. A beautiful young woman, with chestnut hair and iodine skin, is standing on the passenger seat, her upper body protruding through the sunroof. Alongside, a man has climbed a telegraph pole. He is attaching a flag, which has a red background with a green diagonal cross beneath a white cross. The girl notices us with alarm and begins speaking urgently to the man. He clambers down quickly, exchanging a few sharp words with the female.

"Hola!" I call out, hoping to put them at ease.

The man tosses the flag at the girl and nervously lights a cigarette. He is about 30, of medium height and build, with handsome, broad features. His stance is rather effeminate, with one hand tucked into his back pocket, the other pointing the cigarette with understated belligerence. He is unshaven and wears brown plastic-rimmed spectacles with tinted lenses, behind which his small eyes dart quickly. His lips pout rather arrogantly as he regards us suspiciously.

"Gora Euskadi Askatuta!" shouts Eddie.

The man's stern expression breaks slightly at Eddie's words. Eddie sees my puzzled look.

"And I thought you were supposed to be politically educated," he smiles. "It means, 'Long Live a Free Basque Country'. That's a Basque flag he was trying to pin up. It's forbidden."

"Hola," shouts the man. The girl is stashing the flag in the car.

"You speak English?"

"Sure. Ah, you are Scottish? You go to Lisboa for Celtic?"

His voice is rather high-pitched. His hair, which is thinning a little on top exposing a high forehead, is slicked to one side with oil and combed down into long sideburns. He wears a tan-coloured leather jerkin which tones with his corduroy flares, and a white roll-neck sweater.

"Yes!"

"Ah, very good. We met a bunch of you in San Sebastian yesterday."

"Our car has broken down, just back there. Is there a village nearby?"

"Ispaster. It's less than a kilometre. There is a garage there. It is very small but they may be able to help."

"I don't suppose you could tow us?"

"No problem my friend. You should be able to squeeze into the back. My name is Xalbador. This is Angelu."

We shake hands. The girl smiles shyly.

Inside the car Xalbador pauses, scratches the back of his neck distractedly. "My friends, I believe you saw . . ."

"The flag? You can count on our discretion, my friend," I assure him.

"It is very important."

"In Spain it is a serious business," says Angelu rather timidly.

"No bother," says Eddie in a soothing voice. "We know all about flags and symbolism . . . the fight for self-determination. We live in hope for the day when the Six Counties are reunited with Ireland."

"I salute that noble goal!" says Xalbador.

"Me too," says Angelu, flashing a smile of brilliant white teeth at Eddie.

"Up the flying columns!" declares Iggy.

~~~

Most managers look back on their playing days with nostalgia. Life was simpler, then. They turned up, ran about a bit during the week, checked the notice board on a Friday to see if they were in the team, and then finished their working week with a game. After the game, a few pints with the boys and then the cycle began again on Monday morning. Footballers are creatures of habit and there was a comfort in the monotony. They knew where they were, had a set position and that was it. Simple. For a few, like me, it was plain dull. I hated the repetitiveness of it. Ploughing round a cinder track, playing the same position week-in, week-out, it bored me to tears. I wanted to try out new things. But, as a player, nobody wanted to listen. As a manager, you could make them listen. Encourage them, inspire them, command them.

Playing or management? Give me management any day of the week. Some people go to college or university to learn. My football education started to accelerate when I took my first steps into coaching. Learning fired my imagination. I wanted to immerse myself in different football cultures, break free from Scottish and British football, to gain a more rounded education. The memory of the great Hungarian team still burned brightly. I knew there were different things, great things, happening in Europe and I wanted to be part of it.

It was in November 1963, while manager of Dunfermline, that an opportunity presented itself. I was offered the chance to travel to Italy and study the methods of Helenio Herrera, the legendary Argentine coach of Inter Milan, who had won the league the previous season for the first time in nine years.

Herrera was a small, serious-looking man with a huge presence. He did not walk into rooms. He entered. When he did, the atmosphere changed. Tall, bronzed footballers suddenly stood to attention when he addressed them. He spoke to them with a brutal clarity. His philosophies were pinned up around the training ground.

Who doesn't give it all, gives nothing.

Class + Preparation + Intelligence + Athleticism = Championships.

He was obsessed with building a winning mentality. His players were trained to deliver positive messages to the media.

We have come to win . . . we have the players to be victorious.

If any deviated from the script, they were fined.

Discipline was top of his agenda. Smoking and drinking were forbidden. The players' diets were strictly controlled. Three days before games he took his squad to a country retreat to prepare them.

I looked around the walls of his office and saw box files packed with personal profiles of every player at the club. Thorough, meticulously researched, Herrera was taking things to a whole new level.

On the training field, he broke the mould. He carried out drills I had never dreamt of. He laid out his philosophy, explaining his concept of mounting lightning-quick attacks from deep and the value of overlapping full-backs. He was thinking thoughts no-one had before. The players were well-drilled athletes, clean-living and open-minded, diamonds polished by his militaristic regime.

It made me think about Scottish football; the closed minds, the rivers of alcohol, the clouds of tobacco smoke and the betting dens. How would Herrera survive in Scotland? He wouldn't. He would take one look and leave. I had to find my own way to get the best out of players who had grown up in one of the most densely-populated, heavily-industrialised corners of Europe.

I watched how Herrera talked about football, broke it down, analysed it like a science experiment, or a mathematical formula. Herrera was most famed for developing the *catenaccio*, the stifling 'door-bolt' system with its close man-marking and its rigid line of defenders. He spoke passionately about the role of attacking full-backs. He picked out Giacinto Facchetti as the prime example of a defender he had converted into a rampaging full-back and spent just as much time in the opposition's half as he did his own. It was inspiring.

Herrera had happened upon a winning formula, but I began to wonder if there was a gaping hole in his master-plan. I thought about the players that made my pulse race, Patsy Gallacher, Georgie Best; players whose individual genius could light up a game and get the crowd buzzing. Where would they have fitted into Herrera's vision? They wouldn't. He would have run them out of town. It occurred to me that Herrera had most of the jigsaw but there were pieces missing, and I suspected that those pieces were the most important to me. Despite all the talk of attacking full-backs, there was no denying that defence was at the core. His method was more about his players stopping opponents rather than expressing their talents. He had built an impenetrable system, and he had done so with a level of professionalism that would surely lead to even greater success. He was light years ahead of his contemporaries, but I left believing that his system also seemed too rigid, too inflexible. Maybe one day somebody would crack the code, and then where would he be?

But I never forgot his presence. Herrera removed any doubts over the importance of complete authority in management. After that trip, I knew a great manager had to be like a dictator. He was not there to be liked. He was there to command respect and to demand that his orders be followed. Everything else flowed from that point.

~~~

We introduce Rocky and Mark to our new friends and get out the tow rope. The little SEAT valiantly takes up the strain and we glide solemnly the short distance to the village. It's a pretty little place, a cluster of buildings with veined-pearl walls and terracotta roofs, nestling at the foot of a hill. The garage is a dilapidated wooden shed, peeling red and white paint. A rusty petrol pump sits on the oil-stained forecourt bearing the letters *CEPSA*.

Rocky emerges from the gloomy interior shaking his head. He is followed by the silver-haired proprietor, who wipes his greasy hands with a rag as he chats in Basque with Xalbador.

"He's gonnae have to order the part from Bilbao," Rocky informs us. "We're stuck here till the morra I'm afraid chaps."

A concerned grumble emits from the group.

"Well, while we're here we might as well treat Xalbador and Angelu to a beer, to thank them for the tow, like," suggests Eddie.

~~~

Hibs came calling in early 1964 and the job was too big to resist. I had turned Dunfermline around from relegation candidates to cup winners. I had restored respectability and even made a mark in Europe. I could go no further. It was time to broaden my horizons and Easter Road was the place to do it. They had a bigger fanbase and substantially more money than Dunfermline. It was a step up, another test of my credentials but one that I was sure that I needed. I had ideas, but I needed the players to execute them. Hibs were struggling, 12th in an 18-team league but they had good players. And they had Willie Hamilton. Hamilton was the key to everything. Quick, two-footed, skilful, a joy to behold; he was also a loose cannon. Name a vice and he had it. If I was to achieve anything with Hibs, I had to get Willie playing. Some players respond to a hard-line approach. Willie did not. You could scream at him all day and he would nod his head solemnly . . . and then wander off and into the nearest pub, spraying around his wages like the passes he made on a Saturday. Willie took risks every day of his life. He also took risks on the football field. That was the key to his greatness. He lived on the edge, but he gave Hibs their edge. He needed to be indulged, cajoled, occasionally shouted at, but mainly looked after. Man-management was the key to being a leader of men and no-one challenged me more in that respect than Willie Hamilton. Sometimes he was a liability, but other times he was a hero, and for those times, you had to just sit back and marvel; for at those times, the world looked a beautiful place. The grass looked greener, the birds sang in the trees and God was in His heaven when Willie Hamilton was in full flow.

One such day was the second leg of our semi-final Summer Cup tie against Kilmarnock. We were 4-3 down from the first game but Willie took the second leg by storm, inspiring us to a 3-0 victory. When we beat Aberdeen 3-1 in the final, after two legs that had finished all square, it marked the club's first trophy in a decade.

The season started poorly. We lost to Hearts in our opening game, but recovered well to inch up the league. One day I spoke to the chairman.

"How would you like to get loads of good publicity for the club and entertain the fans in a way they've never been before?" I said.

"Sounds great, Jock, where do I sign?"

"Well, you'll need to stump up £12,000 but it is a small price to pay for bringing the great Real Madrid to Edinburgh for a friendly."

He looked at me as if I was mad, but I knew it could be done. And we did it. On October 7, 1964, the great Real, with Di Stefano, Puskás and Gento, brought their talents to Scotland. Football gods descending from their heavenly realms. Thirty-two thousand turned up for the game and there was a carnival atmosphere. Before the game, I put the players in the picture.

"Listen to the fans outside. They are excited. They are about to witness some of the greatest players that ever pulled on a pair of boots. Not one of you can afford to treat this game as a friendly. This is a chance for you to prove yourself against the very best. I'll be watching you all closely, judging you. Don't fuckin' let me down."

They didn't. After 20 minutes, 17-year-old Peter Cormack signalled his talent with the opening goal. Then Willie Hamilton started unpicking the Real defence at will. I watched him sway past Di Stefano and chuckled at the absurdity of it all. It taught me an important lesson, that wayward talents had the ability to perform at the highest level if harnessed in the right way.

The Press were spot on the next day: "Hamilton, the man discarded by so many clubs, was worth six of Puskás."

October 7, 1964.

The day Willie Hamilton taught the great Real Madrid a football lesson.

~~~

We sit at the bar inside a little cantina. Large cervezas are being set up tantalisingly in front of us. The foam froths over the edges of the frosted glasses. It seems right to wait until all seven are served. Then we drink thirstily.

"I like these Spanish beers," says Rocky.

"Sody I," agrees Iggy.

"Soda water," says Rocky.

"Eddie. Tell us the one about Iggy knocking the polis car," I suggest. I'm not sure why I make this request; for some reason I want Eddie to be the centre of attention. Maybe it's something to do with Angelu.

"You mean 'The Greatest Story Ever Told'?" says Eddie.

"Aye."

"Or, alternatively, 'The Miracle of Gorbals Cross'."

"Aye. G-go on!" says Mark.

"Naw, no the now lads."

"Go on," says Rocky.

"Aye, go on Eddie," I urge him.

"Aw, alright then. Iggy's most famous dalliance with car theft was when he stole a polis car. This is a true story, gen up.

"It all started one night in the Smiddy public house in Plantation Street. There was a lock-in, a highly irregular affair, and one that soon came into the ken of the local cops. They rapped the door and gained entry, but no before all the revellers had taken refuge in the cellar leaving just the landlord – a wily old Irishman – and a few choice patrons at the bar.

" 'We've had reports of after-hours drinking here,' said one of the polis.

" 'Just a private party officer. A few quiet drinks for friends.'

" 'No cash sales?'

" 'None at all.'

"The filth nosed around, their radars on full alert. One of them was top brass.

" 'The Inspector here, ahem, he's – we've all had a bit of a rough time in the line of duty tonight. Could you provide him with a dram?'

"Not one to offend the local constabulary, the landlord poured the assembled coppers a large one each, on the house. Then another one. Then another. On the third dram the revellers, tired of being cooped up underground with the rats, started to drift back into the bar. The polis couldn't complain – they were all after-hours drinkers now.

"Meanwhile outside Fate played her mischievous hand in proceedings. Who should be passing by but the bold Iggy. He himself was full of the drink and happened to spy the parked-up squad car had been left unlocked. To Iggy it would have been an effrontery to his very nature to have walked on by.

"Five minutes later and I'm speeding along Ballater Street, driving a van on the early morning breid run. I'm still half-jaked from the night before, hungover, late and have no had too much in the way of kip. I know I am driving too fast but who's on the road at this time of the morning?

"At Gorbals Cross a polis car, blue light flashing, siren blaring, suddenly bursts into view to my left. I barely have time to touch the brake pedal before I've broadsided it. I have right of way but it won't matter. Not when the polis are involved. My heart sinks.

"Then it happens. The Miracle of Gorbals Cross. The driver of the squad car clambers out. Then bolts. Like an Olympic sprinter. My jaw is on the floor. I'm no sure what the bloke is wearing but it sure isn't the uniform of Glasgow's finest. In fact, it has a passing resemblance to one of Iggy's loud suits.

"The cops were so mortified by events that they covered it up, and no heat came my way. But they made sure the Smiddy was shut down after that, the bastards. They were convinced that one of the patrons had knocked the car and they just hated the idea of the Gorbals finding out that night what a bunch of tubes they truly are."

We laugh and sink our beers.

"So, Iggy. You stole the police car, even though you didn't have any key?" enquires Xalbador.

"I certainly did," says Iggy, proudly.

"He's an expert," says Rocky.

Xalbador looks thoughtful.

~~~

Celtic v Dundee, League Cup, August 1965

"He'll get me the sack. I'm telling you, Sean. He'll get me the fuckin' sack. It's players like that who do managers in . . ."

Two defeats in the first three games of the season. 2–0 down at home against a superb Dundee side and the wee fucker is trying to take the piss out of the full-back. Bobby Murdoch shows for it, but the wee man turns away, tries to beat his man for the second time.

"Release it. Fuckin' release it."

This time, the full-back gets him. The wee man spins into the air, comes down with a crash, looks expectantly at the referee. Nothing. He trots past the dugout.

"Don't fuckin' dare moan at the ref. It wisnae a foul. Why the fuck didn't you pass to Bobby?"

He looks at me as if I'm mad, like I'm talking Swahili. Did he even see Bobby? Maybe not. Maybe he's so caught up with his parlour tricks that he can't even fuckin' see what's in front of him.

Soon after, he's done his man again, the cross is on. But what does he do? Foot on the ball, waits for the defender to come back at him . . . just so he can beat him again.

"Never a team player," I say to Sean.

Next week in The Celtic View, *a shot across his bows.*

"Some of our forwards' play against Dundee was just plain stupid. Some players had persisted in going their own way, not doing as they were told in the pre-match planning. Steps will be taken to ensure that Celtic come first and individuals second . . . One change that will be made for the next game is at outside-right, where Steve Chalmers will be brought in again."

The phone starts ringing, the grapevine twitching. Bobby Howitt at Motherwell is interested in the wee man. Eddie Baily, Bill Nicholson's assistant at Spurs, has been watching him too, as a possible replacement for Cliff Jones.

"The wee man is sweating, Jock," says Sean. "Thinks he's on his way out. One of the boys was saying he was in tears the other day, talking about going back to the Juniors."

"Let the wee fucker sweat, Sean. I'll decide on him in my own time."

September 10th, 1965, a friendly match against Clydebank. I'm running the rule over a couple of Brazilian trialists. They've probably got no chance of a deal, but it's a nice wee titbit for the Press. Keeps us on the back pages. The crowd is big for a reserve game. Quite a few of the journalists are here, too.

The wee man's at outside-right. Five minutes in, he picks it up. Bobs, weaves, drops the shoulder and he's away. The centre-half races across to cover. Wee tap through his legs and he moves up another gear. The crowd responds. A murmur sweeps round. Something's happening. Now he's in the box. There's another defender in front of him. But he's got Yogi Hughes free inside him. What's he going to do? He weighs it up. His instinct is to take on the defender. Every fibre of his being wants to drop that shoulder again, go round the outside. I'm ready to blast him. But, suddenly, he stops. Foot on the ball. Square pass. Yogi meets it on the run. 1-0. My jaw drops. Sean swings round. Arches his eyebrow.

Midway through the half, he hits the byeline, sends over a first-time cross. 2-0.

"What about that?" says Sean.

"He's been listening. I can't believe the penny's dropped!"

Forty minutes gone, he gets the ball, outfoxes the full-back and cuts inside. A nutmeg, sidestep and suddenly it all opens up for him. But then he does a funny thing. He lifts his head, looks for a team-mate. Then, he realises that he's on his own. This is his moment. It's time to be selfish, to take the glory. And he hits it low and sweet, watches it fizz into the corner. 3-0. Half-time.

I've seen enough. I take the stairs three at a time, burst into the dressing room.

"Jimmy, get those boots off, you're not going out for the second half."

He looks up at me in horror.

"And wipe that soppy look off your face. It's to keep you fresh for Saturday. You're staying. But always remember one thing: you play for the team, or you play in the reserves."

~~~

Xalbador and Angelu don't seem to be in any hurry and convey our things in their car to where we will camp. We follow them on foot, through a pleasant forest. We see the ocean, which is about a mile away from the village, brilliant blue though the trees. The coast here is formed as a bight that stretches considerably to the east, but less so, yet more steeply, to the west, where it gives way to the sea in dramatic slate cliffs below which lies a wrecked fishing vessel, stripped bare like a whale's ribcage. The deserted beach itself is rocky and primeval, but interspersed with swathes of comfortable sand. It is upon this sand, and against where the red earth of the pine forest drops away abruptly, that we set up camp. I listen to the crackle and spit of the fire and the surf crashing in the middle distance. I can smell kelp and smoking driftwood. Eddie and Angelu, who are sitting nearby, begin chatting.

"Is Xalbador angry with you?" asks Eddie.

"I embarrassed him. With the flag. I was supposed to keep watch. He cannot tolerate mistakes . . . he wants all of us to be professional guerrillas. He says there is a war coming. Not just in Spain, but the world over. The fight for justice."

If Xalbador's voice is peculiarly high-pitched, Angelu's is unexpectedly low in tenor. That, and the way she carries her frame, are at odds with her otherwise delicate, feminine demeanour. She holds her shoulders in a hunched fashion that conveys a sense of being uncomfortable in her own skin, like a permanent self-effacing shrug, and her big hazel eyes roll in mock despair of herself as she talks. Her shyness is all the more becoming because she is, in fact, utterly beautiful.

"You seem to think a lot of him, his ideals. I hope he doesn't get you into trouble."

"I guess all little sisters worship their older brothers."

"Oh, you are . . . brother and sister."

She smiles at him coyly.

"Earlier . . . you knew that slogan, 'Gora Euskadi Askatuta'."

"Well, I know a little about revolutionary politics myself. In fact, my uncle served here on the Republican side."

"Your uncle fought in the Civil War?"

"Yes, for the International Brigades. He was a member of the Communist Party. He was wounded at Ebro."

"He sounds like a courageous man."

"He was the finest man I ever knew." He steals a look at her. "No Pasaran!"

"No Pasaran!" she smiles.

"Angelu, Franco . . . the state. They'll come down hard upon you."

"We will be prepared. We will be ready for the next phase. No more just sabotage, painting pointless slogans."

"So it will be bullets and bombs instead?"

"It is inevitable. Unavoidable."

I open my eyes and watch them from behind. He offers her a cigarette, takes one himself, lights hers, then his. I am struck by how cool he seems. He is lost in thought, then speaks again.

"It's a hell of a thing to see a person die of violence. It stays with you. Nothing can ever erase it from your mind."

"We have no choice . . . your uncle knew that the only way to defeat fascism was with armed struggle."

"Aye, perhaps. As long as you realise where it all ends. With innocents being killed."

"So be it."

"I hope you have enough steel within you." He takes a draw from his fag and exhales. " 'Cause violence, doling it out . . . it gets you."

I begin to feel as though I am intruding by listening in, so I go for a wander a little further along the way where Xalbador and Iggy are chatting in lowered tones.

"Alright lads?"

"Tim! I was just instructing Iggy here about our struggle for a Basque homeland."

"How interesting. I must say Xalbador, your English is excellent."

"A good education my friend. That is the primary means of fighting back. I learned English and German in the UK, at LSE, alongside political studies. The first thing a revolutionary must be able to do is read Marx in the original text."

"Then what does he do?" I ask bluntly.

"We are activists, inciters, aggravators, urban guerrillas. We exist to cause as much disruption to the fascist power as possible."

As he says this I fancy that I notice him making a conspiratorial wink at Iggy.

"Where are you travelling from?"

"Over the border. Getting materials."

"Materials?"

"Flags, literature. And something else."

"Oh?"

Xalbador laughs condescendingly.

"Don't worry Tim. Something far mightier than the gun."
He takes out a little vial and waves it slowly from side to side.
"The drug of truth."

"Is that . . . LSD?"

"Yes. You have tried it before?"

"No."

"This drug expands the consciousness. Gives one perspective upon one's condition. Sometimes I dream that the
masses will imbibe this substance, and recognise how they
are shackled by the oppressor. Also, it breaks down the
barriers of ego, allowing us powerful insight."

"Insight into w-w-what?" asks Mark, who has joined us.

"Truth."

"I don't need to swally a chemical to know t-truth."

"The brain is governed by chemicals. You are merely
temporarily adjusting the balance."

"What is y-y-your view of t-truth, Xalbador?"

"Truth has always been there, but we have been made to
lose sight of it, in our imperialist age."

"But what about the n-n-new truth that came into history
at a specific t-time, 2,000 years ago?" argues Mark. "A new
c-c-covenant."

"Ah, I am afraid I take a differing view. My view is that
truth exists eternally and pre-existed us. You see, the task of
learning is actually a matter of recollecting. Because the
really important truths are ones we originally knew, in a
previous life. So we must tune into Nature, in order that she
can teach us."

"And how do we do th-th-that?" asks Mark.

Xalbador lifts up the vial again and smiles.

"You have a spare day, after all."

"Yeah, let's, let's!" exclaims Iggy.

"I must say, I am very curious," I say, perhaps recalling Delphine's acid experience with a dash of childish envy.

"Haud the bus, don't forget me," says Rocky, who has arrived with an armful of firewood.

"Aye, I'm gemme," says Eddie, who has wandered over with Angelu.

"I'm no so s-s-s-sure . . ." says Mark.

"Perhaps you should not partake if you are not sure," Xalbador says patronisingly. "It is powerful stuff."

"I've heard the Mexican Indians do it for religious enlightenment," says Eddie.

"Okay then," says Mark. "Let's give it a p-p-pop."

"First I must go back to the village," says Xalbador.

Iggy trots after him like a little dog.

"What for?" I shout after him.

"Sugar cubes!" he replies.

~~~

A Prague hotel room. 10.30pm. I glance at my notebook on the bedside table. Flick through its contents once more. That afternoon I had watched Dukla Prague, our next opponents, take on Hradec FC.

Dukla had beaten Ajax in the previous round, the team fancied by many as the surprise package. The Dutch side may have played superior football but the Czechs had hung in there and eventually got the winner through an own-goal.

Ivan Mraz, their leading scorer, had recently switched back to Sparta Prague but they did not lack firepower. Josef Nederost and Josef Vacenovsky showed enough to suggest they will pose a threat to our defence, Ivo Viktor, the talented right-winger, also looked capable of scoring as did the excellent Stanislav Strunc. Then there was Masopust. Josef Masopust. The great Masopust. European Football of the Year in 1962, the same year he scored for Czechoslovakia in the final of the World Cup, losing to Brazil. When Masopust played, Dukla played. He is the axis in the revolving wheel. He is world-class. He is also 36.

As I watched him that afternoon, I noticed an edge missing. The spurt of speed that used to take him away from opponents had gone. Against Hradec, he was caught on the ankles a couple of times by younger opponents, snapping around him, eager to make a name for themselves by leaving their mark on the great Josef Masopust.

He was not the only old head. Half of the Dukla team were 29 or over and it showed. They looked leaden-footed at times, particularly in defence. We could get at them. Our speed and stamina could harass them, stop them building up rhythm.

I thought of Vojvodina and the titanic struggle in the previous round. I could not let go of the feeling that, in beating the Yugoslavs, we had overcome a better team.

I put my notes down and switched off the light. I dreamt about Lisbon.

"How you feeling Stevie? Any niggles or anything to be concerned about?"

"Nothing, boss. Fit as a fiddle."

"Very good."

I catch Sean looking at me. Tomorrow night we play Dukla Prague in the second leg of the European Cup semi-final. We have a 3-1 lead from the first match. Two goals from Wallace – whose signing in December has turned into an inspired piece of business given McBride's injury – and another from Johnstone gave us a two-goal cushion.

But it is a dangerous scoreline for any manager. At home, the Czechs will throw everything at us. How will we respond?

"You thinking about playing Stevie up front on his own, Jock?"

"I am, Sean. It's a tall order, but if anyone can do it Stevie can. He has the stamina and the discipline. We need to make sure we have men behind the ball and don't lose this two-goal advantage."

"I think it's a sensible policy," says Sean. "Ideally, we fight fire with fire, but imagine not being in Lisbon next month, Jock? Imagine coming this far, achieving all that we have this season, and not being able to top it off by making the final?"

"That's my biggest fear, Sean. I've said from the start that this could be a season to remember. It already is. So many things have gone in our favour. We have made our own luck, but we can't afford to leave anything to chance. You're right, not being there would be a fuckin' disaster. We can express ourselves in the final, but we need to get there first. And let's face it, those Czech bastards can hardly complain after trying to chop Jimmy in half at Parkhead."

Sean nods quietly and silence hangs in the air. Neither of us have mentioned the 'D' word, but we both know that the way we will play tomorrow night is not the way we have ever played before or will ever want to play again. It's a fuckin' dirty word. Makes my skin crawl. It goes against our own philosophies and those of the club. But it is a means to an end. We have to be in Lisbon. We have had enough of moral victories and glorious defeats. We'll have our critics. The snipers. Snidey fuckin' snipers. Parasites. Fuck them. Fuck them all.

Three years ago, Celtic were 3–0 up on MTK Budapest after the first leg of the Cup Winners' Cup semi-final. They had already beaten Basle, Dinamo Zagreb and Slovan Bratislava to get there. The final in Brussels seemed almost guaranteed. What happened? They only went to Budapest and lost 4–0. Most of my team played that night. McNeill, Gemmell, Johnstone, Murdoch, Chalmers and Clark. Even now, mere mention of that game brings them out in a cold sweat. Not so much the night a team died as the night they committed *hara-kiri*. How much was it down to them and how much was it down to the tactics, or lack of, they were sent out with? I'm not sure but I am sure about one thing: semi-finals are different beasts. You need to approach them with extreme caution. You need to win them at all costs. You need to be in the final because that is when everyone is watching you.

I have to be careful how to pitch it to the players. I do not want them to change their mentalities, or feel that they have to play in a way that is unfamiliar to them. Most of all, I do not want to mention the 'D' word. I spend two hours with them, spelling out their roles. Wallace is to shadow Masopust everywhere he goes.

"I want to see you inside his shirt," I tell him.

Gemmell will provide cover in central defence, beside McNeill, to cope with the aerial threat. Chalmers will run his legs off, chasing and harrying their defenders, not allowing them time on the ball. Johnstone and Lennox will retain possession as best as possible by taking the ball for a run into the corners. That's the plan.

In the early stages, they flood forward and should be in front. After half an hour, I turn to Sean. "We're going to be alright. They've resorted to chucking balls into the box and big Billy will deal with them all day."

But it is dire to watch. I watch as we get pushed further and further back. Lennox and Johnstone don't even get across the halfway line. Sometimes, Chalmers is the only player in their half. It is embarrassing.

"Never again, Sean. Never a-fuckin-gain."

But then the final whistle goes and all the tension and the embarrassment ebbs away. I enter the jubilant dressing room and spot him sitting grinning in the corner.

"Stevie, you were immense tonight. Thanks for everything you did. I know it is not your game, but you played your part for the team and I really appreciate it."

Just then, Masopust enters the dressing room. As the players had left the pitch, he had refused to shake hands such was his bitter disappointment at missing out on perhaps his last chance to reach the final. After calming down, he has clearly had a change of heart.

"I just want to apologise for not shaking hands before," he says. "You are a great team and deserve to win the cup."

The players jump to their feet and offer him their hands.

After he leaves, I say to the players: "Let Masopust be an example to us all. 'Humble in victory and gracious in defeat,' that's what true sportsmen should be all about."

The excitement has died down a bit by the time I meet the Press men. They expect me to be over the moon, but there is something nagging at me, dampening my enthusiasm.

"Jock, were you pleased that the players managed to perform well in an unfamiliar system?" one of them asks.

The question hangs in the air like an unexploded bomb. The 'D' word. Bastards. Why did they have to bring it up? It brings it all back to the surface. I didn't set my team out to sit as far back as we did tonight, but neither did we intend on attacking in the way we usually do. I curbed my players' instincts and the result was that we spent most of the game with our backs to the wall. The outcome was successful but that was all there was to be said on the matter.

"I am delighted with my players tonight. I asked them to perform as a team and every one of them stood up to be counted. But I'll never resort to tactics like these again – never."

I stare out of the window of the coach and into the Prague night as we journey back to the airport.

"Cheer up, Jock," says Sean. "We're where we want to be. Now, we can show what we are about."

I smile. The road to Lisbon. A season to remember.

~~~

I am drawn through the searing heat by the sonorous tolling of the iron bell, the meadow seething with insects. Time is elastic now, or else the intervals between each peal are truly long, to signify the particular importance of the forthcoming sacrament. Important for me, anyway, as I intend on taking the opportunity to pray for Celtic's victory. I stop to turn 360 degrees, and I am flooded with a wave of joy as I regard the cheerful beauty that surrounds me. I unscrew the cap on the bottle of cola I am carrying and flick some of the contents into the air. Cartoon globules of black liquid rush upwards and explode ecstatically in the sunshine like an oil gusher. I gaze up into a vast sky, the perfect blue blemished only by the odd wisp of playful cloud, and by something else: vapour trails, slashed in glorious arcs across the stratosphere by jet planes purposefully, majestically negotiating the way westwards to Lisbon. The passengers will be merry with drink, enthralled by the novelty of the transportation, thrilled by the prospect of the match. Winking at the hostesses and singing.

We'll be running round Lisbon when we come!

Here I stand in an obscure pasture in Spain, alone and mildly insane. Yet I feel as though I am momentarily occupying the kernel of the universe.

The Mass unfolds in its sacred poetry. It is in Latin, or perhaps it is Spanish. It seems to alternate between the two languages, depending on which one I am pondering at a particular moment, even though I have only a rudimentary knowledge of the latter.

The priest wears a chasuble that is of a most vivid jade, its silken patterns shifting and mutating, in rapture at their very greenness. This contrasts with the brilliant white of the deacon's surplice. The vestments are billowing, alive. The altar screen is the colour of ivory, above which the ceiling is painted in gorgeous sky blue, with deep-crimson lettering: AΩ.

For a minute the flow seems to go awry; one old woman's face contorts and lengthens into that of a gargoyle, then melts back into its original form before mutating again into a new ghastly grotesque. The darkness. So I focus instead on the priest's face; raven black, arched eyebrows; olive, weathered skin. His countenance is profoundly solemn as he focuses utterly upon the sublime rituals. The visual effects are phenomenal, all obeying a slow, rhythmic pulse. The crucifix expands, then retracts, then rotates slightly to the right, slightly to the left, then centres, then throbs majestically. The monstrance stretches into a golden ellipse, first vertically, then horizontally. The priest moves in and out of focus. The flames on the candles grow and grow into vast infernos, then instantly retract to pinpoints. My feet are swallowed up by the liquid floor. Every movement leaves a rainbow of tracers.

The priest and congregants make the ancient petitions in perfect unison. There is total precision to the narrative; symmetry, ceremony, focus. There is also communion; with one another, with the Almighty. We are unified in a single consciousness, bolted together in deep mystical contemplation.

Who is 'we'? The priest, deacon, server, sacristan, a dozen Basque peasants, mostly elderly women . . . and Mark. Hadn't noticed him. After the Eucharist he gazes heavenwards as though in ecstasy. Me, I only watch, yet I can barely dare to think. I close my eyes and see an image of Billy McNeill, standing against a marble colonnade, like a gladiator in the Coliseum, his sweat-streaked face serious, etched with the magnitude of the moment, focused as he lifts up the greatest prize in club football. Savour this moment. Then a picture of my father's face, smiling kindly, worn but handsome, his Donegal eyes still sparkling. I open my eyes and the tears are streaming down my cheeks. I can't stop them. I'm not sobbing, it's just a constant uncontrollable flow of water.

Outside.

"Mr Stein?"

Nothing.

"Mr Stein?"

A long pause. Then that heavy Scots voice, low and authoritative, coming out of the nothingness. Like someone dragging a heavy stone across gravel.

"Aye, lad."

"How's everything going?"

"Inter better be ready for us."

"Why?"

"Because Thursday is the day."

"What day?"

"The day that everything comes to pass. Everything I've worked for."

"What will happen?"

"Something that the world has never seen before."

"What?" I implore.

"We are going to attack them. Relentlessly. Attack after attack after attack. Inter won't know what's hit them. Catenaccio or no catenaccio. We are going to tear them to fucking shreds. They will talk about it for years to come. Forever."

I feel my feet go cold, the hairs on the back of my neck stand up, a rush of ecstasy surge through my nervous system.

"Mr Stein."

"Aye son."

"I'm tripping out of my nut."

"Just be, lad. Just be."

I enter the forest. It is cool and shaded and endless. The little people hide in the deeper shadows. The darkness lives there. I kneel down and rip up some turf, raise it to my nostrils, drink deeply of its rich, soily odour. Life crying out for life. I want to become a part of it, a part of the forest, a part of nature, a part of the land. Another glade. I detect redcurrant blossom, it transports me back to a golden age, a kaleidoscope flickering with the sunshine of my infancy, 1947, two years after the trauma ended; austerity, yes, but relative safety and the imminence of the National Health, a braver, better world, the triumph of decency, maternal warmth and paternal protection; the odour of my father in his prime, pipe tobacco and fresh sweat, *unthinkable* without him. I meditate on him for a while. On my love for him. On his goodness. In further now. The ground gives way here, a sloped and shaded grove, the incline littered with grey-green rocks, angular and dry and cool. Elm trunks and boughs are verdant with lichen, and amid the carpet of moss, herbs and primeval fern sit Eddie and Angelu, their arms around one another, their heads resting upon each other's shoulders, their eyes closed as though in a deep and restful sleep.

It is by the shore that I find it. A pearl of wisdom, utterly pure in its clarity and obviousness and simplicity: *of course* Rocky and Debbie had to be together. They were *meant* to be together. Anything else would be an obscenity, a crime against nature. What purpose would it serve for them to remain apart, simply to spare my feelings? I sit in my pleasant reverie and hear a voice calling me, perhaps in gratitude towards my revelation. After all, surely they all must know of it? Hasn't this substance we have imbibed fused our consciousnesses?

It is Mark. Smiling, benign, beautiful. I call out to him.

"Your benevolence surrounds you like a halo!"

Without speaking he comes to me, smiling. We embrace, feel the life strength within each other's bodies. He begins kissing me, my face. Tries my lips. I am not repelled, I do not rage; only laugh good-naturedly. I see things clearly now. There is no place for severity, no need for it; only understanding. Only love.

"I can't be like that for you. Ever."

I am smiling.

"I understand."

He is smiling. But he wants to walk away. I won't let him. I hold him. I make it okay. I understand things now. How the ego acts as a barrier between people. How we put up defences and question each other's worthiness because we're not sure of our own worthiness but right now I can see my own worthiness and everyone else's.

Most of all I can see Delphine's worthiness. Her gentleness, her vulnerability, the purity of her intentions. Her profound beauty as a woman and as a person. For a moment I feel unworthy of her, then I tell myself: 'You are worthy of her.' And I believe it. I know it.

I look round; Mark has left. So I withdraw my sketch of her and gaze at it and then I ask it out loud, to the sea, to the rocks and the sand; the seabirds are my witnesses: "WILL I SEE DELPHINE AGAIN?"

And the birds and the forest and the waves and the sand and the sky all return together, on one single ecstatic communal beat: *'YES YOU SHALL!'*

The rhythm of nature. The ocean continues to gently lap the shore; relentless, eternal, cathartic. The interconnectedness of everything. The pure truth of beauty. The truth in the way things are; the meaning of things, under the surface of things. God-ness silently vibrating in every tissue of the universe.

The effects diminish. Still strong – still incredibly strong, but in relative terms less so. I am able to perform basic tasks: lighting a fire and positioning the pan, organising the camp, eating fried bread. The Rioja is a myriad of subtle flavours. It is like drinking liquid sunshine. I smell the salt and listen to the ocean swell in the Bay of Biscay. The rushes are mellower. I feel pleasant and at peace. The firewood crackles comfortingly. The shadows lengthen as the sunlight becomes lateral. The sky glows a slightly darker shade of cobalt.

But something is happening in the forest. Something terrible. The sound of the little folk making merry with some cruel sport. I enter. I can hear Iggy's inane giggling and a violent sound of breaking glass. Then a *thump, thump, thump* sound of wood striking a metal panel.

It takes me a few seconds to take in the scene. In a clearing at the end of the forest track are Iggy and Xalbador. They are both stripped to the waist like savages and smeared in places with black paint. Xalbador has a fence post gripped between his hands and is bringing it down in a violent rhythm upon the front end of a saloon car. Iggy is standing on the roof, leaping up and down like a monkey as he splashes the paint from a tin over the vehicle. The car is dark green with a white bonnet. Along the side are inscribed an emblem and two words. I take a moment to focus my eyes: GUARDIA CIVIL.

I fall to my knees, my stomach fills with fear, but worse than ever before, an insane dread, the dread of something evil and out of kilter with the rational universe. This cannot be happening. Why is this happening? Why did he have to do this? Why did he have to ruin everything? He is tripping, yes, but I can detect the madness in his eyes beneath the chemicals. The madness that got his wee brother killed, a tragedy that in turn awoke the same madness in Iggy like a genetic chain reaction. Sent him into a spiral of guilt and self-destruction, all hidden under the guise of the pursuit of fun and anarchy. Hidden from everyone but me, that is. I look at him giggling like an eejit, and a wave of the darkness descends; a living force, swelling within my limbs, mocking me with the extent of my friend's ability to wreak self-havoc. And I feel a sickness, a terror in the pit of my being, the inability to contemplate my losing him. Suddenly he slips on the wet paint and falls on his arse, slides down the wind-screen and lands on top of Xalbador in a heap. The two of them are hysterical with laughter. Eventually Iggy composes himself. I stand up and somehow manage to light myself a cigarette.

"It's the Miracle of Gorbals Cross all over again!" Iggy announces gleefully.

Xalbador is grinning like a devil, his beady eyes flickering beneath his stupid tinted spectacles. I could gladly go up and tear them off his face and stamp them into the dirt.

"Miracles don't strike twice ya balloon!"

"Don't worry – Xalbador knows a joint where he's gonnae dump it. Thump it – bump it – clump it – dump it."

Machine-gun laughter from Xalbador as he glances up from daubing Basque slogans on the car, looking like a malevolent clown.

"Is this acid no amai-zing Tim?" enthuses Iggy. "I'm gonnae get a hold of some back in Glasgow. 'Cause it's the FUCKING BERRIES!"

"Iggy. You've fucked us. You've really fucked us."

"Come on Tim, the polis here are fascist bastards. We've made a political act! In fact – political art! Ha, ha, ha, ha, ha!"

I go over to Xalbador, grab him roughly by the shoulder.

"You, ya bampot. Did you put him up to this?"

"My friend – "

"DID YOU?"

"Oh *f-f-f-f-f-fuck!*" Mark too has followed the commotion to its source.

"You have surpassed yourself this time Iggy," I say. "You have fucked it for us."

"Fucked what?"

"Lisbon."

My legs are turning to jelly. Thoughts suddenly spinning out of control, the darkness threatening to overwhelm me. I

expect to see policemen and demons loom out of the shadows towards us.

"Oh, f-f-fuck," says Mark, pacing up and down.

"Ach, give us peace," says Iggy. "We can dump it further
into the woods or off a cliff. They'll no know it was us that
knocked it."

"Are you kidding? Five foreigners just happen to be in a
wee village and a fucking polis car goes missing. They will
read this with their eyes closed."

"Oh, f-f-fuck," says Mark.

"Will you stop fucking saying that!"

We congregate around the fire, the others drifting out of the
woods like lepers. I tell Xalbador to get to fuck. I comfort
Mark with whisky, coax him away from the darkness. A
slight squall rises and we bed down, close our eyes, try to
ignore the weirdness, and drift off to sleep.

~~~

I listen to the chirping of the crickets and the soft rustle of the
leaves in the trees. The warm night air wraps around me like a
blanket. I gaze out towards the sea and see the lights of an ocean
liner glinting in the pitch darkness. I am tired from the flight, but
tiredness does not always mean sleep for me, particularly this
week. If only I could turn my mind off, close my eyes and not open
them again until the alarm clock sounds in the morning. If only it
were that simple. One a.m. has been and gone. I have done my
night patrol three times already, stalking the corridors, listening
for any signs of life. But the boys are asleep. They know better
than to pull any tricks this week, the biggest week of their lives.
Then I hear a shuffling sound from above. My antenna twitches.
I lean over the edge of my balcony and look up. I can make out a
head poking over the edge, breathing in the night air.

"Who the fuck's that?"

"It's me, boss, Jimmy. I can't sleep."

"What's up, Jimmy?"

"I'm worried, boss. Every time I close my eyes I can see all the great Inter players in my mind. Then I run through all their names in my head. Facchetti, Burgnich, Mazzola. These guys are absolute stars, boss."

"You're right, Jimmy. They are stars. They have been there and done it. But it doesn't mean that they will do it again. Here's a wee exercise for you. Every time you close your eyes and think of those guys, picture one of your team-mates. So every time you imagine Facchetti ploughing up the flank, think of big Gemmell belting up the other side. When you think of Cappellini or Corso sniffing around our box, think of Stevie hovering, ready to pounce on any slip-up at the other end. Then, think of Burgnich. Think how close he is going to get to you. So close you'll be able to smell his aftershave. But think about spinning away from him, leaving him trailing in your wake. I'm not saying they don't have great players, Jimmy, but look at what we have got. Is there one player in our team that you don't totally trust and believe in?"

"You're right, boss. We've got everything. You know me, I'm just a worrier. I'm just concerned we won't get what we deserve."

"Jimmy, only worry about the things you can control. Football is unpredictable. They'll get breaks, so might we but we can't control any of that. We can control how we want to play."

"I'm just so desperate to do well, myself, boss. It's completely taking over my mind. I really want this to be my stage. I want people to remember this game and remember how I played in it. That may sound selfish, but it's what my game is all about. I take people on. These boys are all about stopping players like me. They aren't interested in anything else. I know I'm good, but I can't take on a whole team myself."

"I'm not asking you to, Jimmy. This game is not all about you. Sometimes, even for the real individual talents like you, it is about contributing to the team in other ways. Remember that every time you pull Burgnich away from his area, you have started to disrupt their system. And if they haven't got their system then they haven't got anything. If you manage to pull their defence out of position, it creates space for other players. I'm not asking you to take on their eight-man defence. Think about it like a dam. Every time you pull them out of position, you punch another little hole in that dam. It may take a while for that dam to burst, but something will have to give at some point."

"Aye, you're right boss. I'm just so used to being the man who is relied upon to do something different. It's hard, y'know?"

"Here's a question for you wee man. What do you remember about the Scottish Cup final against Dunfermline a couple of years back?"

"Well, the first thing I remember is big Billy smashing home that winner. What a feeling. I remember the Celtic fans going absolutely mental. And I remember thinking that maybe things were starting to turn."

"What else do you remember?"

"I remember Bertie scoring twice to bring us back into the game. We played well that day, boss. I remember being proud of us, even though I wasn't playing myself."

"Well, I'll tell you what I remember. I remember thinking that we were starting to go places, that the team really turned a corner that day. I remember feeling really proud, too. But if you asked me for one moment in that game, it wouldn't be big Billy and it wouldna be wee Bertie. It would be John Clark clearing a ball off the line when it was 2-2. I remember Dunfermline's John McLaughlin beating John Fallon to the ball and thinking: 'Shite, we're done for now.' Then I remember Luggy hoofing it clear. I can't describe the relief I felt in that moment. And at the final whistle, as everyone ran over to Billy to celebrate, I grabbed Luggy and gave him a bloody big bear hug. I told him I'd never been so glad to see a man on the line in my life. The next morning, I bought all of the papers and I spread them out on the coffee table. Big Billy's face grinned out at me from the back pages. I read all the match reports. You know, some of them didn't even mention Luggy's clearance. Not one fuckin' tiny reference to it. It was as if it never happened. It had been forgotten about. But I hadn't forgotten. And I knew Luggy wouldn't either. I knew he'd be sitting in his house with his feet up, looking at his medal and happy with playing his part in a job well done. And I said to myself: 'That's the type of player that every team needs.' So when you're running your socks off and keep bumping into big Italians, just keep reminding yourself that you are doing your bit and that your team-mates appreciate it."

"Aye you're right, boss. It helps me to think about it like that. I'll need to be patient. The whole team will need to be. Anyway, all this talk of dams bursting has left me desperate for a pee, so I'll leave you to it! And try and keep the noise down, I need my beauty sleep."

"Away, ya cheeky wee bastard!"

Silence descends once more. I shake my head and smile. The wee man. I may sound like the voice of calm and reason, but anxieties prey on my mind, too. Hence the reason I'm standing on my balcony in the middle of the night. Maybe myself and the wee man have more in common than I would like to admit. But it is not only shared anxieties that bond us. It is the fact that, in the heat of battle, they will all disappear. When it arrives, we will be ready to seize the moment. That's what we both want just now – the moment to come, the battle to commence.

The final bend in the road.

Day Six

Wednesday, May 24th, 1967

Breakfast at the Palacio Hotel. The sun is shining, Jimmy Johnstone is singing and all is right with the world. The players are loving it, the waiters are cracking up.

"Go on yersel' wee man!" shouts Bertie Auld as holidaymakers at nearby tables look up from their plates of croissants. There is a relaxed mood in the camp. The Press and some fans drift around the lobby, chatting to the players. A few of the boys are tucked away in the shade beside the pool, immersed in a card school. And me? I am in the thick of it, playing the part of the ringmaster.

"I hope Celtic are getting a cut of the collections at 10 o'clock Mass," I tell the Press men. "I hear the takings are up 50 per cent!"

Gales of laughter billow around the hotel.

"I hear there's a game on tomorrow," Sean whispers to me.

I smile. Sean knows how carefully I have worked to create this atmosphere.

"Keep them relaxed, keep the mood light," I told him and Neilly every day for a week before we arrived. The plan is working perfectly.

As I sit in the lobby, watching for anyone doing anything they shouldn't be, I catch the peals of laughter, the raised voices and the arguments.

"You're at the cheatin' . . . show us your hand then!"

Bluff and counter-bluff. These players hate losing. Even at cards. Their competitiveness never far from the surface.

Everyone is relaxed. Well, not everyone. Another sleepless night for me. Eyes out on stalks. Every ounce of tension that is banished from the players is absorbed by me. I laugh and I joke and I play the part, but behind the mask there are concerns, doubts, worries, fears. If the confidence is real then so are the anxieties. There is no conflict between the two. That is life. I am only human. The confidence that courses through my players stems from many things; from their relationship with success, from self-belief but also from their youthful ignorance. They are young men on the brink of an achievement that will live forever in the history books. They do not realise the full significance of the occasion. And I do not want them to. I want them to play with their usual carefree expression, unburdened by the weight of history.

But, for me, it is different. For me, the journey has been too long, the sleepless nights too many to fail to appreciate the significance of this moment. No British club has ever won the European Cup. By God, no club from northern Europe has won it! We can become the first. An achievement that would live forever, that would be a source of pride for generations.

Tactics occupy my mind more than anything. This is my greatest challenge. How to break down an eight-man defence? I know how I will approach it. I am confident that it will work, but I cannot guarantee anything. I have watched Inter strangle the creative juices out of great teams before.

The players know their jobs. Jimmy Johnstone and Bobby Lennox will play centrally in an effort to draw their markers with them. Wallace and Chalmers will take turns of dropping deep and drawing the centre-backs out of position. It will be a thankless task but their endeavours will hopefully allow us to hurt them on the wings. The focus will fall on Auld and Murdoch to feed the full-backs, Gemmell and Craig. It will be a game of tactical chess. We are capable of executing the plan to perfection, but they have the grandmaster. Helenio Herrera. The image of the Inter boa constrictor will haunt me until the final whistle blows tomorrow.

~~~

The seabirds herald a beautiful morning yet trepidation hangs over the camp like a pall. I go for an invigorating dip in the ocean. As I walk back I can feel the blood coursing through my veins. The boys are all busying themselves with various chores. We have lived months in five days. All of this – packing, driving, stopping for the night, unpacking, waking, packing again, then hitting another unfamiliar open road; its very unfamiliarity is normality to us now. Five previously untravelled boys are now hardened veterans of the highway.

A figure at the edge of the woods. We all look up, apprehensively. It is Angelu.

"The police, they have arrested Xalbador," she tells us plaintively. "On suspicion of stealing the police vehicle."

"Fuck 'im," I mutter, under my breath.

"They'll be searching the woods soon," says Rocky. "Better get to the garage and see about the Zodiac."

"I'm going to leave you now," says Angelu.

"Why not hang around with us for a bit," protests Eddie. "We'll look after you."

She walks over to Eddie. Takes his hands in hers. Looks into his eyes.

"No. I am known to the Guardia. If they see me in your company it will make things bad for you."

She kisses him goodbye. We make our farewells and I watch Eddie as he watches her clamber back up to the tree line and out of sight forever. His expression is sad, yet determined. I half-expect him to grab a drink but he doesn't.

We finish gathering our things together and then walk towards Ispaster. We approach the village like a gang of outlaws in a Western, our nerves fretted with tension, camping gear *chinking* like spurs, the sun already beating down fiercely.

At the garage an enamelled 7-Up sign flaps in the slight

breeze. A puddle of hosewater smells sweet and damp as it evaporates in the sunshine. A mower chatters in the near distance. Other than that the place is silent.

"It's quiet. Too quiet," says Iggy with movie gravitas.

"We're out in the open now," I say. "You boys head to the cantina and act natural. Rocky and me will find out what's going on with the car."

We go round to the back of the garage and find the proprietor in his tiny office. By pointing at the map and the clock he conveys that his brother will arrive from Bilbao at 10 o'clock with the throttle cable. He doesn't mention a missing police car and his brother arrives more or less on time. The part is fitted straightforwardly and at a low cost, and by half-10 we are delighted to be back on the road, the tension finally starting to recede.

The acid has all but worn off; only a slight afterglow remains. Mark seems a bit pensive. The others seem to be hooked upon the humour of the whole experience, which I find a wee bit disappointing. I feel as though I have crossed the Rubicon. I don't know how or why but I know that nothing is ever going to be the same again.

The road to Lisbon. It is blocked by the Guardia Civil.

"I'll do the talking," I tell the boys as I depress the clutch and begin gliding the Zodiac to a halt at the side of the road. "Hold your nerve fellas."

"Shite, Iggy," exclaims Eddie. "Your hands are covered in paint ya tube!"

"J-J-J-Just like Xalbador's will be," says Mark.

"Keep them hidden, but be subtle," Rocky commands.

Two teal-uniformed cops approach the car, fingering their gun-belts. Oh fuck.

"Buenos dias, senors," I say, with surprising confidence. *"¿Usted habla inglés?"*

One of the policemen shouts over to his superior, a tall,

stern man, salt and pepper hair. He approaches the car, removes his aviators.

"Where are you going?"

"Lisbon."

"What for?"

"To see the football. Celtic v Inter Milan."

He is unimpressed.

"Did you spend the night in Ispaster?"

I know that he knows we did.

"Yes. On the beach."

"Why?"

"Our car broke down."

"Who did you have dealings with?"

"Well, there was the man who gave us a tow, there was the man in the garage, oh, and the barman in the cantina."

"The man who gave you a tow. Is this him?"

He produces a mugshot of a younger Xalbador, moustachioed and with a thicker head of hair.

"Erm . . . yes. I think so. Salvatore I think his name was."

"You," the cop says, suddenly turning his attention to Iggy, who happens to be sitting at the rear window. "We believe this man is responsible for stealing an official car. You know anything about this?"

"No, officer. We just got a tow from him, then we bought him a beer in the little cantina. To thank him, like. Then we just kind of made our excuses and left." I glance at Iggy in the rear-view, his face a perfection of innocent charm. "To be perfectly honest with you sir, we didn't particularly like him. He was a bit of a bore."

The cop begins chatting with his colleague in Spanish. I can't pick out a word.

"Okay," he says, turning to us and rapidly rapping on the roof of the Zodiac. "Get moving."

I pull away, slowly exhaling in profound relief.

"Thank God!"

"Sweet Jesus!"

"I'll say one thing for Xalbador," says Rocky. "At least he didn't grass us up."

"I'm just glad Iggy has so much experience of chatting up the polis," I say.

~~~

Sean pops his head round the door.

"He's coming, Jock."

"Who?"

"Herrera. He's coming to Ibrox on Saturday. Thought you might want to know."

Helenio Herrera. Meticulous, thorough; it was to be expected that he would want to see us in action before the final. What better time than in the league decider against our old rivals? We only need a point to win our second successive title. And so, amid the Old Firm chaos, he will be sitting, filling his notebook with every detail, pinpointing strengths, searching out weaknesses. Fuckin' Herrera.

How much insight do I want him to gain? Maybe I should try to keep my cards close to my chest, send him back to Italy with an empty jotter; or at least a false sense of what kind of team we are. That would allow us to surprise Inter in the final. But it is risky. It would mean abandoning our usual style, asking the players to perform in a way that is alien. The disappointment I felt after our second leg against Dukla Prague is still fresh. We might get away with it once more, but I would hate to abandon my principles again, so soon after Prague. Anyway, our best chance is to play the way we always do, to attack them and to try to win the match. And this is no ordinary game. This is the league decider against Rangers at Ibrox. How sweet it would feel to clinch the league there.

We have come this far playing attacking football. We know it works. We have a cabinet full of trophies to prove it. Take Herrera out of the equation and there would be no debate. We would attack. If we play in our usual style, Herrera will undoubtedly return to Italy with a bulging file. He will take copious notes on Johnstone's mazy runs, on Murdoch's precision passes, on Gemmell and Craig's lung-bursting overlaps. But he will also board the plane with more than a few worries. Our constant attacking will be sure to plant seeds of doubt in his mind. He will return with more than a few missing answers. So what will we do? We will attack, we will try to win the league and we will show Herrera what we are made of. I stand on the cinder track with my hands thrust into my overcoat, raindrops trickling down my neck and soaking my shirt. Behind me, the crowd throbs with anticipation. On the pitch, my players are ready, their pristine white socks and shorts standing out against the greyness and glaur of Ibrox Park. A scrum of photographers race up the track but as they draw level with me they keep going. Instead, they point their lenses into the main stand.

Sean whispers in my ear. "Herrera."

I do not turn around. I do not acknowledge his presence. Fuck him. Simply another face in the crowd. Jimmy Johnstone looks over to see what all the commotion is about. I clench my fist then point straight at him. He winks. Rascal. The conditions make it difficult but we pour forward in search of the opening goal. Rangers attack us, too, and the match swings from end to end. Jardine scores after 40 minutes but we reply instantly through Johnstone. 1-1.

Jimmy Johnstone. The rain gets heavier and I look at him, socks at his ankles, looking like the runt of the litter, but he refuses to get bogged down. He is on his toes constantly, skating over the gluey surface. Then it happens. Seventy-four minutes. Chalmers takes a throw-in and finds Johnstone. He picks it up on the right and starts to make a beeline across the penalty area. I sense something is about to happen. I clamber out the dugout. He runs splashing through the mud. I am at the edge of the park now. I watch as he taps it out of his feet.

"HIT IT WEE MAN," I scream.

And Jimmy hits it . . . boy does Jimmy hit it. The ball leaves his boot like a missile. I am in the air before it hits the net. Sean grabs me and we embrace. Suddenly I feel it all ebbing away, all the tension, the fear and insecurities. My shoulders slump and I feel as if a huge weight has been lifted off my shoulders. Roger Hynd equalises soon after and the game ends 2-2 but the league title is ours. The entire bench run on to greet the players but I remain on the touchline and shake every player's hand as they come off. Then I turn, slowly, and look up. I scan the crowd a couple of times. Suddenly, I see him; staring straight at me, his face expressionless. Herrera. I meet his gaze and hold it for a few moments. Long enough to say: 'Fuck you Herrera. I know you're here. I've known all along. But it didn't make any difference because this is about us, Celtic Football Club . . . and you're next.'

I stop off briefly in the dressing room to add my congratulations to the players and head straight to the airport for my flight to Turin. Tomorrow I will take in the Juventus v Inter match and have my own chance to assess the opposition's strengths and weaknesses. Unsurprisingly, Herrera's offer to fly back with him on his private jet has been withdrawn, but I purposely never cancelled my original booking. Never try to kid a kidder, Helenio.

The next day Herrera is there to greet me, all smiles and back-slaps. I, too, greet him like an old friend. He assures me that a car has been booked to take me to the stadium where there is a ticket left in my name. Neither materialises so I have to swing a Press pass. The Scottish Press boys are livid but I order them not to report a word of it.

"Mind games, boys, it's all mind games. You can't let things like that upset you. That's playing into his hands."

The game is stale, Inter camped behind the ball and Juventus finally winning by a solitary goal. The league title, secured in three of the preceding four seasons, could yet move to Turin if Inter lose to Mantova in their final game of the season, after Lisbon.

The home fans are in full voice, the same refrain filling the night air over and over.

'Vecchia Inter, vecchia Inter, vecchia Inter.'

"What does 'vecchia' mean?" I ask someone.

"'Old'. The Juve fans are singing 'Old Inter'."

I smile to myself. Is the most sophisticated defensive system in the world a smokescreen for an ageing team? Do Herrera's players sit behind the ball so much because they don't have the legs to play the game in the opposition's half?

"Vecchia Inter, vecchia Inter, vecchia Inter."

~~~

The phone rings.

"Jock, it's Bill Nicholson at Spurs here. I want to speak to you about buying Jimmy Johnstone."

"Not interested, Bill. He's part of my plans."

"Oh, right, Jock . . . it was just that I heard on the grapevine a while back that you wanted him off your hands."

"That was then, Bill, this is now. Thanks for phoning, but Jimmy is going nowhere."

I put the phone down. Smile to myself. Poor Bill, six months too late. I have now accepted my fate.

Jock Stein and Jimmy Johnstone, for better or worse, for richer or poorer, in sickness and in health.

A marriage made in heaven, but with frequent trips to hell and back. What the fuck have I taken on?

Just as well I like a punt. This is a player who I dropped from the Scottish Cup final victory over Dunfermline in April. On the day we ended the club's trophy drought, Jimmy did not even get a kick of the ball. I had proved then he was not indispensable. If Bill had phoned me the morning after that victory, the answer might have been different. I might have packed his fuckin' bags for him. I thought then he was a luxury, a player more content to do his own thing than be part of a team. Individuality is one thing, but greed another. He crossed that line too often for my liking.

But he gets under your skin, the wee man, he burrows his way into your affections. There's the child-like enthusiasm, the vulnerability. What could he become with a firm hand and a shot of self-belief? Anything he wants, was the answer I arrived at. A manager is like a doctor. He is meant to make people better. It is impossible to change characters completely, but you can craft them, sand off the rough edges, polish them to a shine. A good manager is able to do all that. What he can't do is give people talents they don't possess. I could coach some players for a lifetime and they would never be able to lace Jimmy Johnstone's boots. How to channel that talent into a team framework, that is the biggest challenge I face. It will not be easy, it may not even be possible. But I know one thing: if I pull it off, it will be my greatest achievement in the game.

What makes a top player? Skill, vision, consistency. Determination, too, but something more. Courage. Moral and physical courage. The courage to show for the ball when the chips are down, when it would be easier to drift out of the action, when the crowd are baying, ready to condemn, to abuse. Physical courage, too. The ability to absorb all kinds of punishment. Then, get back up and take it all over again . . . I watch him bounce back to his feet like an inflatable punch-bag, gravel stuck to his cheeks where he has been sent spinning onto the track. I watch him demand possession once more. I watch him make a beeline to beat the same player who has just kicked him. Courage.

But, lurking beneath that spirit, something else. A vulnerability, insecurity, an inferiority complex. He needs to feel valued, to feel loved. He needs attention. He needs the ball.

I watch him in games when he is starved of possession. I watch his shoulders slump and frustration kick in. Some players hang about on the fringes for 89 minutes and then win the game with a moment of magic. He is capable of that but it is not his character. He is impatient. He is irrepressible. He has the attention span of a goldfish. He wants to be central to everything. He wants the ball. He needs the ball.

I could have sold him. I didn't. Now, if I was going to use him, I had to make him the centrepiece of the team. I had to throw my weight behind him completely, cash in all my chips, harness that talent in a way that had never been done before. It was all or nothing.

And so I tell the players: "Give it to Jimmy at every opportunity."

Then I tell Jimmy: "You want the attention? You want the adoration? You want the glory? You want the ball? Well, son, now you've got it. Now you've got it all. Don't fuckin' waste it."

~~~

By early afternoon Iggy is at the wheel and the leather upholstery of the Zodiac is scalding hot. The Kinks' *Waterloo Sunset* gives way to a news report. I make out from the occasional understood word that war is impending in the Middle East.

Iggy lights a Woodbine from the one he has just smoked.

"For a kid who spent a year in a TB sanatorium you sure smoke a lot," I tell him.

"Sorry mother."

We have already made headway into Castille and León; we are well on the way to Salamanca. The powerful Ford chews up the miles, leaving slower drivers in our wake. Increasingly we come across members of the Celticade, and we pass them with much flag-waving and cheering.

Beetles, Imps, Minxes and Minis. Morris Minors, Morris Oxfords – even a rusty old Morris 10. An Austin Cambridge and a salmon-pink Somerset. Fords: Consuls, Zephyrs, Cortinas, Prefects and Anglias. The Vauxhall Velox and Victor. The Humber Sceptre and Hawk. A portly Wolsley 1500 and a stately 1560. A Simca, a Citroën, a Volvo, a couple of little Fiats. A Rover 2000, two Rover 80s. A two-toned (green and white!) Triumph Herald. Vans: Commers, Bedfords and Ford Transits. Motorcycles, sidecars and an E-Type Jag. A Leyland double-decker and several motorcoaches: three Albions, a Bristol, a Seddon – even an ancient Vulcan. Caravans and campervans – even an ice cream van!

"This has never happened before," Eddie says wistfully.

"What?" I ask.

"This amount of folk going abroad to see a gemme."

He's right. Another first for Celtic. A sense of history. A sense that people will talk about this for years.

One convoy numbers at least 20 vehicles and pulls in at Valladolid, which allows us to pass. We overtake a VW camper van, custom-painted with peace signs and hippie imagery. The longhairs inside give us the thumbs-up and one of them waves an Irish tricolour at us. The dry and dusty road, straight and true beneath the vast Iberian sky. The shimmering horizon, the relentless sun; the purposefulness of our motion now, hurtling towards the edge of Europe, towards destiny, towards tomorrow.

Tomorrow. May 25th, 1967.

Mark is still quiet. I catch a glance of his dejected eyes in the rear-view. Poor boy; he must feel odd. Confused, maybe. I guess I feel a wee bit odd too, but nothing else. Need to cheer him up.

"Rocky. Your favourite-ever Celtic match."

He steers with one hand and uses the other to light five fags.

"Only one contender and I wasn't even at it. Hampden. October 19th 1957. Scottish League Cup final. Celtic v Rangers. I mind listening to it on the wireless. Seven past Niven. 7-1. *Seven*-one. Celtic goalscorers: Wilson 23, Mochan 44, McPhail 53, 69, Mochan 74, McPhail 81, Fernie 90 – penalty. The BBC commentator fucking choking as he described the fifth and sixth and seventh goals. Barely able to get the words out. The television division were worse. They tried to kid everyone on that they had – purely by accident of course – no recorded the second-half footage. No visual record for posterity. Aye, right. Queen Margaret Drive – no Catholics need apply right enough. My big cousins were at the match. There to witness history. Outside the cops whipped their legs with batons but the boys didn't give a fuck. My big cousin Gerry – a poet of a man from County Sligo – told me how he just lay there on the deck smiling up at the bastards with a look that said: *'You can number every one of my bones but nothing will alter what has happened here today. Paddy has just fucked you seven-one.'"*

We eat fine tapas in Salamanca, take a little time to browse the shops, to check out the spectacular Renaissance architecture. The locals eye us with fresh familiarity; our species is known to them now. I buy a battered old top hat from a second-hand store, and two lengths of ribbon – one green, one white, from a haberdashery. One hardware shop is of particular interest to the keen street-fighter. It is stocked with an assortment of awesome weaponry: airguns, swords, flick-knives, knuckledusters, machetes, truncheons, crossbows. The boys stand in silent wonder, dreaming of the kudos such arms would give them back home. Me, I'm glad to have left all that shite behind.

Iggy acts furtively, leaves suddenly; he's up to something. I follow him outside.

"What's the score?"

"Nuthin'."

"What the hell are you up to Iggy?"

"I'm up to fuck all!"

He walks off in the cream puff to the next corner, lights a fag. I light one too. Gaze up at the cathedral. Feel bad.

"How are the preparations going Mr Stein?"

"Fine, lad. Our hotel in Estoril is right swanky. The players love it."

"Mr Stein."

"Aye, lad."

"Sometimes I think I'm too hard on folk."

"Nobody's perfect, lad."

"But I even think the worst of my pals, and they are very dear to me. I never seem to give them the benefit of the doubt. Then they do something great. Prove you wrong. Make you feel rotten to the core."

"I'll wager you have done some fairly great things your-self. You spoke about your father – are you a good son to him?"

"I think I am, now."

"There you are then. We've all got our faults, lad. We need to work at them, aye, but in the grand scheme of things are they really that serious?"

"No . . . I suppose not."

"We're all wired in different ways. All we can do is to try our best lad, to overcome that. But sometimes we will fail. And when we do we must be gentle with ourselves."

~~~

The vultures had begun to circle. It was to be expected. If my work at Dunfermline had commanded attention then bringing success to Hibs had taken things to another level. My name was now known, not just in Scotland but further afield. The sacking of Stan Cullis from Wolves in September led to that club making contact. They wanted me badly and while the attention was flattering, I had my eyes on a prize closer to home. "You'll be back at Celtic Park some day," people used to say to me. I dismissed it with a hearty laugh, but I still had a strong connection with the club and a close relationship with the chairman Bob Kelly. It was to Bob I turned during Wolves' courtship. I wanted his advice but, deep down, I wanted something more. There was an inevitability to my departure from the club before, but much had changed. I was now a successful manager in my own right with a proven track record. Success is a powerful drug. It can force people to look beyond their prejudices, open their minds. Bob asked me if I really wanted to move to Wolves. I said I was flattered, but was still some way from accepting their offer.

"Would you consider returning to Celtic?" asked Bob.

"I would . . . but it depends what was on offer."

A couple of days later, we spoke again.

"How would you like to be assistant to Sean Fallon?" asked Bob.

Sean was a close friend and an admirable man but had no serious managerial experience, certainly in comparison to what I had built up with Dunfermline and Hibs. Taking on such a role would have been totally unworkable. My disappointment ran deep, but it was no time to wallow. With Wolves still interested, I was in a perfect position to negotiate.

"Bob, thanks for the opportunity. I appreciate it. Wolves are still very keen, and it is tempting, but my preferred option would be to work alongside you again. However, as I said, it all depends what is on offer. And I don't feel I can accept this proposition."

"Alright Jock, leave it with me," said Bob.

A couple of days later, the phone rang again.

"Jock, I have another proposal. How about becoming co-manager with Sean?"

My mind drifted back to the trip to Italy and the image of Herrera, striding around the training field like a martinet, laying down the law . . . the all-seeing eye, the judge and jury, the lord of the manor. Instinctively, I knew then that I wanted to achieve that degree of independence, which would be considered revolutionary in British football. I knew it would not be easy. It would require a foundation of success, and equal measures of courage and diplomacy. It would also require the right platform. When the moment arrived, I hoped I would be able to seize it.

"Bob, thanks for the offer but, again, I'll have to politely decline. I've got my own vision, and it's a big, exciting one. It can't be achieved by committee."

"Alright Jock, I think I know what you are asking for, but it's not something I can click my fingers and grant you. There are paths to be smoothed, as I'm sure you understand. I can't give you an answer just now because I don't know what the answer will be. But I will do my best for you, Jock."

Several days passed. The phone didn't ring. I began to wonder if I had pushed it too far, if they were not yet ready to take such a major step. On the other hand, the team was underperforming and crowds were falling. They had not won a major honour since 1957. I knew they needed me and now they knew the only way to get me. It was a gamble, but I calculated the odds were slightly in my favour.

The phone eventually rang.

"Jock, we would like to offer you the job."

"Bob, I would like to accept your offer, but I have one condition . . . I want full control of team matters. Anything less and I am not interested."

The silence seemed to go on forever, then he finally spoke.

"Alright Jock. Alright."

"You won't regret this, Bob. Mark my words."

In March 1965, I left Hibs near the top of the league to start my revolution at Celtic Park. I looked around the dressing room and saw a group of players who had been underachieving. I knew the core of the team from my spell as reserve team coach, and I soon made it clear that I expected much more from them. Most of all I expected them to listen to me and follow my orders. Anybody who didn't would be out. It was a simple approach and most of the players embraced it from day one. But the club was mired in depression and change was needed. We won our first game 6-0 v Airdrie but lost to St Johnstone, Partick Thistle, Hibs and Falkirk.

The place needed a lift and what better way to raise spirits and dispel the gloom than by winning a trophy. The Scottish Cup was our best chance and, after a replay against Motherwell, we made the final against Dunfermline.

The signs were not encouraging when we lost to Thistle on the Saturday before the final and were booed off the field. In the programme that day, I had not held back.

"Consistency of performance must be the first priority. And several of the players are not providing that. They have had their chance and they should know that I have been in England, looking."

Before the game, I took the players to Largs instead of the usual Seamill retreat. The atmosphere was upbeat and I did everything possible to keep their minds off the visit to Hampden.

Bertie Auld cancelled out Harry Melrose's opener before John McLaughlin gave Dunfermline the lead again just before half-time. In the dressing room I told the players to keep doing what they were doing and the breaks would come. Auld made it 2-2 then, nine minutes from the end, Billy McNeill met a Charlie Gallagher corner to win the cup. In the dressing room, I told the players: "Remember this feeling. This is how success feels. Not many of you have felt it before, but if you stick with me, you will feel it again."

In the close season, it was all change. I released 20 players, all of them youngsters, dumped the third team and told the coaching team to concentrate on the first 11 and the reserves. I introduced two daily training sessions and an evening one to accommodate the part-timers.

I brought in Joe McBride from Motherwell as the rebuilding process continued. I quickly realised that I didn't need a flood of new players.

Square pegs in round holes, everywhere I looked. John Hughes, a bulky, strong-running player was at centre-forward when I arrived. I moved him to right wing and it was like releasing a greyhound from the traps.

"Watch the big bastard go," I used to say to Sean as he bulldozed past full-backs.

I took Bobby Lennox aside after training one day. I lined up 10 balls a few yards out from the goal-line. I crashed the first one into the net.

Tssh.

"You hear that, Bobby?"

"No, boss. What?"

I hit another. *Tssh.* And another. *Tssh. Tssh. Tssh. Tssh. Tssh.*

"That, son. The sound of the ball hitting the net. Get used to it because I want you doing that more and more. I want you playing through the middle more, getting on the ball and streaking past defenders. Then, when you get to the goalkeeper, just have one thing on your mind. That sound. You do that for me, son, and you'll be a fuckin' legend."

Then there was John Clark. Luggy. I knew him from the reserves. Understood his strengths and weaknesses. So did he. That's what I liked about him. He kept it simple. Never did anything out of the ordinary. Managers appreciate players like that. So do players. Fans don't all see their value, but that's okay. Luggy listened. He didn't just nod his head at you. He thought about what you said, analysed it and applied it. Every team needs players like that. But not at left-half. I watched him shuffling up and down the flank and shook my head.

I tried him beside big Billy in central defence. Before the game I told him straight: "Let Billy deal with all the headers. Just you concentrate on sweeping up on the deck. Pick up any scraps. Keep it simple."

He did more than that. He read everything. Before it happened. I turned to Sean. "We've found Luggy's position."

We had a trophy behind us but other markers had to be laid down. We had to prove ourselves to be physically strong and able to cope with intimidation. The League Cup final against Rangers in October 1965 was a brutal affair due, in no small part, to my insistence that we had to win every 50–50 and impose ourselves physically.

Before the game, the chairman came into the dressing room and spoke to the players about the importance of good behaviour. He said he did not want the club's reputation tainted by foul play and that the eyes of the world were upon them. As he turned and walked out, I keeked around the door, just to make sure he was gone.

"Right, don't listen to any of that crap. Get stuck in. If anyone, *anyone*, jumps out of a tackle, shites themselves, that's it. They'll be finished at this football club. You hear me? Fuckin' finished. Don't even come back into the dressing room. Just go right up the tunnel and straight home. 'Cause I will have seen what you did and I'll fuckin' run you out of town. And I'll make sure every manager who thinks about buying you knows you're a fuckin' shitebag, too.

"I want to see big tackles early in the game. I want to see Willie Johnston sorted out. We will stand tall. We will fight to the death. We will help out our team-mates and be united. But, most of all, we will fuckin' win."

The 2–1 victory was not one for the purist – we kicked and scrapped our way to a win – but it sent out an important message that Celtic could mix it with the best of them. It was a physical victory. The first League Cup final triumph in eight years. My first trophy in an Old Firm match.

On the final day of the season we only needed to avoid a 4-0 defeat by Motherwell at Fir Park to win the league. In the end, we won 1-0 to secure the title.

~~~

We approach the border crossing, Rocky at the wheel, the atmosphere pregnant with significance. A Portuguese official wearing a tall peaked hat flags at us to pull over.

"Look at us," I say. "Driving through the sunshine on our way to Lisbon, to the European Cup final."

"Anything to declare?" asks the customs officer in a heavy accent.

"Aye," says Rocky. "We're here to bring back the European Cup!"

We all laugh as Rocky puts on the indicator, pulls back onto the road.

The road to Lisbon. Its final stretch.

Those last miles to our destination are like a dream. We have reached a new level of consciousness, of heightened awareness. What we talk about no longer matters. All that matters now is the experience. To drink deeply of it. To savour it. I glimpse the Tagus, I know we are almost there. Rising in the Albarracín mountains she flows ever westwards, filtered pure by the limestone ravines of Guadalajara. Fortified by the Jarama and the Alagón she fires the hydroelectric schemes that power central Spain, irrigates the fertile plains of Iberia's heartland, drains the filth and silt from its vast alluvial basin; before cascading through Portugal and sculpting Lisbon's majestic harbour.

The capital itself is sublime. Fine boulevards lined with handsome blond buildings link splendid squares. The city is teeming with Tims, adding a dash of Glesga style to the pavement café culture. Wearing their suits they swelter in the

evening heat. Polite and cheery, they seduce the Portuguese
with easy Garngad charm. Evidently Herrera's plea to locals
to support their fellow Latins has fallen on deaf ears.

We pull in at Praça do Comércio where King José I has a
tricolour wedged into the crook of his bronze arm. We sound
the horn, disembark, are mobbed by locals who want our
lapel badges and Celtic fans who place cigarillos and bottles
of *tinto* to our lips. Some of the lads are Gorbals bhoys.

"There were 500 fans watching the training today!"

"Aye, and those Tally chancers stayed behind to watch us!"

"You'll no believe this – we were drinking in this English
pub yesterday, out beyond Estoril where the team is based,
and guess who walks in? Tam Gemmell, Bertie and Wispy –
out for a sly pint!"

Rocky gets down on his knees and kisses the flagstone in
papal style. Ten-dozen excited conversations at once. I turn
to Mark. I raise the bottle to him, fix his eyes with mine.

"To my dear, dear pal Mark Halfpenny."

I drink to his honour. The strain seems to dissolve from his
face. I pass him the bottle and he takes a swig.

"Th-th-thanks, Tim."

We install ourselves at a hotel in Belém. Escudos are
converted from pesetas, which had been converted from
francs, which had been converted from pounds and shillings.
The arithmetic leaves us weary. Two adjoining rooms,
shaded, dusty and cool, the dark-varnished furniture ancient
and imposing. The Eire flag is installed as the centrepiece of a
shrine on the wall, necks are washed, bottles of Super Bock
opened, fags passed round.

"Okay lads," begins Rocky, drawing numbers from his
trilby. "Sweep time. Eddie. You're up first."

"2-0 Celtic. Chalmers and Wallace will score."

"Mark?"

"3-1 Celtic. S-S-Stevie, Wispy and J-Jinky."

"Iggy?"

"5-0 to the Celts! With a Wispy hat-trick!"

"Get to fuck!"

"Away you go ya tube – against the meanest defence in the world?"

"No chance!"

"Me," says Rocky, "I'm gonnae plump for 1-0. We'll struggle to break them down, but I believe we will score, maybe from a less usual source. Now Tim, there's just you."

I take a draught of the strong beer, chew the matter over in my head.

"Nobody's got 2-1 Celtic yet?"

"No."

"Okay, 2-1 Celtic. We'll go down early. Inter will resort to form: they'll dig in, try and frustrate us. But then Celtic will batter them, again and again. Eventually we will breach them in the second half. Twice. Inter will be exhausted. They'll be pleased to hear the final whistle."

"You seem to have a lot of detail."

"I should do. Big Jock himself told me it in a dream!"

~~~

When we arrive at the Estádio Nacional, Inter are training.

"What the hell is this? We are supposed to be training at this time," says Sean.

"Stay calm, Sean. It's just another attempt to unsettle us."

They eventually spot us and scurry off like mice into holes in the wall. Then, as we emerge from the darkened tunnel for our session, I look around and there they are again. Freshly showered, sitting cross-legged on the perimeter wall, waiting for us. I feel a wave of irritation at this breach of etiquette. Herrera. Sneaky fuckin' bastard. Then, I brush it aside, or rather absorb it with all the other pressure.

"Would you believe it, Jock," Sean says. "They've come to learn a thing or two about attacking football."

"It's too late for that, Sean," I reply.

But the challenge is there. I look over at the bronzed figures, half-smiling as they huddle together in the afternoon sun. Then, I call the players together.

"Let's make this a good session, boys."

That is all I say. The players know. We begin with a passing drill in which the players line up in two rows 15 yards apart. The player at the front of one row pings the ball to the man at the front of the opposite one, then runs to the back. It requires concentration and discipline. It is easy to get it wrong. If one player fails to control a pass then the momentum is broken. Shuttle runs would have been a less risky policy with 13 of the greatest defenders in the world watching us, but this is our chance to win the mental battle. The players respond. Every pass zips across the lush turf with laser accuracy. Their control is instant, their movements purposeful. I walk up and down, saying nothing, just watching it happen. I look over at Inter and smile.

The players never let up; every pass, every flick, every header that reaches its destination making another little dent in the confidence of our audience.

"Well done, lads. Very well done indeed."

I look at my watch. We have trained for half an hour longer than I intended, but the players don't want to stop. Drenched in sweat, their faces flushed with enthusiasm, they know what this means. The Inter players start to drift away.

"Is it just me or do they look worried?" I ask Sean.

"It's not just you, Jock."

I call an end to the session with the players still buzzing from the thrill of their mini-victory. Twenty-four hours to kick off. Inter 0 Celtic 1.

~~~

We walk through the city at night, shaking hands with Portuguese well-wishers and our Celtic compadres gathered in throngs in plazas and parks. Coco Costello and his pals, Mickey Zamoyski and Co., the Murphy brothers and their entourage, even Jack Palance and his Tongs buddies; dozens of others. We exchange travel stories, pass the bottle, join in the odd song or chant, take in the sights of pre-match festivity. Iggy bungs a wee guy from back home who is broke. Some of the tales are priceless. A fellow who lost his job a month ago then sold his house without telling his wife so that he could use the deposit to fund the trip. Folk who came directly by yacht all the way from Fairlie. Guys who hitchhiked the entire distance. A contingent from Sligo whose ancient car gave up the ghost near Burgos but who were rescued by an Austrian coach party on a pilgrimage to Fatima. For some reason we don't relate our adventures. We just kind of smile knowingly at each other or gaze absently up at the moonlit Castelo de São Jorge; perhaps our memories are too precious to be bandied around as banter. We ease ourselves into a relatively quiet bar near the waterside, local to our hotel. There is tomorrow for more socialising with the rest of the support. For now it's just about us.

~~~

Outside, darkness has fallen. I sit alone at the desk in my room, crumple up another sheet of paper and toss it towards the bin. It bounces on the edge and lands among all the others. I start again, pencil poised, patiently waiting for inspiration. The team-talk, a few well-chosen words . . . but what words and in which order?

A good team-talk should inspire, motivate and inform. I have delivered hundreds in my time but nothing on this scale. There is no point in discussing tactics. That has all been done. Their minds should be uncluttered, totally focused. I think of my mother's wisdom, "If you have nothing sensible to say you are better saying nothing." But there is something I want, something I need to convey. I'm just not sure what it is. Do they need a rallying cry? This is the European Cup final, the biggest moment in all their careers. Motivation, inspiration is surely not needed at this stage.

What do they need to know? The years of praising, encouraging, criticising, fighting; all the different elements that went into forging this team, have come down to this one moment in time. The work has been done. There is nothing left to be said, or at least nothing that will fundamentally change the character of the 11 men who will take the field tomorrow.

Maybe I should just speak from the heart. No mind games, no chest-beating; just let them know what I think of them. My team. My wee team. I pick up my pencil and turn the notepad on its side. I write five letters in big, bold capitals. I tear out another leaf and write another five-letter word. I stick them to the mirror.

PRIDE   TRUST

Players need to know what's expected of them, but they also need to be in a frame of mind to execute it. A football manager is a mood-setter as much as a tactician. I need to step inside the players' minds and make sure they are clear. Footballers like what they like. Sometimes, they like what they like a bit too much. That is where my spies come in. But they are grown men and must be treated as such.

After dinner, I round the players up and take them for a walk. Off we go, out of the hotel and turn left up a country road which winds into the far distance. We hit a good pace. As I look behind and see the players strung out behind me, bantering away, not a care in the world. The Pied Piper of Parkhead, I trail them further into the countryside. We reach the abode of Brodie Lennox, a Scottish businessman and golfer who has been in Portugal for years. He had extended an invite to the whole squad to visit if we wished to get a break from the hotel. Now seems the perfect time. What else are we meant to do, sit in our hotel rooms and let anxiety build?

Lennox is the perfect host, giving the boys the full run of his villa, and letting them play snooker and watch the England v Spain international on the television. The night slips past and darkness falls. I've never seen the players look so relaxed but they also need proper rest, so we set off back to the hotel. Neilly offers to lead us back in the darkness.

"Don't worry, Jock, I've got a sixth sense when it comes to walking in the dark," he says.

"Nae bloody sense, more like."

A while later, as we make our way back along the country road, we spot the lights of the hotel to our right.

"Boss, boss, there's our hotel there," shouts Jimmy.

"Aye, but this is the road we came from so we should stick to it. We can't go wrong if we do that," I reply.

Then Neilly chimes in.

"The wee man's got a point, though, Jock. The hotel is just there. I know a shortcut."

"Shortcut?" I splutter. "Neilly, I wish I had a shilling for every time you've led us round the houses on one of your bloody shortcuts!"

"Aye, aye, I know Jock, but time's cracking on. We want to get the boys to their beds before midnight. It'll save us time, honest."

"Alright, alright, Neilly, but this is all on you. If anything happens, I'll fuckin' claim you."

So, off we go, creeping through the undergrowth, trying to find our hotel the night before the biggest game of our lives.

"Ahhh, I think ah just stood on a badger!" shouts Jimmy to peals of laughter. I'm not laughing.

I'm thinking about what Herrera and Inter are doing. They've probably had an early-evening team meeting, just to finalise tactics and go over one or two small details. Then they will have turned in, about two hours ago. Probably all sleeping soundly. Expecting and looking forward to victory tomorrow. Herrera might have stayed up for a bit longer, poring over his tactics one more time. He might have finalised his schedule for tomorrow. Every moment of the day planned to the most minute detail, none more so than the 90 minutes they will spend trying to suffocate us. He might be asleep by now. One thing's for certain, he sure as hell won't be leading his players on a midnight expedition in search of their bloody hotel!

Suddenly, we halt.

"What's up Neilly, why have we stopped?"

"It's a fence, Jock. We'll need to climb it."

"Christ Almighty, Neilly! Call this a fuckin' shortcut?" I scream. "We've got a group of finely honed athletes with a big game tomorrow and you want them to climb a bloody fence!"

"It's no that big, Jock."

I can hear the players giggling like schoolkids in the pitch black behind me.

"Right, looks like we've no bloody choice. But I'm first over. Neilly, give me a puddy-up."

Fifty yards later, we stop again.

"Em, Jock, we've hit a wall this time."

I can feel my blood pressure rising. First a fence, now a wall!

"And, em, there appears to be a bit of a slope on the other side," he adds.

"Neilly, if we get out of this intact, I'm gonnae murder you with my bare hands."

"Are you gonnae bring on the sponge when one of us gets injured tomorrow then boss?" shouts Jimmy.

"Johnstone, I can't see but I can hear you. You're for the fuckin' high jump, too."

I'm fuckin' livid now. But the players are not even trying to hold in their laughter now. The angrier I get, the more they laugh.

"Right. We can't exactly back out now. So every one of yous be careful. If there's one twisted ankle among yous I'll have you shot like a lame racehorse."

I'm first over. Then the slope. I can't see where I'm going so I hunker down and slither down it on my backside. I reach the bottom and can make out the vague outlines of the players dreepying down the wall.

"Right. Everyone on their arses and slide down the slope. No-one try to run down it or I'll fine you."

A chorus of whoops and yells follow as some of the greatest footballers in the world negotiate a slope in the pitch black the night before the European Cup final.

"Right, is everyone okay?"

"Yes, boss," is the cry.

"Okay, let's get into the hotel. But one more thing – Neilly . . ."

"Yes, Jock."

"Start running, because I'm going to murder you!"

Neilly turns on his heel and takes off. I'm after him in a flash, bad ankle and all. After 50 yards, I give up and stop. All I can hear is the players' laughter. Then it hits me, too. Wave after wave of laughter. And once I start I can't stop. I'm hysterical now. Neilly trudges back and taps me on the shoulder. We embrace and then he starts laughing, too. We walk back into the hotel lobby, a bit muddy and with bits of grass sticking to our clothes, arms around each other's shoulders, laughing like drains. Neilly turns to head for his room. Then he stops.

"Boss."

"Yes."

"I've heard a rumour. There's a game on tomorrow."

I hear his laughter tinkling all the way to his bedroom.

But the pressure never leaves for long. When the laughter stops and the lights go out, it returns, like a storm cloud drifting back to obscure the blue sky. Temporary relief is all you can ever hope for in these situations. Anxiety is a strange condition. It creeps over you in unusual ways. Sometimes it throws problems into your mind, problems that don't exist, others that do but are not worth spending time thinking about. It is scary, but experience teaches you to ignore these thoughts. Trust the ones that you know you can rely on. Trust yourself.

Other times it is physical. A tightness in the chest, a shortness of breath, a cold sweat, a sense that the world is bearing down on you; that everyone is analysing you, judging you. They are. A team is an extension of the manager. This is my team and I will be judged on it. I slip under the sheets and glance at the mirror before I turn off my light.

PRIDE   TRUST

~~~
</div>

The bar is a pleasant enough wee howff, intimate, smoky and softly lit by shaded lamps and candles set in empty port bottles. Its wood-panelled walls are decorated with maritime paraphernalia. Samba music plays on the wireless and the *clack* of billiard balls comes from an anteroom. Salazar smiles down at us from the gantry with conditional beneficence.

"You guys from Scotland?"

"Aye."

A Yank sailor.

"I was stationed at Holy Loch."

"Okay. So you'll know Glasgow then?"

"Yeah. A great place, my friend. My kinda town."

"That's nice of you to say so, pal."

"Joe's my name. I'm from Brooklyn, New York."

"Good to meet you Joe."

I buy him a beer and introduce the boys, chat about Glasgow for a while. Some other sailors amble through from the billiard room. Joe seems like a nice fellow, but one of his pals is drunk. A squat, tough-looking character with a round head. He chins Iggy.

"What you wearing that button for, buddy?"

Eddie intervenes.

"It's for peace, my friend. Means we're against the war in Vietnam."

"You want to be ruled by Moscow?"

"Not particularly."

"Then why don't you support the boys over there?"

"We've got nothing against them, just against the war itself. The politicians who wage it."

"Yeah, well fuck you, pal."

"Hey, hey, Max, Max, Max. Take it easy buddy," urges Joe.

"Yeah. Listen to your pal, Max," says Eddie.

"Make me."

Max grips the pool cue he is holding with both hands, and shifts it over his right shoulder as though he is about to swing it at Eddie. Then Iggy does something that could be considered daft even by his standards. He withdraws something at double-quick pace and points it at Max. It is a stiletto knife. My mind flashes back to the hardware shop in Salamanca; he must have stolen it. At that moment, as I watch my wee pal with an inane grin on his face and a deadly weapon in his hand, a realisation dawns on me: Iggy will not see middle age. I have to give it up. I can't protect him all the time. I can't protect him from himself.

"Time to let it go, Max," says Rocky.

Max glances round. Silence.

"Looks like you're facing the whole team, pal," I say.

"What team?"

"The Cumbie," I say. "Pure, mad, mental. And don't you forget it."

I wink at Eddie and he grins at me.

"Aren't you forgetting something? There are only five of you, there are eight of us."

"Look, I'm telling you, this ends now," says Eddie, calmly.

" 'Cause you are out of your depth. We will wipe the floor with yous."

Slowly, Max lowers the cue. We collect our fags and leave. Outside Iggy has to shout some smart-arse comment over his shoulder.

"Away home, your mammy's got your tea on."

"That's enough, Iggy – shut your face! And how come you ended up with that chib?"

"Big Vinnie asked me to get one for him. You can't get them back home."

"Can I see it?"

He produces the knife and hands it to me. I walk to the dockside and throw it in to the dark, silent water where the Tagus meets the mighty Atlantic.

"What the fuck did you do that for?"

"You don't need to act the eejit all the time Iggy. Nobody blames you."

At that moment someone calls out, Iggy ducks and I am aware of a brief image of Max, his face contorted with rage. I hear a *swish,* then there is an explosion of light and pain inside my head. Now I am falling, falling . . .

So this is drowning. This is what it feels like. A momentary pretence that it isn't happening, then the rapid descent into a panicked struggle as the irresistible power of water, which it has carefully concealed from you all these years, suddenly becomes dreadfully apparent. The realisation that you aren't going to escape, that you are going to become one of them, the prematurely deceased. The realisation that you weren't anointed for greatness after all. Faces come to you. Da, Ma. My sisters. My nieces and nephews. Debbie. Delphine.

I can see the Angel of Death. Sweet Jesus, have mercy on me.

Then Rocky grabs you. Hauls you. Drags you. Saves you.

# Thursday, May 25th, 1967

Sunlight streams into the ward. The walls are painted baby blue, the bed sheets are crisp white and the place has a reassuring odour of bleach. My head throbs a bit, and I felt nauseous and dizzy when I got up to use the toilet earlier but the nurses don't seem too worried. I can't resist coaxing a smile out of one of them, a pretty African girl.

Rocky comes in.

"Alright?"

"Alright?"

"Thanks for saving my life."

"Don't mention it. That stick was meant for Iggy. Joe and his pals say they are really sorry. So is Max. Apparently he has not long since lost a brother in Vietnam. He's taken it really bad."

"Poor bastard."

A pause.

"Rock."

"What?"

"I just need to tell you. It's . . . okay."

"What is?"

"You and Debbie . . . getting together. I mean, one day. It'll be okay by me."

He pulls up a chair and sits. Sighs as though a great burden has been lifted.

"And it isn't 'cause of . . . what you did. I had already decided it."

"I know."

"We're getting older, Raymond. We've got to grow up. You realise that you will have to get out the Cumbie?"

"Aye. Deep down I suppose I knew that you were right to get out. You are a fine man."

"And you are too. Except I never give you the credit. It's just that . , ."

"What?"

"Things can't be the same, between us. When you two are . . . together. We have to be realistic."

His eyes well up.

"I understand," he says, his voice breaking slightly.

He looks sad. I mean a lot to him. At this moment, finally, I realise that he does to me too. He gets up to leave.

"Where the fuck do you think you're going?"

"It's one visitor at a time. The boys are waiting outside."

"Bugger that, I'm coming with you."

"Are you kidding? You're in no fit – "

"Rocky. Celtic play in the European Cup final this afternoon. And I'll drag myself there if it's the last thing I do. We're going to the gemme. All of us. Together."

He helps me up from the bed and I pull on my shoes.


Corpus Christi. The priests' vestments are brilliant white, in honour of the feast. Standing room only. Packed with Portuguese families, Celtic fans, the odd Milanese. Jack Palance, of all people, notices my bandage-swathed head, gives up his seat for me.

Raise my eyes up to the big cross. No need for the words now. He knows what I mean.

~~~

The road to Lisbon. It leads us to the altar. A wing and a prayer. I stand at the back of the room listening. To the silence. I look at the heads of my players bowed in prayer. I gaze at Father Bertie O'Reagan holding the host aloft. Ten o'clock Mass in the Palacio Hotel in Estoril. The Feast of Corpus Christi. A Holy Day of Obligation.

I may not be a religious man but there is something moving about the rituals and the ceremonies involved in religious practice. If there is a God, and he has the power to determine something as insignificant as a football match, then surely he must be on our side! If there's no deity, or he has bigger things on his mind than us beating Inter Milan, then there is still something powerful happening in this room. This time spent by the players – the Catholic ones, anyway – collecting themselves, focusing their minds, is invaluable. What better way to start the most important day of your life than with some moments of peace?

The battle for hearts and minds has been won in the chapels, they tell me. Herrera's attempts to get the locals to support Inter have fallen on deaf ears, swept away by a wave of piety. The Celtic supporters have all congregated in the plaza in the city centre, winning over the locals but it is their attendance at Mass which has further endeared them. As a Catholic nation, the Portuguese locals have been impressed by the devotion of their Scottish visitors.

The boys all go for an afternoon nap. I don't even bother trying. A knot is forming deep in my stomach and my mind is beginning to race. I am sweating despite the cool, air-conditioned corridors of the Palacio. I go to the lobby and make the trunk call I had promised Jean. It is good to hear her voice. She can detect the strain in mine.

"John, take care of yourself."

"Ach, I'm fine love."

I go up to my room and lay out my things. Suit, new for the occasion, crisp white shirt, polished shoes. Sunglasses, chewing gum, my faithful notebook.

I strip and take a shower, the powerful jet of water temporarily blasting away my anxiety. I think back to my Albion Rovers days, standing shivering under a temperamental spray after a hard match. I think about how far I have come. I dry myself and dress, the nerves building again. I inspect myself in the mirror. Check my watch. Take a deep breath. Time to go downstairs.

The players are feeling well rested when we all meet up before boarding the bus. I take Gemmell aside.

"Tommy, this is a big day for you. You are up against Domenghini. He's good. Lovely tricks and flicks but he's lazy. He's not interested in chasing back. If you push up the field, he'll let you go. You'll get more room today than you'll have had against any team in the competition. Their system is all about snuffing out the threat middle to front, but it's not designed to stop rampaging full-backs. This is a big day for you, son."

Gemmell beams from ear to ear.

"You know me, boss. I never need a second invitation to get forward."

Jimmy is next for a quiet word.

"We need you today Jimmy, more than we've ever needed you. But you'll not get the space to attack the way you like. They know about you. You'll have been the first name on Herrera's chalkboard. 'Stop Johnstone and we'll stop Celtic,' that's what he will have told his players. I'm asking you to sacrifice yourself for the team. Keep on the move, constantly twisting and turning, dragging them out of position. It'll be so frustrating at times. You'll feel like greetin', but keep the head up. Everything that you do will be making space for others. That's the only way we can get through them, Jimmy."

Jimmy nods. "I'll do it, boss."

I have decided to give the team-talk before we leave for the stadium. I want their minds clear when we get there. I look at their faces and feel a surge of pride.

"I am going to keep this short because everyone in this room knows what this occasion is all about. Every achievement boils down to one key moment, one big occasion which decides who is the winner and who is the loser. But let me just say this. It has been a wonderful season. We have won every competition we have entered. We are already winners. Now we have the opportunity to make it an even better season. This can be a season that we can all look back on with great fondness. It can be the best season of our careers. We have a chance to make history. The opportunity is there for each and every one of you to be remembered forever. We know about all the great players of the past. We don't want to live with the legends, we want to become legends ourselves. Just remember when you take that field that I am proud of you all and trust you to meet the challenges ahead."

~~~

We walk to Rossio Square where the troops are congregating for a bevvy and a sing-song. A massed sidey breaks out. Twenty-five-a-side; Scots, Portuguese, some Inter fans. Yank sailors and tourists – Jerries, Spaniards, French, English, Aussies, Japs – stop to watch. Today, Lisbon is the centre of the world. I take it easy and view proceedings from the shade with a cheese baguette and a lemonade. It is hot. So hot.

I tell the boys I need to buy some fags but really I'm making a beeline for a post office I had noted earlier.

Inside I nod at a seated row of aged Portuguese women who smile pleasantly back at me, then chatter approvingly to one another, presumably about how impressive these northern interlopers to their city have proved to be.

There is no queue for the telegram booth.

I take the blank form from the clerk. I pick up the little pencil and carefully copy my cousin Nicky's London address in block capitals. Then I write:

FAO Mlle Delphine Marie Robin
    STOP
September is coming soon
    STOP
Yours
    STOP
Timothy Mario Lynch

I pay the requisite number of escudos, then leave and rejoin the boys.

It is time.

We decide to go to the ground on foot. My head hurts less now and the saltwater nausea has passed; just a wee bit weak-feeling.

"Mr Stein."

"Aye, lad."

"This is it."

"It is that, aye."

"What will you tell them?"

"To enjoy themselves."

"Just that?"

"Only that. Everything else is in place. They have the belief; they know they can do it. It's up to the players, now."

"And for me?"

"Everyone reaches a point in their life when they have to stand up and be counted. A crossroads. A life-changing moment. When it comes along, seize it with both hands. Step into the brave new world."

"Mr Stein. Just one last thing."

"What's that, son?"

"Thanks."

"What for?"

"For taking us to the stars. No matter what happens out there today, thank you for showing us the stars."

"Tim! Tim! Tim!"

"Eh?"

"You're away with the fairies."

"Och, sorry Rocky. What's up?"

"You've never told us."

"Told you what?"

"What *your* favourite-ever Celtic game is."

"Och, that's easy. Scottish Cup final, April 25th 1965. Celtic 3 Dunfermline 2. The Big Man's first trophy as Celtic manager – Celtic's first trophy since 1957!"

A vivid image of Hampden on that glorious day comes into my mind.

"Stein had shown that he was a force to be reckoned with in the same fixture in '61, when his Dunfermline side done us to win the cup after a replay.

"In '65 they led from early on, but after about half an hour Charlie Gallagher cracked a pile-driver from outside the box. The baw hit the bar, spun up in the air, and wee Bertie was waiting to head it in. But just before the break Dunfermline went ahead again, after some shite defending at a free-kick.

"The spirit in that second half was all about Big Jock. First, Auld got his second; a cracker after a one-two with Lennox. 2-2. There was something strange about the atmosphere now as the game raged from end to end. We all roared the team forward; we sensed that something had changed, that something was different now."

I suddenly feel self-conscious and look at the boys. They are hanging on my every word so I continue.

"And so it proved. In the 82nd minute, Cesar rose majestically to meet a Gallagher corner. He seemed to hang in the air for an eternity, just waiting to connect with that baw and send it crashing into the net. We all celebrated like crazy, not just because we had scored a goal that would win a cup, but because we knew the significance of that goal. After years in the shadow we had finally stepped into the light again."

There is a reverent silence, only the sound of our marching.

"Well telt Lynchy," says Rocky. "Here, have a daud of this fizzy wine."

I get torn in, sickly sweet, my first bevvy of the day. Hope the bubbles aren't premature.

"You know the queerest thing of all?" says Eddie.

"What's that?" I ask.

"The team that played then – in '65, and even before then. Most of them will play today."

"Aye," says Iggy. "We had the players but we were shite. Except we weren't shite, no really."

"Aye, everyone knew we had potential," says Rocky. "Maybe no how much, but we knew we had potential."

"All it took was Big Jock to unlock it," I say.

~~~

The road to Lisbon. It rarely runs straight. The greyness of the morning has given way to glorious sunshine. The atmosphere is buzzing as we board the bus at 3pm.

Hail, Hail the Celts are here . . .

The boys are in fine voice. Myself and Sean sit at the front of the bus. Time passes and then someone points out that the traffic is moving in the opposite direction.

"I think we might be going the wrong way," says Sean.

I grab the driver by the shoulder.

"Estádio Nacional," I say, pointing in the opposite direction. He looks at me blankly.

"Estádio Nacional, that way," I shout, gesturing to the hundreds of cars travelling the opposite way.

The driver looks sheepish as he pulls over and prepares to cut back on himself.

"The biggest day of our lives and this fuckin' idiot is driving us in the opposite direction," I say to Sean.

The players have noticed.

"Boss, what's up? Are we lost?" shouts Jimmy, stopping mid-chorus.

"Lost? Are you joking? This kindly fellow has just taken us the scenic route. He wanted to show off his fine city to us visitors. In fact, why don't we all give him a cheer."

The players stamp their feet and burst into another chorus of *The Celtic Song*. Sean looks at me and laughs.

"Nice one."

"Aye, well let's hope we make it in time, Sean. This traffic is murder."

The minutes tick past. Four o'clock comes and goes. The singing is louder up the back of the bus. My heart is pounding. I ask Sean the time again.

"It's two minutes later than the last time you asked me."

"Christ, Sean, it's less than 90 minutes to kick-off."

"I don't think the boys are particularly worried, Jock."

"Boss," shouts Bobby Murdoch. "Put it this way, they can't exactly start without us, can they!"

Another deafening cheer and a chorus rises up as I sit down in my seat and try to disguise my anxiety with a smile.

The stadium is a reassuring and inspiring sight. I feel the hairs on my neck rise as the concrete giant looms into view. The Celtic fans, strung along the main drag to the ground, part like the Red Sea when they see us approaching. Their songs fill the late afternoon air.

We're gonna win the cup, We're gonna win the cup.

Jimmy bangs the window in recognition as we speed past. Not

a shred of tension. Apart from me. I straighten my back against the seat, feel the dampness on my shirt and become aware of a slight feeling of nausea. I fix my gaze straight ahead. *Please, please, let's get this game started.*

~~~

The approach to the Estádio Nacional is wooded with eucalyptus trees. A pleasant mini-forest walk. The air is fresh here, strange for inside a city. I am wearing a crisp, white short-sleeved shirt I saved for the day, a fake-silk Celtic scarf, and I have a bottle-green V-necked jersey tied round my waist. I must look a sight; my bandages are crowned by the top hat I bought in Salamanca, replete with green-and-white ribbons. As we climb the slight ascent I look over my shoulder to witness the tide of humanity behind me, making the last leg of this great pilgrimage. The fans are too nervous to sing. But I feel kind of at peace.

"Do yous realise it's a new cup?" asks Rocky. "I mean, the actual trophy itself. They let Real keep the original one last year."

"Aye," says Iggy. "It's a new shape and everything. It's ginormous."

"I hope this heat isn't gonnae affect our boys too much," says Eddie.

"Aye, and Inter will be u-u-used to it," says Mark, his brow furrowed. He nervously fumbles with a cigarette. I reach over and light it for him.

"Mark. It's gonnae be okay."

He smiles thinly.

Iggy is wearing a kilt he scored out of Paddy's Market. Christ alone knows what tartan it is. On his chest he wears a white T-shirt with the words JOCK STEIN scrawled in childish lime-green crayon. Eddie wears his suit with collar and tie, and is draped in our Eire flag. Mark is wearing a green-

and-white hooped jersey, onto which is pinned a giant Celtic rosette. Rocky is wearing flannels and a green-trimmed tennis shirt he had saved for the occasion; his trilby and shades make him look like a movie star.

Iggy, Mark, Eddie, Rocky. I feel a wave of tenderness for them. Yet I feel a sense of sadness because our time together is passing. And then I remember what I had said to Eddie three days earlier, about Celtic always being there for us, as a focus for our love no matter how well or badly they are playing, providing us with a sense of identity no matter what else changes in our lives.

I think of the enormity of the task that faces us. Internazionale. *La Grande Inter*. The *Nerazzurri*. Their third final in four years. Twice winners.

But somewhere out of the darkness must come light. My generation coincided with Celtic's worst period. Yet they still occupied a special place at the edge of my imagination, as a powerful, strange force that always somehow held the promise of a sense of meaning. And now, incredibly, that promise finally threatens to be delivered. So savour this moment. Remember this place. Remember the way it looks and sounds and smells. Remember the way the moment feels. Savour it when life gets tough. Because if this can happen – if a football team that contains Catholics and Protestants, a set of players who all hail from the Glasgow area, a club set up to feed the hungry children of despised immigrants – if they can become champions of Europe, then anything is possible.

I take out Barney's St Anthony medal. Kiss it.

Estádio Nacional is downright odd. In fact, it is beautiful. An entire side of it is simply open space, but for a temporary stand erected for the occasion, making for a sense of the surrounding forest encroaching in. Beautifully manicured hedges and shrubs are landscaped into the arena. The ends sweep away majestically from the main stand. It is

constructed of pale stone and marble, and is like a benign
Roman amphitheatre. The pitch is like a bowling green, the
turf looks lush. The precious match tickets, priceless at 10
shillings, so carefully stowed away, dog-eared and grimy from
being checked and double-checked a hundred times, are produced. 4.21pm. Just over an hour until kick off. In we go.

The Celtic fans inside have rediscovered their gallusness,
aided no doubt by the sale of bottles of lager and carafes of
cheap Portuguese *tinto*. We get a double round in, and Eddie,
Iggy and Mark also buy some of the paper sunhats scores of
our fellow fans are wearing. They look like merry Glaswegians crossed with Chinamen. We walk round to take up our
positions in the southern end of the ground, about halfway
up the terrace, slightly to the eastern side. As we climb the
steps we meet more and more folk we know from back home.
Everyone seems to have developed a skill for arts and crafts.
Novelty green-and-white stovepipe hats, replica trophies,
club shields, giant rosettes – all fashioned from coloured
foolscap and card, foil and crepe paper. There are all sorts of
flags. Some fans wear bunnets and woollen tammies, just like
you would on a January trip to Dens Park – they must be
roasting! The Inter fans have air horns and seem to occupy
most of the temporary stand, which they have draped with
enormous black and blue banners covered in slogans. There
are hundreds of dignitaries, occupying the temporary stand
and the area round the plinth in the main stand.

The vividly lined running track is a constant hubbub of
activity. It is patrolled by stewards in berets and boiler suits,
and policemen in peaked caps and smart, braided uniforms.
Handicapped guys putter in on little motor trikes and photographers grab the best positions behind the goals.

We are chatting nervously, singing, chanting. In front
of us are a few boys from Duntocher who are wearing
sombreros. They have palled up with a bunch of amiable

Portuguese fellows who seem totally taken with all things Celtic. Behind us is a church group – male and female – from Wyndford, led by a young curate. There are lads from Ireland to the left, and kilted boys from Barra to the right, brandishing a beautiful big saltire. These are the strangers we will share the most significant 90 minutes of our lives with.

The main stand is to our left, the tunnel opens in the ground behind the faraway goal, the benches are to our right, in front of the temporary stand. The team comes out briefly. A roar of approval. John Clark points as he chats to Tommy Gemmell. They seem truly stunned by the number of us who have made the journey. They wave at us as they return to the dressing room. They love us. We love them.

I think of my cousin Nicky watching the television pictures, probably with Barney and the other Irishmen at the pub in Camden. Maybe Albie, Austin, Barbara and Margaret-Mary will be with him. I think of Scots and the Irish diaspora all over the world tuned in on televisions and wirelesses. I think of Da back home. Of everyone back home, but especially Da. He'll be sitting there in his favourite chair, his eyes sparkling, a wee dram in his hand, a grandchild on his knee. He'll be delighted by the novelty of the television set, quietly thrilled at the magnitude of the event. He'll be fussing, making sure everyone is comfortable, has a drink, can see the screen. He'll have read the bit about Lisbon in his tattered old encyclopaedia. He'll be looking out for me. He'll pretend to himself and the assembled that he caught a glimpse of me, shout my mother through from the kitchen.

"Teresa! Teresa! I'm sure I just saw our Timothy! I'm sure it was him!"

Everyone will play along, just to keep him happy.

I'll see you soon, Da.

~~~

It is 4.40pm when we arrive. Fifty minutes till kick-off. The diversion has worked in our favour. It has given the players less time to think. They stroll into the stadium, up the tunnel and onto the pitch. A quick wave to the Celtic fans then back into the changing room. I leave them to their own devices, let them relax and enjoy each other's company in these crucial moments. As they change, I slip outside and hand the referee our team-lines.

"Where's Inter's?" I ask.

He shrugs.

"It's your job to get them," I shout. "We are not taking the field until we have seen their team-lines."

He scuttles off. Five minutes later, he arrives clutching a sheet of paper. I scan the names. My heart leaps. Suarez is out.

Suarez is oot, Suarez is oot, Suarez is oot.

Luis Suarez. A £124,000 signing from Barcelona in 1961. A world-record transfer: signing-on fee said to be around £60,000, annual wage around £7,000; arguably the greatest playmaker in the world. A superstar, but a superstar with a thigh strain. A thigh strain that I suspected was a ruse by Herrera. "He'll play, he'll play," I kept telling the boys. I called that one wrong.

I hand the sheet back to the referee.

"Thank you for doing your job. And I hope you have taken notice of what just happened here. The game's not even started and they are trying to bend the rules. You need to watch them closely; because, be sure of this, I'll be watching you just as closely."

I turn away. Smile. Suddenly, I feel the tension ebbing away. I take a moment and listen to the Celtic fans in the stadium singing their hearts out. I feel the warm sun on my neck and, for the first time in days, weeks even, I relax properly. Tactics sorted. Players ready. The stage is ours. I glance at my watch. 5.10pm. I walk into the dressing room. I casually swing my foot at a bit of mud on the floor. Then I stand in front of them. The room goes silent. Then I speak. No fist-pumping, no battle cries, just simple words spoken from the heart.

"Right, lads. You've made history. Go out and enjoy your-selves."

The players leap to their feet, more ready than they will ever be.

The darkness. The darkness of the mines. The darkness that envelopes everything, that seeps into your soul and claims a part of you forever. The hand goes out. Taps the man next to you. Comradeship.

The tunnel stretches before us. The air is cooler down here. It is dark but there is light ahead. Glorious sunlight. I watch the shafts pouring in, illuminating the concrete steps. I look down the line. Impatience. Jimmy is hopping excitedly from one foot to another. Big Billy twists his neck, loosening up. Bertie looks like a caged animal. Then they appear, gliding past like prize thoroughbreds entering the paddock. They do not so much as look at us. Do not acknowledge our presence. The strip. That famous strip. Blue and black vertical stripes. Football royalty. Hair slicked back, muscles oiled. Slow and purposeful movements. The battle lines drawn.

"Jesus Christ, they look like film stars!" says Jimmy.

"Is that big yin there no married to Sophia Loren?" chips in Bertie.

The players laugh. Nervously.

The wait continues. The tension building. Then it starts. Bertie leads it off.

Hail! Hail! The Celts are here . . .

The Celtic song.

What the hell do we care now?

Jimmy joins in, then Billy, then Stevie. Suddenly they are all at it.

For it's a grand old team to play for, for it's a grand old team to see,

And if, you know, your history

Inter are looking at us now.

It's enough to make your heart go: o-o-o

The walls are shaking now. My spine shivering, heart swollen, feet tapping.

For we only know that there's gonnae be a show, and the GLASGOW CELTIC will be there!

Then at last we are off. The click-clack of studs on concrete. Up the stairs.

Out of the darkness and into the light.

As we get to the top of the stairs I shout to John Fallon.

"John – claim the bench nearest the halfway line before them."

John sprints off down the touchline and plants himself on the bench. Inter are raging and tell John to move. John is not for moving. Quite right; we have been allocated the home bench. But Herrera and his back-room team are not letting it lie. They drag over the Portuguese police and demand that they move us but the local constabulary have clearly been converted to the green side.

"No. This is Celtic!" they tell them, as myself, Sean and Neilly stroll up and take our seats, grinning broadly.

I take in the vast arena. The pitch is lush and green, flatter than a bowling green. If we can't play on this then we should give up. The sun is beating down but starting to lose the worst of its heat. Green and white as far as the eye can see. I think of the supporters who have travelled across land and sea; the sacrifices they have made, the friendships they have formed. This is a defining moment in their lives. This is their team. They feel a part of it. They are a part of it. We knew they would come but we didn't know they would come in these numbers. This is an invasion. How can anyone not be inspired by this sight? The running track separates them from the action but, even before kick-off, it still feels like they are right on top of us, inspiring us, driving us on. The strips look different, incandescent in the sunlight, in contrast to Inter's dark attire. Light versus dark; attack versus defence.

~~~

Before we know it it's 5.20. Some figures emerge from the tunnel, then the teams, the green and white of the Celtic strips brilliant in the late-afternoon sun. The black and blue of Inter is impressive, intimidating.

"Look fellas – the flags!" says Iggy. All around the ground the Celtic fans have raised their colours above their heads as they welcome the players with a spine-tingling cheer.

The teams slowly walk in two files into the centre of the pitch, led by the match officials. The gait of the Celtic players betrays strain, but determination, as though they can't wait to get started. All except Jimmy Johnstone, who is fooling around, grinning and nattering as he gestures manically to the Inter players.

"What's Jinky giving it?" asks Eddie.

"He's taking the pish out of the Inter guys!" says Iggy. "Showing he's no scared."

~~~

Jimmy is already noising up Giacinto Facchetti. I can't hear what he's saying but he's tugging at his top and pointing at him. Maybe he's saying, *Take a good look because this is as close as you'll get.* Or, *Does your mammy know you're no coming home for yer tea tonight?*

He's like me, is Jimmy. Itching to get started, for the phoney war to be over.

~~~

The teams line up in a long single row.

"Check all the photographers!" says Rocky.

Billy McNeill and Armando Picchi take care of the formalities with the referee, Kurt Tschenscher.

"Big Billy will command everything in the air, the Brush will deal with everything on the deck," says Eddie.

"Celtic are going to sh-sh-shoot away from us in the first half," says Mark. "What time is it, Tim?"

"It's . . . 5.29."

The players begin to take up their positions. Inter will kick off.

"Well boys, this, as they say, is it," says Rocky.

We all look at each other for a moment, rather at a loss at what to do. Then I shake Mark's hand, then Eddie's, then Iggy's, then Rocky's, saying, "Fellas, it has been a pleasure."

The boys respond likewise with warm handshakes all round. We turn towards the pitch. One moment in time. The whistle sounds.

We are off.

"Go on Jinky!" says Iggy. "Who's the Inter number 2?"

"Burgnich," I say. "He's going to shadow Jinky everywhere."

~~~

Jimmy's first touch. He knocks the ball down the right wing. Tarcisio Burgnich is breathing down his neck. No surprise that they've chosen to man-mark him. Burgnich will follow him everywhere. Jimmy swivels and turns inside. Burgnich is on him. Jimmy spins again and goes back where he came from. Still Burgnich is there. Then Jimmy reverses again and moves inside once more before laying it off to Bertie. Bertie shuttles the ball down the right wing, but I keep my eye on Jimmy. He has dragged Burgnich into the middle now. He keeps spinning and swivelling. The ball is 50 yards away but still Jimmy twists and turns. Burgnich mimics every moment faithfully. The big Italian looks like a Labrador chasing a bit of paper in a gale. I see Jimmy smile up at him as if to say, 'Enjoying my game, Big Man?' But Jimmy is not playing at little games. Minutes later, he picks up the ball on the right edge of the box. Burgnich shadows him but Jimmy flicks the ball inside. Burgnich slips to the turf as Jimmy spears in a low shot which the Inter goalie Giuliano Sarti blocks.

Then Bobby Lennox hits the byeline and floats the ball over. Jimmy is up highest, angling in a header which Sarti tips over the bar. I catch Jimmy's eye, give him the thumbs-up. He smiles.

~~~

Inter make some ground over to our left.

"Well in Jim Craig!"

The West German referee's whistle sounds shrilly.

"N-never a free-kick!"

"He's saying Mazzola was pushed in the back."

"Garbage ref!"

Mazzola's free-kick is easily picked out of the air by Simpson.

"Well taken Ronnie!"

Inter attack again, on their left this time.

"Shite, Corso's skinned big Tam . . ."

"Oh, Christ."

Corso crosses perfectly and Mazzola bullets a header downwards; Simpson saves, then clutches Cappellini's follow-up.

"That was c-c-close!"

"I'm no sure Ronnie knew all that much about that header."

"COME ON CELTIC!"

Good play by Celtic now. Jinky beats his man, turns two defenders inside into the box to make a gap.

"Go on Jimmy, GO ON!"

He shoots! Saved, spilled, caught by Sarti the Inter keeper, clad entirely in black.

"Great stuff!"

CEL-TIC, CEL-TIC, CEL-TIC.

Lennox on the right now, hits the byeline at lightning pace.

"Go on the Buzz Bomb!"

He somehow manages to fire a great cross back towards the penalty spot. It is met by wee Jinky, of all people, who rises to force a great save from Sarti, who touches the ball over the bar.

"Oooh, g-great header wee m-man!"

"Wee Jimmy must have springs in his heels!"

Mazzola drifts left and threads a marvellous ball through to Cappellini in the penalty area, taking out most of the Celtic defence. Jim Craig checks the run. The Italian goes to ground, very easily. Every pair of eyes turn to the referee.

He points to the spot.

"He's given it," I whisper. "Jesus Christ he's given it!"

"Ach away, n-never a penalty!"

"He's rolling around like he's been poleaxed – GET UP YA CHEATING BASTARD YE!"

"BOOO!"

"Tschenscher – you are a fucking HUN!"

"Who got at you ref? How much are they paying you?"

"FIX! It's a fucking FIX!"

"REFEREE! REFEREE!" shouts Iggy. "YER MA WAS A VIRGIN YER FAITHER WAS A FUCKING MAGICIAN!"

A ripple of defiant laughter, but sickness in everyone's stomachs now. The Celtic players' protests die down, all in vain.

~~~

I'm off the bench, screaming blue murder, looking for blood. Never a penalty. Never a fuckin' penalty. Never. Never. Never. Never. Never. The referee was looking to give it almost before Cappellini hit the ground. It was all there in the casual way he pointed to the spot. He wanted to give it, was desperate to give it. Why? Because it is Inter. And Inter always win penalties, always win games, always win cups. That is the natural order of things.

Giving Inter a penalty is the easiest decision in the world for a referee. The Italians have history, too. Inter's 2-0 win over Borussia Dortmund in the second leg of their European Cup semi-final in 1964 was a perfect example. A few months after the game, the referee was on his holidays in Italy allegedly at the expense of Inter. Not to mention Shanks' Liverpool getting robbed in the '65 semi. Even in their semi-final play-off against CSKA Sofia last month, they offered the Bulgarians two-thirds of the gate money to play the game in Bologna instead of Austria. It worked. They won 1-0.

I'm screaming at Herrera now.

"Cheats. Fuckin' cheats. Diving, cheating bastards!"

Herrera looks at me, confused. Mazzola steps up and slots home the penalty. I kick the bench. I kick the ground. I turn back to the pitch. Bobby Murdoch comes over.

"Nothing's changed Bobby," I tell him. "Keep playing exactly the same way. We know what we need to do."

Bobby nods, turns and spreads the word. Jimmy looks over. I gesture with my palms downwards. Keep it calm. Jimmy nods.

It's a test of nerve but we have been here before.

~~~

Celtic probe, but through-balls from Auld and Clark catch the forwards offside. And whenever a midfield man is beaten a full-back is waiting to put the challenge in. Got to be patient, boys.

CEL-TIC, CEL-TIC, CEL-TIC.

For a moment the curtain of Inter players stand too far off our midfielders. Auld goes past two, into the box – chips the keeper – the ball slaps off the face of the bar!

"Oooh, Sarti was beaten!"

"Good God, we can hurt them!" says Iggy. "We can score!"

Hope springs.

Bobby Murdoch now, great defence-splitting ball to Lennox, Wallace shoots – well held by Sarti!

"We're getting at them Tim! We're getting at them!" shouts Rocky. He's right. We are playing really well. Our heads haven't gone down at all.

A sublime one-two between Johnstone and Lennox takes out the Inter defenders on the left-hand side. Tackle made. Corner-kick.

"We're getting change out of them over there."

"L-Lennox is looking g-great!"

"The whole team is looking great!"

Corner headed on – what a chance – headed just wide!

~~~

How will Inter respond to going a goal in front? Sarti bounces the ball. Bounce. Bounce. Bounce. Bounce. He rolls it to his centre-half, who rolls it back to him. He picks it up. Bounce. Bounce. Bounce. Bounce. The ref, to his credit, trots over and tells them to get a move on. I look at my watch. Fourteen minutes. Fourteen minutes into the 90 and they are already wasting time. We are creating chances. Lennox, Wallace and Johnstone have gone close already. Inter are the top scorers in the Italian league with 59 goals in 33 matches. My team had scored 59 goals by Christmas. I watch Sarti roll the ball out and pick it up. Then I look to our half. Not one Inter player in it. They have pulled down the shutters. Without Suarez, they have no idea how to build attacks; some of the most talented players in the world shackled by a system designed to rob football of all its beauty and unpredictability. It is up to us to break them down now.

The game settles into a familiar pattern. Us dominating possession and creating chances but the one-way traffic is not all to do with Inter's negativity. Our fitness is shining through brighter than the Portuguese sun. Every time they get the ball we are onto them, blocking passes, snapping at their heels, denying them space. It is little wonder they have retreated into their shell.

Bobby Murdoch trots over to the bench.

"You okay, Bobby?"

"No really boss. I took a sore one on the ankle a couple of minutes in."

I look down and his right ankle has swollen up like a balloon.

"You able to carry on?" I ask.

"No question, boss. My right may be loupin' but that's why God gave me a left peg!"

The midfield area is key to our pressing game. We need to have Murdoch at his best. I watch him closely for the next 10 minutes, for any sign that he's struggling. Nothing. He is everywhere. Winning tackles, spraying left-foot passes. If only people knew. If only they could appreciate the genius of a man who is dominating some of the best players in the world on one foot. His 'wrong' foot. That is what this team is built on. Courage. Mental and physical courage, running right through its heart.

~~~

Sustained pressure from Celtic; a shot by Chalmers from outside the box!

"Oooh – just over!"

Great effort from Stevie.

Whenever Inter get the ball they can't attack as there are no forwards to pass to. Celtic's players seem to dispossess them at will. But when we attack they generally defend effectively. Their sweeper, Picchi, tucks in behind their back line. The *catenaccio* in all its strangled glory.

"HOW'S THE SUNBATHING RONNIE?" shouts Eddie.

Faither's had nothing to do since the penalty. He turns round and gives a wee smile. A roar of approval from the fans.

~~~

The play rages but Gemmell is on the ground injured inside the Inter area after a rampaging overlap. Less than 20 minutes gone and one of our key men is down. Shite. Inter break but Clark cuts out the danger. I am still looking at Gemmell. He is limping back into position now. Simpson rolls the ball back to him again. Clark advances. He spots Gemmell, now partially recovered and loitering on the left touchline. He pings it to him. A pass that says: 'We need you Big Man. Do your stuff.' Gemmell kills it and moves inside. Pulls it onto his right foot and lets fly. It slips past the post and hits the side-netting. Some fans cheer, they think he's scored.

"He's alright," says Sean.

I breathe a sigh of relief. The full-backs, Gemmell and Craig, are key. Inter know how to defend against attacking teams. They know how to shut down the channels and deny forwards space. Gemmell and Craig are so important because they present a different threat from a different area. With them, our 4-2-4 formation becomes something altogether different, something alien to Herrera and Inter.

"You're awfy hard on the wee man."

Even my dear old ma thinks I take it too far. But she doesn't know him like I do. He needs to be kept on his toes. He wants to be kept in line. He needs it.

March 1967 and the players are drained after our late win over Vojvodina a few days earlier. Five minutes left against Queen's Park. Jimmy's been getting a hard time all game. He snaps. Lashes out and picks up a booking. I see my chance. The final whistle goes and I'm straight over.

"You're a fuckin' disgrace to the club with antics like that. This club is built on discipline and fair play. You think you're above all that, do you? You think you can disrespect me and the chairman with your disgraceful antics?"

The players are all looking over. I keep going, right up the tunnel, the wee man fuckin' cowering.

"This is not over. I want you in the boardroom in an hour."
He pitches up, sheepishly takes a seat.
I give the chairman a wee nod to start proceedings.
"Jimmy, you have been warned time and again about your conduct. You have gone too far this time. We see no alternative but to suspend you for seven days."
"But, chairman, that means I'll miss playing for the Scottish League team against England . . ."
"Not my problem, Jimmy. You've had enough warnings. That is all."
He looks at me, willing me to intervene. I stare straight ahead. He troops out, shoulders sagging, looking like someone whose tyres have just been let down.
The chairman turns to me.
"Were we a bit harsh there, Jock?"
"Chairman, this is not about a booking. This is about getting under the wee man's skin. He needs a rocket. It keeps him on his toes. He plays well when he's angry, when he's got a point to prove. We've got a big couple of months ahead. We need him up for it. We need him angry. We need him at his best. Just you watch the wee man over the next couple of months. He'll be a giant."

~~~

Johnstone is terrorising Inter on the right-hand side, crosses it into the box.

"Referee!"

"Surely that was d-dangerous p-play!"

No foul given for a bicycle kick in the area, although it would have been indirect. Instead, a free-kick but for a different foul, on the left-hand edge of the box. The ball in is just too high.

"We need to make the crosses count better," I say.

Auld makes a bold run from midfield – shoots – just over!

"Great effort Bertie!"

Twenty-five minutes on the clock. What a performance this is. Celtic are completely outplaying them.

"Every Inter player is behind the ball," says Eddie.

"An 11-man defence!" I say.

"COME OUT! COME OUT YA BORING SHITEBAGS!" screams Eddie.

It's all Celtic. Constant pressure. Stroking the ball around with ease. A Johnstone shot is charged down in the packed box. Then Murdoch shoots after a free-kick.

"Oooh! I thought he was going to score there."

The ball is deflected for a corner.

Craig supports Murdoch on the right-hand side, the ball comes over to Gemmell, who blasts a great first-time volley that is brilliantly saved by Sarti! A gasp of disbelief as it is touched just past.

"That's the closest we've come," I say.

"Magnificent Tam. MAGNIFICENT!" shouts Eddie.

"Their keeper's on f-fine f-form," says Mark.

"Do you think he's one of the Sartis who own that chippie in Thistle Street?" asks Iggy.

"Away you go ya daftie!" says Rocky.

Auld and Murdoch are imperious in the middle of the pitch.

"Bertie and Boaby are directing the entire match!" I say.

"Aye, and do you notice that Craig and especially Tam Gemmell are more and more coming forward to support their attacks?" says Rocky.

CEL-TIC, CEL-TIC, CEL-TIC.

The Portuguese have got the hang of our chants now and join in, totally won over by our attacking flair. All the Inter fans can muster in response is the depressing tone of their air horns.

An Auld corner – flicked on – just missed. Inter counter-attack with a high ball – Simpson has advanced right out of his area!

"Oh mammy-daddy," says Iggy as he covers his face. "I can't watch!"

Then, something marvellous happens. The Celtic keeper does a spontaneous impression of Pelé, back-heeling the ball to Clark, totally outfoxing the advancing Domenghini.

"Olé!"

"I can't believe my eyes – did he just do that?"

"Beautiful Ronnie! B-b-beautiful!"

Chalmers threads the eye of a needle to feed Johnstone, who energetically chases the ball to the byeline and is fouled by Picchi.

Mauro Bicicli kicks the ball, which had gone out of play, away.

"That's pure terrible you!"

"Play the game!"

"B-b-behave!"

"BOOO!"

Rocky whistles in derision, the referee has a word with the Italian.

A hopeful shot by Murdoch flies over, then the half-time whistle sounds.

~~~

The players walk towards the tunnel at the bottom right-hand corner of the stadium. I do not look at them. My eyes are fixed on one man. Tschenscher. An Inter player tosses him the ball. He catches it and they exchange a joke. The linesmen trot over and flank him as he follows the players towards the tunnel. A couple of my players rub their thumb and forefinger together.

"Was it Lire or dollars they paid you to give that fuckin' penalty?"

Tschenscher looks away. I am matching him stride for stride now, just 10 yards to the right of him. As the tunnel approaches, suddenly, I am on him. In his face. Finger jabbing furiously. "You're a Nazi bastard," I scream. "A cheatin' Nazi bastard! That was never a penalty. I know it and you know it."

He looks at me in disbelief. The colour drains from his face.

"You gonnae get your villa out of this then, eh? Cut into the cliff somewhere on the Adriatic? Nice wee hide away for a cheat like yourself, eh?"

He tries to ignore me, skips down the stairs two at a time. I take them three at a time. Always one step ahead.

"If we lose this game then it will be down to you. You will have cheated us out of what is rightfully ours. And if that happens then I'll drag your fuckin' name through the mud."

The linesmen are between us now but Herrera has become involved, too. The Argentinean is wildly gesticulating, jabbing his finger in my chest, ranting in Spanish.

"And here's another cheat. What's the collective noun for a group of cheats, eh?" I shout, but Herrera is giving as good as he gets.

"Your players are dirty, cheatin' bastards. And you're a cheat. You and your big German pal there," I shout, pointing to Tschenscher. "Cash changed hands, has it? I know your history." Herrera is ready to swing for me now. My dukes are up. Burnbank v Buenos Aires. But now the linesmen are dragging him away. He disappears into the dressing room. The officials vanish, like rats into the sewer. Then it is quiet. And I am suddenly aware that I am alone. In the darkness. I take three deep breaths. Smile to myself. Job done. I turn the handle on the door of the dressing room and enter.

Half-time. My time. I look around. Animated chat but no raised voices. The penalty has upset but not demoralised them. I'm actually beginning to suspect it was a penalty. It certainly was a stupid challenge. Part of me wants to strangle Craig, but this is not the time or the place. The time for the truth will be later. When the cup is heading back to Celtic Park and the pressure is off.

I stand stock still for 10 seconds. Let them become aware of my presence. When I speak, it is in measured, unhurried tones.

"Cairney, it was never a penalty. I know that, you know that, we all know that. It is gone. We cannot dwell on the one negative when there have been so many positives. We have created plenty of chances. We are dominating the best team in the world. Luck has not been on our side at times but the breaks will come. Let's not forget what we talked about. It is not easy to get past that wall of defenders, so make sure we cut passes back from the edge of the area. That will help tease them apart. We have a great threat from those areas; guys like Tommy and Bobby who can move onto balls and strike them cleanly. Most of all, don't get frustrated. That's what they want. Keep our heads up, our chests puffed out. Suck the air in through your noses and out through your mouths. Keep driving at them. We can do that because we are younger than them, fitter than them, better than them. Look boys, I think today can be our day. Go out there and win."

Jimmy takes me aside as the players leave the dressing room: "Boss, I feel I'm not doing enough. Burgnich is all over me."

"Jimmy, you are doing exactly what I've asked of you. If Burgnich is inside your jersey then it means that one of their best players is taken out the game. That leaves space for others. Bobby, Willie and Stevie are running riot. Tommy and Jim are tearing up the flanks. Bertie hit the bar, Bobby's dictating play. That's all down to your good work. You're creating space for us to play."

Jimmy nods. He gets it. He always gets it. He just needs to be reminded all the time.

~~~

Eddie and Rocky disappear on bar duties while Iggy and Mark score some ice-creams. I am left alone for a minute, time to loosen my collar, take my hat off for a moment and scratch under my bandages, spark a fag, survey the scene, drink in the hubbub of excited voices, laced with anxiety.

"Mr Stein, I'm worried the heat will start to sap us. All that fantastic play and no goal."

"It will come, son. It will come."

Before we know it, the teams re-emerge. Celtic start the second half strongly and win a free-kick on the left edge of the Inter area as we look down. The ball is plopped into the danger area, two Celtic players header it – a great chance; then Bedin makes a clumsy attempt at a clearance.

The whistle sounds.

"PENALTY!" shouts Rocky.

"HE'S G-GIVEN IT!" shouts Mark.

"YEEES!" shouts Eddie.

Everyone is jumping up and down excitedly. Apart from me. The ref is, in fact, signalling for an indirect free-kick, inside the area.

"Boys, boys – it's no a penalty."

They settle down, disbelief etched on their faces.

The free-kick is tapped back by Wallace to Lennox, but the ball is blocked. It spins out to Gemmell just outside the area – he shoots into the ruck of players, the ball takes a deflection and bounces towards the line – goal!

"YYYEEE–"

But Sarti has somehow reached behind him to clutch the ball! Did it cross the line? All eyes on Tschenscher – play on!

"He's not given it!" says Eddie. "He's not given it!"

"Oh Jesus bloody wept!" exclaims Rocky as he turns and sinks to his knees, only to catch the eye of the curate standing behind us. "Sorry Father, excuse me."

What a start to the second half, and what an atmosphere there is now, a constant crackle of noise.

"He's given them a foul for fuck all," moans Iggy.

"BOOO!"

Rocky whistles derisively.

"Come on lads," I say, "let's give the Bhoys a cheer."

"Cel-tic, Cel-tic, Celt-ic."

All five of us chant, and then the entire end, then the entire ground, follows suit, in the wistful two-note refrain:

CEL-TIC, CEL-TIC, CEL-TIC.

A moving swelling of noise, all started by me!

"Mazz-o-la, Mazz-o-la, Mazz-o-la" comes the feeble riposte.

"First time we've heard a peep out of you clowns!" shouts Iggy.

I was worried that the heat would drain us, but Celtic seem even more mobile than in the first half, more urgent. They are not tiring at all, just continuing their fast, incisive, confident play. Better crossing into the box now, by Craig, then Gemmell – that's the way!

The Inter number 4 feigns injury.

"BOOO!"

Water bottles come on.

Bedin pulls back Johnstone, who had stolen the ball from him. Johnstone then dribbles his way into the box, but his shot is charged down. Then Lennox puts in a great ball-winning tackle in the middle of the field. Then Clark finds Lennox in the box. We seem to be able to attack from anywhere!

McNeill, Murdoch, lovely chip by Auld – flag's up.

"Never offside!"

"Come on to g-grips ref!"

"BOOO!"

Good, patient, attacking play on Celtic's right. We are winning every 50-50 tackle, chasing down every loose ball.

The ball is out of play for a goal-kick. A photographer is too smart in giving it back for Sarti's liking – he's furious!

"That says it all."

"There's 35 minutes left ya bloody disgrace!"

"BOOO!"

Gemmell now. Craig to Murdoch. Eleven men back. Fucking crowded out again.

Sixty minutes gone. I've never seen a match as one-sided as this. How the hell are we losing it? Mark sits down on the terracing step, puts his head in his hands, a look of despondency on his face.

"What's up, pal?"

"I'm t-tired. We've battered them for an hour. We're never gonnae s-s-score."

I place my hand on his shoulder.

"Don't give up."

He rises with a sigh, takes a swig of the wine I have offered him, smiles grimly.

~~~

It only takes a moment. When will our moment come? They are strung across the middle of the field now. Closing down every inch of space. Still we push forward. Gemmell is tearing forward at every opportunity.

"Tam, pace yourself. Keep it tight, we'll get them in extra-time."

He turns to me: "Fuck that boss. It's 85 degrees out here and we're going to finish it here and now!"

I look at my watch. Sixty-three minutes gone. Then, it happens.

Clark finds Murdoch, who sprays it to Craig on the right of the area. Craig holds onto it.

Tap.

Gemmell starts a forward run. I see him build up a head of steam.

Tap.

Cut it back, son. Cut it back. Just like I told you . . .

And he does. A perfect lay-off for Gemmell. It is as if I am watching it in slow-motion. Gemmell hits it. Hits it sweeter than he has ever hit anything in his life. It leaves his boot like a missile. Explodes past Sarti. Rips into the net. I am off the bench. Sean grabs me. Then Neilly. The stadium erupts.

Craig and Gemmell. Two full-backs. Combining to such beautiful effect.

It only takes a moment. Our moment has come.

~~~

We've broken them.

"Sweet Jesus, we've scored!" I gasp. "Oh sweet Mother of Christ!"

The next minute or so is a blur. I find myself half a dozen steps down the terracing from my original position. I push my way back to my pals, being hugged and kissed by strangers, by the Irish bhoys, by the lads from Barra, by the folk from Duntocher and Wyndford. I reach my friends and embrace them.

We've broken them. Good God Almighty, we've broken them.

CEL-TIC, CEL-TIC, CEL-TIC.

~~~

As my men celebrate I cannot take my eyes off the Inter players. I watch as Sarti picks the ball slowly out of the net. Like an old woman picking up a bag of spilt groceries. He hands it to Picchi. The Inter captain's face is a picture of disbelief. He is looking at the ball and looking back at Sarti's goal. As if he cannot believe how this spherical object reached the back of the net. Their players look around at each other. They look horrified. But they look something else. They look tired. Inter are gone. Mentally and physically crushed.

Vecchia inter, vecchia Inter, vecchia Inter.

I turn to Sean: "I think we have just won the European Cup."

He looks at me as if I have taken leave of my senses.

"There's a long time to go, Jock. I'm surprised at you saying that."

"Look at them, Sean, they are finished. Absolutely fucked. Their entire system is based on not losing goals. Not on scoring goals, but on keeping them out. They are finished. Look at Herrera, Sean. I rest my case."

We look at the Inter bench. Herrera is sitting, hands clasped to his face. His assistants are silent. A couple of players glance towards him, but the Argentinean still does not move. Why? Not even Herrera can fix a broken system in just over 25 minutes.

Their players are over now, getting doused with water by the Inter trainer. Baking heat yet it is the swarthy Italians who are suffering the effects of the sun, not the peely wally Scots.

"We still need to score another, though, Jock."

"We'll score, Sean. We'll score."

~~~

Craig, great through-ball to Murdoch. He shoots!

"Oooh, just over!"

"Twenty-five minutes left. We've got them now. LET'S DO THEM!"

"SHOVE YOUR DEFENDERS UP YOUR ARSE!"

"N-N-NOW LET'S SEE YOUS COME OUT INTER!"

"SARTI - YOUR TEA'S OUT YA TUBE! YOUS HAVE HAD IT!"

"Auld. FOULED! PENALTY!"

No, it's obstruction. Indirect again. Just inside the box.

"WHAT DO WE HAVE TO DO TO GET A PENALTY REF?" shouts Rocky.

"THIS IS NEARLY AS BAD AS SCOLAND!"

Bertie to take. Straight at Sarti. Hoped for a ricochet.

Again we attack. A roar of encouragement. Ball blocked, spins out to Murdoch – oh what a shot and what a save – a left-foot volley from 20 yards just palmed over!

"How the fuck did he save that?" asks Iggy.

"J-J-J-Jesus, Tim. I th-th-thought that was it," says Mark. "I th-thought that was it!"

Then a Gemmell trundling shot is saved – Sarti almost fumbles it and Chalmers was waiting to pounce.

Gemmell on a great roving run, shoots just over.

"What a game Gemmell's having!"

"Aye, and John Clark too!"

For it's a grand old team to play for,
It's a grand old team to see,
And if, you know, your history,
It's enough to make your heart go: o-o-o
We don't care if we win, lose or draw,
What the hell do we care,
For we only know that there's gonnae be a show,
And the Glasgow Celtic will be there!

Auld sends Johnstone down the middle – Sarti just gets there first. Corner-kick.

McNeill's up for it. Too high for the header, but a fierce shot at the back post!

"GOAL!"

"No – it's the side-netting."

Then Gemmell hits the bar with a 40-yard chip! We just stare at each other, our mouths open.

Now Cappellini takes a nasty little kick at Simpson, long after the goalie has gathered the ball.

"OFF! OFF! OFF! OFF! OFF! OFF! OFF! OFF!"

"How's that no even a booking?" says Eddie.

"BOOO!"

The Celtic trainer is on, but Ronnie is okay.

Attack after attack.

The ball loops towards the Celtic bench. Stein, of all people, saves it, chucks it back on.

"Herrera – you're no a genius, you're a tumshie!" jeers Iggy.

"Away hame ya tube!" says Eddie.

Craig finds Johnstone. Burgnich fouls him.

"BOOO!"

The main stand and the flagpoles cast a longer shadow onto the pitch. It's a little cooler now. But for Inter the heat is still on. Celtic are still running them ragged. Eleven heroes. The greatest Celtic performance ever.

~~~

Anxiety is an almost permanent state when you are a manager. There is no escape. Even fans singing your name can seem like a burden. If I cared less, it would be easier.

But something strange happens as the minutes tick towards the 90. As I sit watching my team – my wee team – pouring forward, I feel at peace. I relax the furrows in my brow and I have a wee look around the stadium. Green and white everywhere. And opposite us, the main stand. I look at the huge Roman pillars and then I see it. The European Cup, just sitting there. We are so close to it now; a big lump of metal with a significance which cannot be fully understood; I can see big Billy up there, holding that huge silver jug above his head. I have no doubts now.

What happens next is further proof. John Clark crosses the halfway line.

There are 10 minutes to go when a defensive header lands midway inside the half. Suddenly, Clark appears, desperate for a piece of the action. He controls it. Auld comes up to him but Luggy skips away from him. Auld looks bemused, as if to say: 'Luggy, launching an attack?'

He shuffles down the inside-left channel. He points to the space he wants Chalmers to run into. His pass is measured but it is just cut out. The ball is shuttled to Domenghini who races up the wing. Luggy is miles out of position but he is after him, running like the wind. Domenghini slips the ball inside and takes the return. Luggy is still after him. He is level with him now. Domenghini cuts inside but the danger is cleared. Luggy is back at his station. Hands on hips, gazing straight ahead. Barely a bead of sweat on his brow.

~~~

Wallace wins it well, finds Johnstone. Then Craig, back towards Johnstone, crosses in to Lennox – but the referee blows for a foul on the goalie.

"NEVER!"

Chalmers, such speed and skill all the way to the edge of the area. Stopped.

"Surely that was a f-f-foul!"

"Referee, for fuck's sake!"

Auld shimmies, finds Murdoch on his left, cuts inside, cuts outside, cracks one from the angle – beaten away by Sarti! But the ball finds Gemmell, he rolls it to Murdoch – another angled blast – another marvellous reaction save by Sarti!

"We've played them off the fucking park!" groans Rocky.

Chalmers to Murdoch, to Gemmell. He rolls it across the six-yard line, Wallace tries to steal it from Sarti who takes his legs – actually grabs his legs with both hands and pulls him down, as clear a penalty as you will ever witness – not given!

"THAT'S DISGRACEFUL!"

"A STONEWALLER!"

"CHRIST ALMIGHTY!"

"YOU'VE GOT TO BE FUCKING KIDDING REFEREE!" an unfamiliar voice yells out. We turn round to see the curate, red-faced at his outburst. We smile at each other.

Free-kick as Burgnich again fouls Jinky on the left side of Inter's area as we look down. Auld takes it, headed on by Murdoch – what a save by Sarti – a one-handed catch from point-blank range!

Auld rolls a diagonal ball into the danger area, Wallace is only inches away from connecting as a defender gets the vital touch. Then Auld pings it through to Johnstone but the flag is up.

CEL-TIC, CEL-TIC, CEL-TIC.

"How l-long, Tim?" asks Mark.

"Five minutes. There's five minutes left."

A free-kick for offside just inside the Celtic half is rolled forward to Murdoch, who finds Gemmell on the left-hand overlap as usual. Gemmell holds it up at the edge of the penalty box as the Inter defenders stand off momentarily. He does a little shimmy, rolls it back into the path of Murdoch. Murdoch hits it cleanly with his left foot from outside the area – Stevie Chalmers, who has run ceaselessly all game, is lurking on the six-yard line like a predator.

Chalmers stabs at it.

Sends the ball into the back of the net.

We celebrate as a group, the five of us in a ragged huddle, the odd Portuguese or Celtic fan reaching in to hug us. Every fibre of my being burning with euphoria. I look upwards, into the splendid blue sky.

"Yes!" I say quite quietly to myself. "Yes, yes, yes, yes, yes, yes, yes!"

~~~

I grab Sean, whisper in his ear.

"What did I tell you, Sean? I told you we would score. I told you we would fuckin' score."

~~~

"Let's get down!" commands Rocky hoarsely. "So we can get onto the pitch at full-time."

We begin descending the slope, along with hundreds of others. Grown men are weeping. An elderly man wearing a Celtic scarf grabs me and babbles in Portuguese, clearly delighted. The Celtic fans are already celebrating victory, brandishing their flags and singing:

We shall not, we shall not be moved!

The match has become an irrelevance. Once at ground-level we file along to the south-east corner where Celtic are letting the final minute tick away.

"How long now?" says Iggy, quietly.

"Seconds," I gasp.

~~~

I glance at my watch. Not nervously. We could play here for another hour-and-a-half and Inter would never score. In fact, they would struggle to get out of their own half. All tension is gone. All that is left is the scale of the achievement.

What is a man meant to do when he achieves his destiny?

I start walking.

"Where you going?" asks Sean, as I stand up.

I do not reply. I walk slowly. I'm not sure why. Maybe it has all become too much for me. Maybe the pride I feel in the players is beyond expression; beyond excitement and joy. This is everything I ever wished for. This is my life's work. Maybe I am scared of breaking down. Big Jock, greetin' like a bairn. It could happen. If I let myself get caught up in it all; hugging the players, hailing the fans. No, I need to get away. I quicken my pace. And then I hear it. The final whistle.

~~~

Part of me wants to catch my breath but Eddie and Rocky are already clambering over the barricade and the rest of us follow suit. I stumble clear of the moat. The others race ahead, intent on celebrating with the players. But I slow to walking pace, and watch the four of them dash onwards. More and more fans are pouring onto the field, going berserk. I fall to my knees, weak with emotion, tear up a piece of the lush turf with my bare hands, kiss it, stuff it inside my shirt.

I look to the heavens and say it out loud: "Da. You said Celtic were anointed. You were right."

A figure catches my eye. It is him. Stein. The Big Man. I make a beeline for him, run on a burst of adrenalin I didn't know I had. I fight my way through the throng, am confronted with his broad back and shoulders.

"Mr Stein!"

He turns round. For a single moment in time there is calm within the storm. I reach forward, tentatively. He looks down, extends a giant paw and envelopes my outstretched hand.

"We've done it, Mr Stein. We're the first."

He fixes me right in the eye.

"Aye lad. We are that."

He smiles, lets go of my hand.

~~~

I am at the entrance to the tunnel. I turn and take in the scene. The players fall into each others' arms. Then the fans come on, pouring off the terracing, jumping over the moat. I hear someone call my name. I turn round. A young man.

"We've done it, Mr Stein. We're the first."

I look him in the eye and I see it all there; all the hopes and dreams of every man and woman who has sacrificed so much to be here.

I search in vain for something profound to say.

"Aye lad. We are that."

I turn and slip into the tunnel. I start to jog, but it is chasing me; tidal waves of emotion. I am running now but they pursue me, crashing at my heels. I push open the dressing room door and rush to the toilet. I place my forehead against the cold porcelain wall and let them wash over me. Thoughts race through my mind.

Burnbank. Pope's corner. The Cross. Turncoat. Jump the dyke. Bigotry. Hate. Jean. Love. Blantyre Victoria. Albion Rovers. The mines. The darkness. Death. Greed. Exploitation. Comradeship. Wales. Jimmy Gribben. Celtic. Friends lost. Friends found. Sean. Success. Captaincy. Kelly's Kids. Dunfermline. Hibs. Willie Hamilton. Celtic. The Scottish Cup. The league. Success. Europe. Simpson, Craig, Gemmell, Murdoch, McNeill, Clark, Johnstone, Wallace, Chalmers, Auld and Lennox.

I raise my head from the wall. Dab my eyes with a tissue. Three deeps breaths. Open the door. Bill Shankly is standing there.

"John, you're immortal now."

~~~

I stand by myself on the pitch as Billy McNeill climbs up to the podium like a gladiator. He is presented with the massive silver trophy, which glints in the evening light. He grips it with both hands. He turns to face the world as he raises it aloft.

I wipe a film of tears from my eyes. I look at the treetops, to where the sun is making its way over the Atlantic.

And I know that nothing will ever be the same again.

Bibliography

Jock Stein: The Definitive Biography, by Archie Macpherson (2007)
Mr Stein, by Bob Crampsey (1986)
The Lisbon Lions, with Alex Gordon (2007)
One Afternoon in Lisbon, by Kevin McCarra & Pat Woods (1988)
All the way with Celtic, by Bobby Murdoch (1970)
Thirty Miles from Paradise, by Bobby Lennox (2007)
Undefeated: The Life and Times of Jimmy Johnstone, by Archie Macpherson (2010)
A Bhoy called Bertie: My Life and Times, Bertie Auld & Alex Gordon (2008)
Tommy Gemmell: The Autobiography, by Tommy Gemmell & Graham McColl (2004)
Jinky: The Biography of Jimmy Johnstone, by Jim Black (2010)
Jock Stein: The Celtic Years, by Tom Campbell and David Potter (1999)
Hail Cesar: The Autobiography of Billy McNeill (2005)
Official Biography of Celtic: If You Know the History, by Graham McColl (2008)
The Glory and the Dream: The History of Celtic FC, by Tom Campbell & Pat Woods (1987)
The Story of Celtic, An Official History, by Gerald McNee (1978)
Sure it's a Grand Old Team to Play For, Ronnie Simpson (1967)
The Real Gorbals Story, Colin MacFarlane (2007)